# Adiel

by the Author

Yet Another, 1978

# Shlomo DuNour

TRANSLATED BY
Philip Simpson

*The* Toby Press

First published in Hebrew as *ADIEL*, 1998, Carmel Publishing

First English language Edition, 2002

*The* Toby Press *LLC*
www.tobypress.com

Copyright © Shlomo DuNour, 1998
Translation Copyright © Philip Simpson, 2001

The right of Shlomo DuNour to be identified as the author of this
work has been asserted by him in accordance with the Copyright, Designs
& Patents Act 1988

ISBN 1 902881 32 X, *hardcover*
ISBN 1 902881 33 8, *paperback*

A CIP catalogue record for this title is available from the British Library

Designed by Breton Jones, London

Typeset in Garamond by
Rowland Phototypesetting Ltd., Bury St Edmunds, Suffolk, England

Printed and bound in the United States by
Thomson-Shore, Inc., Michigan

*This book is dedicated to the memory of my mother Hannah-Esther, my father Moshe Zvi, my brother Yehiel and some 120 members of my extended family—all swept away in the flood of our times during the Nazi period.*

# Chapter one

Ten generations have passed and passed away since I came, at my Lord's command, to this earth. I was here when Adam and Eve came, expelled from the Garden, cold and shivering and fearful of the wrath of the Creator. Today I see the last of mankind drowning and perishing in the waters of the flood.

Whole days and nights the Lord has sent unceasing rains to fall. The windows of the heavens were opened at His command, and are open still. From the vantage point of my cave, high in the mountains of Ararat, I see the waters swelling and mounting. And if this rain continues to fall, in a few more days the water will lick the mouth of the cave, and I shall be compelled to take flight and abandon my last refuge on the face of the earth. If the Lord commands me to return to the Garden, there I shall return, and my only consolation will be to meet again with Michael, my brother and my friend. If I receive no such orders, I shall return to the orbit of the sun from whence I came, and resume my service as a junior angel in the Uriels, who push and drag the sun from East to West.

From the mouth of the cave I see the pitiful ark in which all the living things permitted to survive are enclosed and imprisoned. By the will and by the choice of the Lord only one family has been spared, the family of Noah, sole survivors of the family of mankind on the earth. All the others, men and women, young and old, have already drowned in the waters of the flood. Their swollen and shattered bodies drift on the surface of the water, stirring with every breath of wind and every ripple. Their spirit and their soul has left them, and they are tossed about like logs on the water. All the fields are covered with water, and flocks of birds swoop down on man and beast alike and rip their flesh.

From beneath the water, fish nibble at the tide of corpses.

Angels are not supposed to weep, and yet my eyes have streamed with tears at the sights that I have beheld. In the ten generations that I lived among men I have learned many things from them. These have been days when men lived long, long lives, with the generations living side by side, tender infants along with mature men six, seven, eight hundred years old. I have learned to rejoice and to mourn, to laugh and to weep, to hope and despair. It was only hatred that I never learnt, since the Lord's implant in me did not contain the seeds of hatred, the bitter fruits of which I have been given ample opportunity to see with my own eyes in the many years that I have lived amid mankind.

Since the flood began I have seen wretched people weeping bitterly, I have seen mothers mourning the death of their children. Who will weep for the people whose bodies are already distorted beyond recognition? Who will mourn for the children, the last of whom are floating, like balls, in the heart of the great sea that covers the face of the earth?

I saw them fair and strong. I saw them born with the first cry of life. I watched them growing old, storing up years and wisdom, memory and oblivion. I saw them seeking kinship and warmth by night and by day, working by the sweat of their brows, working the land that the Lord had cursed on their account.

What I saw, the Lord has commanded me to remember and to relate. I am the witness, I am the memory of deeds both good and bad, performed by men upon the earth. For this purpose the Lord chose me from among my fellow Uriels, and this I shall do. I shall not deviate from what I saw, neither add nor subtract, not turn aside to right or to left, for I am the recorder and the witness. It is not for me to judge, to suppress, to ignore or to exaggerate. I shall tell only what I have seen.

Will the Lord who sent the rain to destroy every living thing and to crush humanity, not mourn and not weep Himself, seeing the ruin that His hands have wrought? Is it only I, who have lived ten generations in the midst of all these people, that am left to lament their annihilation.

The water is still rising. What I saw yesterday has already disappeared beneath the water, and what I see today will yet be covered and will disappear.

Will the ark endure this relentless buffeting? It is a frail wooden shell, at the mercy of every blast of wind. Within it is the last storehouse of the living things spared by the Lord—Noah and his household and two by two, male and female, every creature of the Lord's creation. This splendid, glorious world, the perfection of beauty and wisdom, without compare in the entire universe for all its myriad stars and planets of the Lord's creation, is borne, here, within this frail wooden shell. How will the ark be able to remain afloat for many more days in these tempestuous waters? Will life be sustained in its cramped compartments below deck? Will the humans survive in the dark, in the stench and the over-crowding? Is there enough food in the ark for all? Doubts begin to penetrate my heart.

I wonder about the actions of the Lord. I ask myself about the steadfastness of His promise to mankind. Has it been in order to restore life to humanity that the Lord has spared survivors in whose memory this calamity will forever be inscribed, like darkness at noon? Is what they are experiencing now not like a chasm gaping before their feet, like the void and the chaos of the days before Creation? And is this state preceding Creation not one to which the Lord is sending His world back? It is hard for me to endure this thought, and I stop myself. I am only the witness and the narrator who records the memory of things that have been, and it is not for me to entertain such doubts or to question the purpose of the Lord's decrees. His wisdom is beyond reproach; His beyond any question. His word I shall obey and His commands I shall fulfil, and my doubts and questions I shall store away deep in the recesses of time, until the Lord may consent to illuminate them with his wisdom. My name is Adiel. It was once Aziel, but I will explain.

I was one of those minor angels assigned to one task and to one task alone. The Kingdom of Heaven is like a ladder, on the lowest rung of which are angels such as I, while the highest reaches to the fringes of the Lord's abode. We, the minors, can attain only a distant echo, coming to us from the infinitude of space. My name was Aziel and I was one of many in the flock of Uriels. The Lord created us on the fourth day of Creation, the day He separated the lights, giving the sun dominion over the day and the moon dominion over the night.

On the fourth day we were created, the Uriels, to serve the great giver of light, the sun. Every morning, when the angels of song have concluded their chorus in praise of the dawn, the Uriels set out for their daily task, guiding the sun along its appointed path. They draw the orb from its scabbard and roll it from East to West. In the instant at which light and dark are still intermingled, a spark is ignited that no eye can see nor any glance discover. But within me and within all the Uriels it heralds the start of a new day. Then each stands in his place, beside the beam of light, and in a fragment of time which is never advanced and never delayed, and to the sound of the beating of the wings of the leader of the Uriels, we set to work. Each one of us holds a beam, mingling with the light emanating from it, combining his strength with its light and setting the radiant sphere on its way, from East to West. This was our daily task, and one we carried out scrupulously day after day, every month, every year, from the day of Creation to the infinitude of time, past, present and future. I had no other quality, no talent other than moving the sun in its orbit, in a never changing rhythm.

The sun shifts from the eastern horizon, clad in gold and purple, citron and turquoise, awakened from its night slumber. In majestic motion, its colours grow ever more limpid until it reaches the apex of the firmament. And then, from the heights of the heavens it descends and inclines more and more towards the fringes of the West, donning once more a gown of purple and gold, turquoise and blue, until it kisses the horizon that bathes in the great, primordial sea. It is in this place that our brothers, the Melanols—those of the black hair and swarthy complexion—await it. They are the night-watch, taking from our hands the giant sphere whose radiance is fading and heat abating, and dowsing it in the chilly waters of the sea, while the last rays of light are still visible between heaven and earth. Then the angels of song chant their paean in praise of the evening, and the Melanols roll the sun into its scabbard, encrusted with all the most precious gems of the universe.

From the Melanols we have heard of their night journey, when they roll the sun through dark chasms to its place in the East. We Uriels fall asleep in the West and waken in the East, not knowing how an invisible hand has transported us to the place where our work begins. I never asked myself how this happened. The stone does not ask where it lies, and why it falls where it falls. I had no urge to ask questions, and since the day of my creation I had neither wondered nor been perplexed. I was a particle of power within a great wave of power, drawing its strength from a source infinitely mightier than myself. The beginning of all of us is in the source of sources. I was so insignificant then, and still am too insignificant to comprehend the source of sources.

This was my lot and this was the course of my existence, until the day when I sensed a change stirring in me. That day, as I waited to awaken with the unseen spark which ignites the first light of the dawn, I was aware of a momentary delay in the instant of time wherein all the sparks are drawn together for the first flash of light. No one but I sensed this most minute of infinitesimally slight delays. Never since I had been first created had such a thing happened to me. The delay became greater, and the leader of the flock, who dictates the rhythm with the beating of his wings, shot me an angry look. In sudden panic, I feared lest I be detached from the wave of power moving the light and become one particle, expelled into the void, left suspended in space. I was gripped by dread of the fearful loneliness of the endless universe. When I was with the others I had clung to them and they had clung to me, and I had had no sense that the universe in which I existed was without beginning and without end. In that fraction of an instant wherein I sensed my detachment from the wave harnessed to the beams of light, the wave which draws the sun from east to west, fear possessed me.

How long this sensation lasted I do not know. I was swept far away from the orbit of the sun. At a dizzying pace I circled stars, touched moons, hovered between worlds, sometimes in numbing cold and sometimes in searing heat, veered between darkness and light and passed from light into darkness, until I lost my senses. I do not know how long I hovered, if I soared or plunged, if my stature was increased or diminished, for on my departure from the realm and the orbit of the sun, it was impossible to determine either direction or time. When I awoke from this headlong ride through space I was in another world.

# Chapter two

The Garden. I call this place by the name that I have learned from its inhabitants. In found myself in the Garden. I discovered that I had been endowed with senses. I discovered smells, sounds and sights—flowers, trees, bushes, shrubs of verdant green which softened the red rays of the scorching sunlight, casting cool and easeful shade about them. I remembered the blazing heat which, from dawn until sunset, had been my destiny and my lot. I recalled the dazzling light from which there is no hiding, the eternal aridity with never a drop of moisture, and I was amazed. I had come to another, more pleasant world, a friendly and welcoming place. I lay down among beds of flowers whose colours were those of dawn and of sunset. Above me stood a big angel, broad of wing, attired in a stately gown of many colours, and he smiled. In the orbit of the sun there had been only grim faces around me, scorched and weary.

-You are welcome, Aziel, said the angel. I am Michael, and the Lord has appointed me your elder brother. You are in the Lord's Garden. You have been chosen to fulfil a mission, the nature of which is known to none. We angels do not question the decisions of the Lord. It is my task to teach you new things, things that you do not know. I am glad indeed to be your brother and your teacher.

Michael held out his hand, and helped me to rise. With the touch of his hand on mine my love for him was kindled, and it has persisted undimmed to this very day.

-What mission is this? I asked, and why have I been chosen out of all my companions?

-When the Lord chooses, the reasons for His choice are not questioned. Why am I Michael and why are you Aziel the Uriel? Why is the sun the great light by day and the moon the lesser light by night? The Lord has chosen you, and this is the only reason for which you have been chosen. Do not ask why, but learn to be worthy. This you may learn from me, and from yourself. I was chosen to be your teacher and I shall learn to be a teacher, and you shall learn to be yourself.

When I stood before him, I saw how minuscule I was in comparison to him. He was tall and strong. There were six wings to his body and when folded, pair upon pair, they resembled a garment of limpid turquoise. The black hair that covered his head impressed me most of all. Uriels are without hair, for the heat of the sun has burned it away. His big eyes, sunk deep in their sockets, were unlike any I had known. My eyes had always been closed, to protect them from the blinding glare of the sun. His eyes were wide open and smiling, the smile whereby my heart was enthralled. For a moment I thought he was the Lord, since only the Lord could possess such splendour and such beauty. Yet, had he not said his name was Mi-cha-el, meaning: Who-is-like-God?

-You are the Lord, I said and sought to kiss his hand.

He withdrew his hand and answered: No, Aziel, no. I am only the servant of the Lord, one of His supreme angels. The Lord is not to be seen. Even you will not see Him.

Saying this he laughed. This was the first laugh I had ever heard, and from him I learned to laugh.

-If He is not seen, Michael, how is it known who He is?

Up there in the orbit of the sun I had not asked questions, for I did not know they existed. On my coming to the Garden, I found it was possible to ask questions.

-Yes, yes, Azi. Suddenly I felt that the way he shortened my name expressed great affection. You are learning, and learning quickly. You have learned one important thing already, without even being aware of it.

I did not know to what he alluded. I looked into his eyes for the answer.

-To remember, Azi. In the orbit of the sun you did not know how to do this.

# Chapter three

It was as if a wondrous change took place in me. From being a particle joined to other particles, working all together, from being a particle whose entire strength and existence was devoted to constantly repeated motion in one direction, in the cycle wherein I was confined—from such a particle I suddenly became a being endowed with memory, with the awareness of time as a freely flowing stream, flowing before me and behind.

Memory is a higher rung on the ladder whose summit approaches the presence of the Lord. As time passed, I too grew another pair of wings. Now I have six wings, like Michael. With two I cover my feet, with two I fly and with two I cover my face when the Lord is nearby. I have also grown in stature, and although I am not so tall as Michael, I can even look into his eyes, and see his smile, without straining my neck. These changes have come about with no awareness on my part. And even the universe that I knew has changed in my eyes. Before this I knew only the way of the sun, from the dawn in the East to sunset in the West. I saw only this, and my brothers the

Melanols, who were exactly like me, only darker, dark as the night.

Once I thought that the Lord was the sun. It I served, to it I was drawn and to it I was enslaved. I could not have known the sun was but a star, one among the myriad stars which fill the universe of the great Lord. I told this to Michael. He evidently detected in the tone of my voice a note of shame and of apology for my narrow and misguided intelligence, which I had brought with me from my past. He took me between his wings as if to comfort and console.

-No matter, Azi. Do not be ashamed of what you did not know and could not know. I will teach you the things that I know.

Even as he was speaking to me I listened to the beating of his heart. To the steady rhythm, measured and clear. In my ears it sounded like the heartbeat of the universe. This was the first heart I ever heard beating, and this is a sound that is never forgotten.

-Michael, I whispered, my head on his chest. Teach me about the Lord.

Michael took my head in his hands, and looked into my eyes, gravely. The smile disappeared from his face, yielding place to a ray of light which came forth from some hidden place within him. After a silence, which had the purpose of removing from his words all that was superfluous, and endowing his words with great clarity, he answered:

-He is the Lord of all. He is the centre from which the universe extends in all directions, He is the Lord of life and of being, by His command you and I are what we are.

I felt dizzy, my thoughts confused, I was not capable, as yet of comprehending thoughts of such magnitude.

-Slowly, Michael, slowly. I cannot follow your words and understand things which are so overwhelming. We must talk of the mission that the Lord intends to impose upon me. What is it? Where to? To whom?

-I do not know, Aziel. When the day comes you will know. As you said yourself, there are many things you do not understand.

-But why me, Michael? Who am I? A little particle, invisible to the eye, scorched by the fire of the sun. With your own eyes you have seen how feeble is my intelligence, all but worthless. And can it possibly be on *me* the Lord will impose a mission? I am small Michael, weak Michael. I cannot bear such a burden.

-We are all of us small and weak, Azi. He is eternally the whole and we are eternally only a part of Him. We shall forever be smaller than His creation, just one breath of wind, one spark in the abundance of light. Do not trouble yourself with questions, when you have no means of finding answers to them. They will only confuse the little understanding that you have acquired. Come Aziel, come wash in the waters of the river.

I looked around, and saw a broad river flowing gently between two banks decked with trees and bushes of all kinds. Even in the water at my feet I saw the sky and the trees and the rest of the vegetation. I discovered the miracle of a thing and its reflection. There was no limit to the abundance bestowed on me by the Lord, my first day in the Garden.

I heard Michael say: You have travelled a long road, and the road before you is longer still. When you bathe in the waters of the Garden, you will draw new strength for new life.

When I rose and stood before Michael, I felt a mighty gust of wind that came from him and pierced me to the core. I was so small beside him and so joyful. Love for him was awakened in me. It was later that I learned the word 'love'. I also learned that a new thing, so long as it is not called by a name, comes into being and disappears, fades and disperses. One moment it is in your grasp, solid and sure, the next it deceives and eludes you. Only the name, the word, has the power to create the thing, to draw it out of chaos and establish it forever. This was love, indeed.

When I was in Michael's company, I grew taller and grew stronger. When I was not in his company, I would seek him out.

I was drawn to him as if I were a part of him, and when he was near me I felt strength flowing from him to me. He furnished me with his wisdom, his majesty and his goodness. In his company I understood that in my former existence I had been a slave, for in his presence I gained freedom. He enlightened me and helped me to grow and to flourish. He uncovered layers within me and planted in them the greatest wonder of all, the gift of memory and of remembrance.

# Chapter four

I will never forget the day that I discovered water. Only one who comes from the fiery orbit, all arid and parched, from the desolation of heat from which there is no escape and from the dazzling light that casts no shadow, will be moved to the distraction of his senses by contact with water. But now, as I write these words the very waters are rising without mercy and in their fury destroying every living thing. Now I am assailed afresh by all the questions that began to stir within me on the first day in the Garden; questions that have multiplied during my ten generations upon the earth. Of a thing and its opposite, of a thing and its contradiction, of the blessing and the curse encompassed in one word, in the same name.

Yet that first contact with water will not depart nor be forgotten, nor be uprooted nor fade from my memory. When I saw for the first time the birth of a child, drawn out into life amid the waters streaming from his mother's womb, I understood what was the Lord's intention when He created the waters above and the waters below. How He *willed* life into being.

It was on my first day in the Garden that I plunged with Michael into the invigorating waters of the stream. I felt them encompass me from every side and direction. I felt its silken limpidity, the way I became part of it, yet moved through it. I shook my wings, struck out with my hands, splashed water on Michael's face and on mine. Michael taught me that what seems to be the very furthest depths of the water, a landscape rich with variegated colours and shapes, trees and bushes, all this is the reflection of what is above. I was transfixed by our reflections emerging from the depths.

From the mouth of my cave now, I am discovering for the first time the destructive power that water is capable of, when unleashed by the Lord. Ten generations have passed since I touched it for the first time. And only today, when it threatens to banish me from my last refuge upon the earth, do I recognise the full extent of its curse.

*Chapter five*

Days passed, and still I knew nothing of my mission. To my frequent questions Michael, would reply calmly and with great patience: When the Lord decides that the time has come, you shall know, Azi. Do not press and do not be pressed. Everything comes in its time. Learn, open your eyes, listen and every day something new will come to you, and every new thing is a part of the universe that you did not know. And in the meantime we are together, we are close, and all is well with you.

So saying, he touched my wing with the edge of his wing. This light touch sent a wave of excitement coursing through my body. I did not know that touching another could overwhelm with such sweetness. I enveloped myself utterly within his wings, which he spread over me and I breathed in time with his breathing, like an embryo in its mother's womb.

-Michael, I whispered. Michael, all the time I find conflicts and contradictions in my new world. It began with touching the water, in the river. This ancient river waters the Garden, refreshes it and renders it fertile. Its banks are crowned with abundance, with flowers and trees and bushes and plants beyond counting. In the place I came from there is not even a scrap of leaf, not a rustle of life, only fiery desolation.

Nestling, safe, against the frame of his breast, I could hear his voice issuing from his beating heart:

-We shall always understand only a part, for we ourselves are no more than a part. Only the great whole understands the whole, and that is the Lord. What seems to us a contradiction is not a contradiction in His eyes, but a thing that completes another thing. Once, so the senior angels tell one another, before the Lord drew the word from its scabbard and said, Let there be light, all things were void and chaos. All things were in conflict, fire burned water, water extinguished the fire, storms raged and winds howled. When the Lord uttered the first words, the conflicts and the contradictions were held in check and harnessed for the work of Creation. Whatever existed before Creation we do not know and shall never understand. Only the Lord keeps this great secret, and only He can encompass it. The root of our existence is buried in this secret.

-Michael, I said, not knowing is painful.

-You are right, he replied. It is painful. This is the price of existence. But there is also pain in knowing, and this you shall learn when you know more, my little brother.

When he addressed me thus, I was moved. I was simply happy to be a little brother to an angel such as Michael. Gladness filled my heart and distanced the pain and the curiosity, silencing the questions that were poised on my lips.

## Chapter six

Once more I survey the desolation of the rising waters and I weep. I remember the faraway days of innocence and I do not understand the purpose of the Lord. Indeed, Michael taught me not to inquire into things too lofty for my understanding.

The deeds of the Lord are not our deeds, he would say and His thoughts are not our thoughts. He creates worlds and He erases them, and does not leave in our hands even the tiniest fragment of them. When it seems to us it is in our hands, all at once it slips from our grasp and is swept away by the torrents of unseen forces. It is through the boundless grace and generosity of our Lord that we are enabled to peer at the miraculous and be stirred by it, but no more than this.

Michael fulfilled his obligation to me precisely and with affection. Love was awakened not only in my heart toward him, it was also awakened in his heart toward me. This I sensed every time we were together. His absence stirred longings in me, I wanted to see him and touch his velveteen wings and hear his voice. Sometimes he used to stand over me on the banks of the river, where I had bathed for the first time, and look at me a long time and be silent. It was then that I learned the power of silence.

-Michael, I whispered, tell me about the Lord. Have you seen Him?

I sensed a vibration issuing from his body and the rhythm of his heartbeat quickened. Something, the meaning of which I did not know, was happening within him. Had my question aroused his wrath, or was he afraid of it? After a lengthy silence he spread his wings, raised his head so he could look into my eyes keenly and sternly, and said:

-The Lord is never to be seen. Sometimes He makes his voice heard from the midst of fire, sometimes He rolls back the wing of a cloud and touches us, sometimes He hovers with the winds that blow from star to star and sometimes His voice is heard from within ourselves.

His answer was beyond my comprehension. When I was an Uriel among Uriels, all that I knew I saw, and all that I saw I knew. I pulled the sun and saw the brightness of the light, and when the sun sank I saw the darkness. I saw my comrades scorched and soot-stained. I knew it was the Lord who commanded us, and the leader of the flock who beat out the rhythm at the Lord's behest. A thing that exists but is not seen was beyond my comprehension.

Michael's answer did not assuage my curiosity. I wanted to know much more than I was capable of encompassing. Later, as I wandered among men when they were banished to the land, I saw them retracing the path I had already trodden. Sometimes they sought the Lord in the fire of the lightning striking a tree, sometimes they sought Him in cataracts descending from the hills, sometimes they sought Him in a dark cave into which they did not dare to venture, sometimes they worshipped a rock resembling the head of a man or a beast. Hard and long is the way to the unseen Lord, hard and full of errors.

*Chapter seven*

From Michael I learned many things about the Garden. It extends without limit until it is swallowed up by the cosmos. Its gates are open in all directions and here the anger of the raging storm winds abates. Here the winds are held at bay, waiting before setting out on a new course. And the Garden is full of flowers, bushes and shrubs and trees, and the singing of winged creatures and the rustle of vibrant life. There are no predators and no hunters, no prey and no victims. The lion and the wolf and the sheep and the goat graze side by side without fear. Abundance satisfies all hunger and quenches all thirst.

Two sturdy trees stand in the Garden, like a pair of central pillars supporting all the richness and the bounty, the landscape, the multiplicity of shapes, colours and forms. Their canopies entwine, high, high above the ground, and in a broad swathe around them nothing grows. Ripening fruit nestles among their branches. The fruits of one tree glisten like tiny suns, overflowing with juice and vitality, boundless strength. When I saw that fruit I sensed a surge of life pass through me, life that has neither beginning nor end, life nourished by the primeval source of eternity.

-This is the Tree of Life, said Michael. And his voice betrayed the excitement and awe that his face radiated.

Facing the Tree of Life, with its straight soaring trunk and branches neatly ordered like the rungs of a ladder, with its fruit glistening brightly amid verdant leaves, stands the other tree. This one is shrouded in dingy foliage, its branches twisted and inter-twined like a dark labyrinth; its trunk twists sometimes this way, sometimes that, as if seeking a way through the void, to arrive at a goal hidden from the eye. The leaves are sometimes round, sometimes square, sometimes straight and sometimes curled, and the fruit is concealed from view. Unlike the fruits of the Tree of Life, which catch the eye with their beauty and tempt with their lustre and wink at the beholder, the fruits of the other tree are enveloped in shade, and only one stopping to look would glimpse their colour, reddish-gray and sometimes a dark shade of blue. The Tree of Life displays its fruits in lavish abundance, but the fruits of the other are out of reach, hidden from the eye of the beholder. When I approached it to take a closer look, Michael hastened to prevent me, almost in a panic.

-Stop Azi, stop! You must not touch nor go near these trees. Anyone who touches them and eats of their fruit shall surely die.

I withdrew my hand, and Michael sighed in relief.

-It is the Tree of Knowledge, Aziel. The Tree of The Know-ledge of good and evil. From both of these trees it is forbidden to eat.

Ashamed and confused I asked him, What are good and evil? And what is dying? There are so many things to learn, Michael.

-You see, my brother, I do not always remember that you are the pupil and I the teacher. You are right. The words sound simple, but are not at all simple. You asked what is death, and I scarcely know how to answer you. In the Garden there is only life. Life is in what is flourishing, growing, stirring, seeing, hearing, feeling, speaking. Death is evidently the reverse of these things. Until we face it, we shall not know what it is. But even without knowing what it is, we know it is something to be feared.

-As to your question, he continued, about what good and evil are, I must tell you that good is what the Lord commands and evil is what He forbids. We do as the Lord commands us. Perhaps in time we shall know more.

## Chapter eight

Lt was beside these two trees, that I heard for the first time from Michael about Adam. Before he told me I did not know who Adam was, for I had not yet seen him. Again I asked, who is Adam?

-The Lord created him, said Michael, He formed him in His image and His likeness.

-Did you not tell me it is impossible to see the Lord and only His voice is to be heard, and that but rarely and from the midst of fire?

-It is true, replied Michael, that is what I said. The Lord is not seen, His image and His likeness are not known, but Adam, so the Lord said Himself on the day He created him, was created in His image and His likeness.

-Surely there is contradiction in what you say, Michael.

-I know, but in this contradiction there is buried a great secret, one that we cannot solve. Of all the secrets of the Lord this is the most closely guarded, and this paradox is only understood by the Lord. He walks amid contradictions and is not harmed. Leave this question, Azi. There is no path leading to its solution. Enjoy the Garden, revel in its fragrance, delight in its beauty, and the Lord will be good to you.

I left the question, but it would not leave me, and from that day to this it has constantly returned to my thoughts, demanding that I face it and come to some resolution. Even now, when my memories of the days in the Garden transport me back to the days of innocence and grace, as I witness the creatures of the Lord drowning in the waters of the flood, my heart is not reconciled to His actions. Are these very humans not creatures in His image and likeness floating on the surface of the water, their flesh torn and corrupted? But then, when I had yet to meet Adam, and had only heard of him from Michael, I thought that he was a Lord, inferior perhaps, less mighty perhaps than the Lord, but a Lord nevertheless. So I thought until I met him and saw him for what he was.

## *Chapter nine*

I loved to return to the banks of the river where I had bathed on my first day in the Garden. I was drawn to the colours, the forms and the scents that were so luxuriant there. I would return to that place in order to restore myself to things that I did not have in my past. By the banks of that river of life, all life was a chant: glory, honor, wonder . . . How beautiful are your works, O Lord, how beautiful! I would sit on an outcrop of rock over-hanging the water flowing beneath me and delight in my reflection.

Then I saw Adam. From the rocky outcrop where I sat, I saw him on his knees, staring into the water. He looked so tiny, helpless, naked; vulnerable. His body was bare and hairless, unlike that of the other creatures in the Garden, gleaming pink through the greenery of the riverbank like one of the flowers of the Garden. Had he not stirred and moved from place to place I would not have noticed him. I did not see his face, for he was kneeling with his back turned to me. When I approached him, hovering, and still he did not notice me, I knew then that he was no angel, for angels see and are seen by one another. His face was reflected in the water. He had been staring at it transfixed for a long while. His wide open eyes scanned the water stubbornly, desperately pleading for something unclear, as if saying, See me, look at me! I saw how his eyes were wide open, expectant, as if prepared for disappointment or joy or something that is supposed to come but does not come.

With intense curiosity and empathy, I waited for Adam to speak. He held out his hand to his face in the water. He wanted to touch it. Cautiously. His hand was open, fingers splayed, ready to caress. In the water, too, a hand appeared. As the one above descended, so that below rose, until they met. All at once he closed his open hand beneath the surface of the water. The other hand disappeared. His face betrayed a kindling of anger. He moved his hand within the water, seeking the hand that had disappeared. In vain. Now he brought his face close to the face in the water. Light ripples moved his liquid reflection, splitting and distorting it. Again he moved his hand cautiously to touch his reflected face, and again it dispersed at his approach. The signs of his anger intensified. His mouth contorted and the look of entreaty in his eyes was replaced by a scowl.

Adam's face no longer said, Come to me, look at me, but it was hard and threatening, as if to say, If you do not come to me, I shall bring you to me by force.

He leaned his whole body forward, opened his arms wide as if seeking to clasp to his heart the image in the water, and the reflected image did the same. A broad smile rose to his face. Again his eyes opened wide with a look of gladness, with excitement, and from his mouth issued an eager, inviting voice. He dipped head and arms into the water to embrace his reflection, and it disappeared from his sight. When he raised his dripping face from the water it was distorted with fury. The reflection appeared again, its face also full of wrath. He rose to his feet, and then I saw his stature. Not large but muscular, legs jointed in the middle, unlike the legs of an angel, which are unjointed, without articulation.

And Adam's genitals, both male and female, were covered in hair. Neither an angel nor an animal, I reflected.

Adam angrily broke off a branch from a tree close by, returned to the bank and saw his reflection standing in the river, head down, waving a heavy stick at him. Furiously he struck at the water, and the other figure likewise brandished his weapon and struck. The branch in his hand descended with great force and the figure in the river was shattered into drops of water flying in all directions. He dropped the branch into the water, and the current carried it away from him. He turned his back on the river, tears of disappointment and humiliation smarting in his eyes.

I hastened to return and find Michael. The thing that I had seen on the riverbank perplexed me and aroused so many questions and musings within me. Who was this creature? Why was his body devoid of hair, as if the Creator chose to remove from him any partition, anything that would separate him from the universe surrounding him? Perhaps He sought to bring him close to Him. Why was he alone and why did he have no mate?

I found Michael waiting for me.

-You saw him, he said, before I had time to tell him of this.

-I saw him, I answered impatiently, who is he?

-I knew one day you would meet him by the river. It is Adam, whom the Lord created in His image and His likeness. The Lord is one, and alone, and therefore He created Adam to be His one and only likewise. Adam goes down to the river in search of some being that resembles him, and he does not find it. He thinks that the reflection in the water is a creature like himself.

-But I have seen him furious at his image in the water, I answered, he thinks that the figure is running away from him.

-Another paradox, said Michael. The Lord who exists is not

seen, and an image that is seen does not exist. It is truly a long road that I must travel before I understand such contradictions. This was my first encounter with Adam, the image and the likeness of the Lord, and I never supposed that he would be the object of my mission.

# Chapter ten

From the day I met Adam on the bank of the river to this day, when I began to inscribe and record his history and that of his family, as I have been commanded to do, my life has been bound to his. In a sense, his fate became my fate, since many of the things that have happened in my life were in many ways an echo of his life.

Today, for example, I was witness to an incident which left me utterly shaken. There were two children left behind, a boy and a girl, clinging onto a tree-trunk, which drifted on the surface of the stormy waves. They had been tied with ropes to the trunk, and this had prolonged their lives, as the trunk was tossed from wave to wave, a mute witness to destruction. I knew the children. Their home had been nearby that of Noah. They and Noah's children would come and go in one another's homes. Perhaps these neighbours had heeded Noah's warnings of the impending flood; it was probably their parents who strapped these children to the tree trunks, in the hope of saving their lives. And here they are floating, and still they show signs of life.

The boy and the girl struck out with their hands in the direction of the ark. It was clear they believed that if Noah saw them he would save them also. They struck out, they struggled amid the waves of the deep. What gave them life? What had been their nourishment for so many days? I did not know how strong is the urge to live when life is threatened. Is it possible that the children had fed on the flesh of the corpses floating upon the water? After all, I had seen birds and other creatures beginning at this time to prey on the weaker ones among them, and even to eat carrion for the sake of survival. This I learned well in the course of the ten generations I spent among men, that they are deterred by no obstacles set before them by Lord or by man.

The children on the tree-trunk cried out piteously to Na'ama, to Shem, and Ham, and Japheth. They called out the names of the womenfolk and the children of the house of Noah, but in vain. The tightly sealed ark drifted this way and that with the waves, like a dark and sealed off shell. The boy had managed to untie the rope, and he clung to the bow of the ark and continued to cry out. Between one cry and the next all that was heard was the sound of the waves lashing the timbers. Alas, if only it had been within my power to save those two children, despite the ordinance of the Lord.

## Chapter eleven

S till the floodwaters are rising, and I must complete my task. I was sent here to record the chronicles of mankind, not to empathise with its fate. I am not the master of my own destiny, but an angel invisible to Adam, his sons and his sons' sons, but instructed to walk in their path.

After the first encounter on the riverbank I could not but think of him, observing what he was doing, seeking him out among the paths and the thickets of the Garden. Every day I would go down to the river, hoping to find him in the place where I had last seen him, and, sure enough, one day I did find him. This time his back was turned to the river. He seemed angry, as if despairing of something which he wanted to attain. Evidently, he had learned that the image in the water would not respond to him and that all his efforts to befriend it were doomed to failure. Now I saw him with the sun behind him and a long shadow before him. Adam stared fixedly at the long shadow lying prone at his feet. He took a slow, cautious step, and the shadow moved in front of him. He leaned over to touch it, and the shadow grew shorter, contracting into a coil. Adam held out his hand, and when he touched the shadow it disappeared. Again he rose to his feet, and with him the shadow lengthened, stretching out before him and touching the trunk of a tree where it stood still, seeming to wrap itself about the tree. He encompassed the shadow that had fallen on the broad trunk, embraced the trunk with a frantic movement, and hurt himself. Adam was stunned at the sight of the blood spurting from his injured hands. Once more his features contorted in fury. The shadow likewise brandished a stick, but was silent. Adam lifted a heavy stone and hurled it right at the shadow's head. The stone struck the ground, but the shadow remained intact. Adam fell prostrate on his shadow and wept. The shadow was silent, indifferent to his tears, and completely shrank away from sight.

I could not go to Adam and say: This is only a shadow, it will go with you everywhere, accompany you on every journey, walking before you or trailing behind you. It will never respond to your cries and your entreaties. Only I hear your cries, but I cannot speak to you.

Among all the creatures in the Garden, Adam was the first that I saw weeping. I, too, learned to weep, in the generations that followed. Adam wept because the Lord created him with the ability to feel sorrow and the ability to give expression to it. Does the Lord weep too, perhaps? Was not Adam created in His image and His likeness?

This was what I asked Michael, when I hastened to him and told him about Adam and his shadow:

-Is this his destiny, Michael? To seek his reflection in the water and chase after his shadow? Why was he created alone? Why did the Lord not give him a mate, as He gave to all His other creatures? Even the angels have companions.

I sensed that my questions made Michael uncomfortable. When deep in thought, he used to fold his wings tight, leaving only his face visible through the dense mantle that encompassed him. Sometimes he gathered me into the mantle, sometimes he enwrapped himself alone, and this was a sign that he wanted seclusion, the chance to sink into his own depths. We were both silent, he wrestling with his thoughts, I awaiting his response. A gentle, easterly wind blew in the Garden. The sun stood high in the sky, and the inhabitants of the Garden were gathered at this hour into herds and flocks beneath the spreading trees, sheltering in their shade. The silence was broken at times by a breath of wind stirring the leaves, a rustling sound that only deepened the silence following it.

-Azi, Michael began, you surely expect me to answer all your questions. I am your teacher, but you should know that I cannot answer many of them. In you there is something strange and different, which does not exist in me and in the other angels. We accept the Lord's world as it is. Many of your questions do not arise at all. What the Lord has done, He has done for the best, and yet you persist in questioning His acts.

-Could this too be His will? I asked.

-Perhaps. I do not have the answer. I do not know why the Lord created Adam to be alone, and I ask no questions about it.

Suddenly a thought came to me, like a flash of understanding. That perhaps the Lord loves Adam just as I love Michael.

I looked around, and seeing no other angel nearby I whispered:

-Michael, perhaps He does not want him to love any other but Him.

Michael did not understand why I had whispered it. He asked, *Who* does not want?

-The Lord, Michael. Perhaps He wants Adam just for Himself.

-Hush, and do not repeat such words in the hearing of others. The Lord loves all of His creation, and what He has done, He has done for the best.

-You are right, I replied, but inside I found it hard to quell the doubt.

We strolled beside the river and Michael told me of the four rivers which split away from the primeval stream flowing through the Garden. He named the lands to which the wondrous waters flow, bringing shade, luxuriance, the iridescent limpid colours of the rainbow—and an abundance of life. He spoke of crystal, of fine gold and of onyx.

He spoke, and his words lilted away from us like a distant gust of wind. I was thinking of Michael and of the question which had troubled me since I had asked about the Lord and Adam. I wanted to know if I was Michael's only love. I wanted to know if he only fulfilled the Lord's command, or if he loved me in obedience to a command from within, from his heart. I was not commanded to love him, yet love for him had blossomed in me. He was the one I saw when I first came to the Garden, his smile had greeted me when I was still enmeshed in slumber, the slumber that lifted in the light of the Garden, in the calm, shady tranquillity. All my memories of my new creation begin with his image and it was in his eyes that the changes that had come about within me were reflected—from Aziel the Uriel to Adiel—the emissary of the Lord, setting forth albeit on an unknown and uncomprehended mission.

Not far from us, among bushes of myrrh and aloes, crouched Adam, his back bent, in his hand a sharpened and shining stone. He was working. The Lord had put him in the Garden to work and to water it. With the stone he was digging a channel in the rich earth, to guide water from the river to the flowerbeds. Today I ask myself: Did the Lord really need Adam's help to work His Garden? He, the Creator of heaven and earth, He who blows the wind and sends the rain? And is Adam the only one of his creatures that must work, while the others graze, feed themselves, pluck and nibble from the bounty with which the Garden is blessed? What secret, what hint is the Lord conveying to Adam and to the earth? Did He know, even then, what the future held for Adam, and was this a preparation for the destiny that he must bear, the destiny in store for him?

I mustered my courage and asked Michael whether I was the only one he loved.

-You are like a son to me, you are like a brother to me, you are my pupil and in your heart I have kindled many sparks. To you I owe the ability I have learnt to give, to bestow, the joy of sharing with you the gifts granted me by the Lord. From you I have drawn your delight in the forms that you see, from you I have borrowed eyes wide open to the wonders of the world, and through them I have seen again things forgotten. In your eyes I read the pleasure of shade from the heat of the sun, the miracles of water, the vault of the sky, the wondrous power embodied within the tiniest of His creatures. You see, Azi, we have both helped each other. You were small, timid and bewildered when you came to me. Now you are tall, alert of eye, overflowing with questions. I am proud of you, my son. I have succeeded in drawing out of you what was hidden and dormant. This is the secret of my love for you, my chosen brother.

So saying he covered me with his wings, and I laid my head on his breast, joyful. I only listened, only breathed, only touched his wings. Then he told me of the two senior angels who were his fellows.

Today I often think of the six days of the world's Creation and of the seventh day, when the Lord rested upon completion of His work. Is it the sight of so much destruction that turns my thoughts towards creation? In order to understand the end is it really necessary to return to the beginning, as one returns to the source of a river to understand its flow, or to the start of the day to comprehend the sunset?

From the mouth of the cave near me I see fearful devastation. Water everywhere. Ranges of tall mountains disappearing, and the day is not faraway when all that will be seen is the high, concave vault of heaven, arching over the plateau of the water and stretching from horizon to horizon. Noah's ark will perhaps still be drifting or perhaps it will sink along with its cargo, and there will be no man left in the universe to witness this. My words are words of grief, and all that I have seen has filled me with despair.

# Chapter twelve

Among the many questions with which I burdened Michael, the one I would return to most tirelessly concerned the question of creation and he, my friend and loved one, would tell me to be patient and wait.

-This is too great and too wonderful to be understood. You will grow, you will learn much, you will store up wisdom, acquire the skill to inquire profoundly and to take upon yourself the burden of the unknown. Only then will you be ready to set forth and discover the limits of knowledge. The wonders latent in the tiniest of insects are beyond even my understanding, my son. Wait. You must be patient.

I waited. Every time I was faced by something that perplexed me, I broke my promise to myself that I would trouble Michael with no further questions. I was afraid of repelling him, but his tolerance was as steadfast as rock. He was never angry, he never rebuffed my curiosity brusquely, never chided me. Patiently he led me down the twisting byways of the cosmos, revealing to me what had been, what was now, and what he knew. What he did not know, he took to be self-explanatory, for these things are the acts of the Lord and His will. How strong is my desire for him today, at this time of sorrow and destruction, when I understand neither His purpose nor His justice.

I see that I have strayed from my purpose once more, my task of recording the memory of past events. The beginning I wanted to remember, since perhaps the end that I observe now is already foreshadowed in it, the end that I now observe from the mouth of the cave in the high mountains of Ararat.

# Chapter thirteen

I particularly recall one night, a night when the light of the full moon and its flawless shape so eloquently offered their praise to the work of Creation, and the heavens told of the glory of the Lord, and the praise doubled and redoubled in the calm flow of the waters of the river as they washed and purified the picture reflected in their midst. The moon in all its splendour, bobbing in the current, and the trunk of a tree drifting away and out of sight, and all that was floating born along with the current, and only the moon and the dark landscape and the ridges of the river banks standing firm and unmoving. I noticed how all things and their opposites did not disconcert me, nor did they pull me this way and that, but rather they taught me to accept and to consent, to reconcile opposites that only appear to be opposites but are actually both one side and the other of the same things . . . And so, it was on that night that the miracle occurred. Michael opened his heart to me and and told of the Creation.

He spoke without preamble to his words, without being asked, for no discernible reason, like something originating in itself or the continuation of what was before, so, from within himself, as if everything that appeared to our view was to be supplemented by something else that had been lacking, Michael began as if filling such a gap, saying: In the beginning God created the heavens and the earth.

He spoke of the six days of Creation, and of the seventh day, the day when the work of Creation was completed in great silence, an outstretched hand, an untroubled gaze on everything that is, that had been created, and how the Lord had given souls to all living things, how his creatures were the crowning glory of the Lord and Creator.

In the beginning God created the heavens and the earth ... Necessarily so, I reflected, for it could not be otherwise. It would be impossible to create in a different order, starting with the earth and from thence to the heavens. After all, the Lord's abode is in heaven and it is there that creation begins. I made not a sound. Michael opened the gate and passed through it, I following him close by, to hear from his lips what had happened then, in the beginning, when God created the heavens and the earth.

Since the day of my arrival in the Garden, since the day that I understood there were other things besides the orbit of the sun, there were open spaces, and stars, and other angels, and the Garden with its dwellings, and the habitation of the Lord, and Adam, and bounty lavishly bestowed ... since that day I had felt an ever more powerful curiosity to know from whence all this came, how everything exists and was created.

-Of the first day, continued Michael, I know only from hearsay. There was darkness on the face of the abyss, and the spirit of God hovered above the waters.

I turned to look at the river flowing near us. The surface of the water was smooth and pure and the moonlight hovered above it—or was it the spirit of God, hovering, as at the Creation?

-Michael, I whispered, see, it is hovering above the water.

Michael hugged me and patted my shoulder. Indeed it is hovering, it hovers over all and it hovers always.

A soft breeze passed above us. An almost silent rustle followed it from the river, and I seemed to hear His voice.

-And after that, Michael, after that what happened?

-After that it was the light. The Lord said, Let there be light, and there was light. We, the senior angels, were created on the second day. The light was created on the first. The word of the Lord split the darkness, and light burst from the breach as if it had been imprisoned there by the power of the darkness, and the word of the Lord broke the chains and set the captive free.

-Oh, I said, Oh. This is the sun that I used to move.

-No, little brother. This is the *whole* light, in all its fullness, in all its splendour. Afterwards, on the fourth day, when the Lord saw that the day was too bright and the night too dark, He curtailed their length and ordained two lights. The moon that is above us, that is reflected to us from the river, is the lesser light of the night. But it is also the heart of the world. It swells up, and declines and disappears. Waxing and waning, like the beating of the heart. It marks out our time, it counts out the days. Dates and festivals will be determined according to it.

-And life, Michael, the most wonderful thing that the Lord created, what happened to life?

-When the waters were divided, when the dry land rose from the depths, when the storms and the tempests were abated, when the void and the chaos were harnessed and with them the angels of destruction who hated the works of the Lord, then harmony and the wonders of life—the grasses and the trees and other plants of their kind—rose up. And when nourishment for the animals was emerging from the earth in abundance, he created them too. On the sixth day the insects were already crawling, the birds were flying, and all manner of beasts were hopping and leaping and frolicking, and the seas teemed with fishes and with whales.

-And what of Adam, Michael? Six days have passed, and where is Man? Surely he was not created on the seventh day, when the Lord rested from his labours.

Michael lapsed into silence. There are silences that cannot be measured, since they make time itself stand still. Such was the quality of this silence.

-The sun on that sixth day was on the point of setting, he said, and all the angels of the Creator stood ranged in a circle. The senior angels stood close to the flame from the midst of which the Lord spoke, around them were the serving angels, Seraphim and Cherubim, every angel standing according to his rank in the hierarchy of the firmament. All things that grow, that crawl, that teem and swarm, all that flies and all that swims in the deep— all held their breath.

I, continued Michael, I stood and waited for the sign that would issue forth from the flame every day of the days of Creation. When the Lord saw that it was good He would bless the sixth day and we would all burst into a hymn of praise for the Creator and His Creation. And then something happened which I cannot explain to this day.

-The flame was burning with red light, a sign that the Lord saw it was good. We waited for the blessing with which He blessed every day of Creation, but instead we heard His voice saying, Let us create Man in our image and our likeness. Silence reigned, utter silence. It was as if the entire universe held its breath. There was not the stirring of an insect to be heard, not the flutter of a wing nor the wriggle of a fish.

-What is Man in His image and His likeness? Will the Lord reveal his likeness to all in the likeness of Man? Can it be that all that has been created in these six days is nothing but degrees ascending, till they attain the degree of Man? Did the Lord conceive of Man as the epitome of His Creation, and would He see him and would He say that it was good?

-Since the day of Adam's creation, I have asked myself

constantly, who and what is he? Is he the last act of Creation or the first step in a process not yet begun? When the Lord took a handful of dust from the ground and breathed His spirit into it, we saw before our eyes a naked creature, his body displaying both male and female organs, but, like us, standing upright and like us looking about him and wondering. Neither angel nor beast. Was this the image and this the likeness of the Lord? Did this creation resemble the Lord, the Creator of all? To this day I cannot understand this riddle.

Michael knew that I could not answer his question, but he wished to express it aloud before an attentive listener. I was proud that he had chosen me and not one of the angels, his companions. I realized that this meant that I had grown and had matured and was worthy of sharing his thoughts.

Suddenly I saw Adam approaching the place where we sat and talked. He walked along the path, from time to time looking up at the glorious and flawless full moon, then looking down at the river and studying the reflection of the moon in the water. He repeated the movement many times, as one who discovers something and examines its nature.

-Michael, I said to my friend, Look, here comes Adam. My words aroused him from his thoughts and his musings.

Observing Adam for a while, Michael shook his head and said sorrowfully,

-He has understood that the moon is reflected in the river, and soon he will realise that the image in the water is *his* image and he'll cease trying to catch it.

-Perhaps he will also stop chasing his shadow, and find peace of mind, I suggested.

-No, Azi. He will be more miserable and lonely. As long as he thought he might attain what he so much aspired to, there was hope in his heart. Now he will miss that hope itself.

We continued gazing at Adam, looking at what he was doing. He stood at the edge of the river, casting stones into the water. Every time a stone hit the water and made a splashing sound, he imitated the sound with his voice. In the deep silence, the echo of his voice was heard returning to him. Time after time he cried out into the void, and when the echo returned he inclined his ear and listened with rapt attention.

-Here is his new hope, said Michael. Now he will search for the one who is making the echo, hoping to chase after him and to find him.

Suddenly we saw Adam fall on his knees and raise his hands to the sky, his eyes gazing at the moon. Sometimes he looked at it in the sky, sometimes down in the river.

-Look, Michael, what is he doing?

-He is asking the moon to come to his aid.

-Surely the moon is not the Lord, I said.

-Of course, but he does not know that yet, replied Michael.

# Chapter fourteen

On the surface of the water float the bodies of men, of cattle, of birds and beasts of the field. They float on the water in chilling silence. I am the only one left to witness what has happened. I am the only one who can grieve over the devastation. Those imprisoned within the ark, that is drifting calmly on tranquil waters, the tempest now abated, have not yet seen this sight, this desolation. At the present, they are confined in their ark, but when they emerge from it, how will they endure this terrible sight? The body of a child floats at the mouth of the cave. I saw him alive, the day he left his mother's womb, and here he is, silent, floating on the water like the branch of a tree.

# Chapter fifteen

At last the flood has abated. The water has begun to subside and is at last below the level of the mouth of the cave. However, the mountain range is still submerged and there is no dry land, no foothold for the humans or the beasts in the ark. An easterly wind blows, a drying wind, but it will be a long time before the waters subside and return to their usual level. Yet, my heart is once again filled with hope, hope that the ark will still be bearing its living burden when dry land appears from beneath the water.

For one hundred and fifty days I have watched the flood day and night, have heard the surging water wipe out all living things from the face of the earth, have seen the ark tossed by the stormy waves, and doubt has been awakened in my heart. Will this frail wooden shell be able to withstand the tempest and not sink, taking the last of life with it?

During these fretful days I have realized how closely, over the course of ten generations, my life has become entwined with the lives of human beings, and my destiny has touched their destiny. I was indeed sent to them as a witness to what they did, and as a chronicler of their story, but my life has become intertwined with theirs and I cannot view their disappearance with equanimity. Whoever has seen life must recoil from its destruction. Whoever has heard the sounds of laughter and of weeping, the cry of a new-born infant, the voice of a mother soothing her child to sleep, the voice of a man loving a woman, the rustling of the wind in the tree-tops or the murmur of insects and birds as the dawn rises, cannot regard the extinction of these things with equanimity

I dare think to myself, I dare ask the Lord whether a world without life will be a better world, a more just world. It is not for me to answer this question, but at the very least I have the right to ask it.

I have loved human beings ... their wonderment, their constant searching, their changes, contradictions. Curiosity. Even their failures, since from failure to failure they have learned to ascend to a higher plane.

In the ten generations that have passed, one thousand six hundred and eighty-five years, I have contrived to strike deep roots in man and in his earth. Memories of the Garden are alive in me and I feel the absence of Michael every day, but man and his earth were a part of me and my sorrow at their destruction knows no respite. It grieves me that the Lord has unleashed his wrath upon them. Did He do this out of love? Or were His expectations dashed? If the Lord can destroy a loved one who has failed Him, what then will men do, being only the creation of His hand?

I find myself constantly asking, constantly wondering, constantly taking the side of mankind. And yet I am not a mortal, whose fate is to dwell on the earth.

# Chapter sixteen

A shaft of bright light penetrating the cave rouses me from my musings. The great sun of noonday stands high in the sky. I look out from the threshold of my cave and I see a great sea bathed in shining light and I see the ark drifting calmly, serenely. The flood has run its course. Beneath the surface of the calm and translucent waters the mountain ranges can be seen. The light and the tranquillity infuse renewed hope in me, hope that Noah and all those adrift in the ark will soon find a foothold upon the land.

A few days hence, if the waters continue to subside and to recede, I shall go down from my cave to the ark, to see how the sons of Adam and the beasts are faring. In the course of these days, so long as I can do nothing else, I will try to complete my story of the creation of man and his history upon the earth.

## Chapter seventeen

The body of the child is still floating on the water by the mouth of the cave. Every time I approach the threshold to feast my eyes on the glorious spectacle of sunbeams dancing on placid waves, and ripples lapping the rocky cliffs of Ararat, I am confronted by his frozen stare. Such a sight cannot be endured. I know that the child is dead and that breath has fled his body, yet I feel that his eyes are looking at me and demanding an answer to questions that have long troubled me. Was this child a sinner and a destroyer, as well? I have indeed heard the Lord muttering to Himself that the inclination of man's heart is evil from his youth—but what was the offence of this child whose eyes are fixed on mine? You, O Lord, created man, so did You not also create the evil in him?

I remember again the times that I would observe Adam in the Garden; from the day that he chased after his shadow and his reflection in the water to the day he was expelled from the Garden, I followed his progress.

The day Michael told me of the creation of Adam, I recall

sensing that I detected the faintest hint of envy in his voice. Until Adam was created, the senior angels had been the beings closest to the Lord, the first to hear His words, the first to speak to Him. When man was created, in His image and His likeness, he displaced them from their proximity to the Lord. I too envied the sons of Adam, but for other reasons. I envied their ability to devise new things, to change their ways of life, to delve deep into the secrets of the ground, the waters and the sky.

We angels, even the most senior among us, understand only what the Lord has decreed that we understand, whereas man has been given choice. When good is done, in preference to evil, this is a measure of the freedom that we angels do not enjoy. Only man, among all the creations of the Lord, walks by a path that he has carved out for himself. Only he and I still bear within us our longing for the lost Garden.

The loneliness of Adam was his greatest flaw. We saw him chasing mirages, pursuing fantasies, hearing the voice of another in the echo of his own voice and seeking to befriend his shadow. This loneliness worried me. I had Michael, and whom did he have? Solitary, Adam was solitary. And I did not envy this solitude.

# Chapter eighteen

For whose sake am I now writing the history of mankind? He who sent me surely does not need my words in order to know and to remember all that has happened. He, who sees what was and what is and what shall be, He will know without consulting my chronicle. Among the angels, there is no one in whose eyes the deeds of man are worthy of the attention of even a fleeting moment. Each has his task to perform, each has his own concerns. Michael is the only one who might perhaps read these words, if he could, knowing that I had written them.

So, for whose sake is it? Only for the sake of man himself. I am writing for him, and this is the Lord's will. Memory, transferred in ten generations from father to son and from son to his son, like layer upon layer, stratum upon stratum, is a thing that flows and does not pass away, like those four rivers issuing from the eternal river in the Garden. Memory, flowing from the Garden, also makes man and the earth fruitful.

Since the flood ended, I have felt a strong desire to go down to the ark and to see the human beings and the beasts confined there. They are the only ones on whose behalf I write, they are the only ones in whom there remains a memory of things that were. How are they faring in the ark? Has hunger afflicted them, or the ravages of disease? Perhaps they have lost their minds, perhaps they have taken their own lives, or the lives of one another.

Again, when I think of the loneliness of Adam in the Garden, and of who relieved him of his isolation, I am reassured. I know that the Lord will preserve Noah. But it is only when I receive the signal from Him to go down to the ark that I shall do so. Such is the nature of angels.

# Chapter nineteen

Even when angels desire to do something, or to refrain from it, it is not their own will power that moves them. The will of the Lord alone determines their actions and their inactions. Michael taught me what is permitted and what is forbidden, although this was implanted in us in our very nature as angels. From Michael I learned of the angels, of their status and degrees, of their tasks and their qualities. From his lips I heard about his fellow senior angels, who stand in the presence of the Lord, as close as they are allowed.

Raphael is the quickest and most agile of all the Lord's angels, he sets out with immeasurable speed for the furthest recesses of the universe whenever some flaw is revealed that is invisible to the eye or intangible to any of the senses. At the prompting of the Lord, he detects it immediately. Day by day, hour by hour, hidden channels are open whereby messages are conveyed between the stars. And if there is a hint of a deviation that has not yet happened, or a schism that has not yet befallen, or a conflict as yet unborn, the Lord signals at once to Raphael to set forth, to repair and to return in the twinkling of an eye. He is the healer, the repairer, the comforter, he is the open eye of the Lord surveying his infinite universe.

The enthusiasm, with which Michael described the work of Raphael, ignited a similar passion in me and I too was excited, perhaps even more than he. Here is an angel who knows the most distant corners of the heavens, the vaults and the cavities, here is an angel who sees all the wonders of the universe, from the most minute to the greatest.

As I grew into maturity, and my eyes were opened and my interests widened, my desires and longings were aroused and many were the things of which I sought to gain knowledge: spaces, distances, faraway suns and wonders close at hand, such as the blooming of a flower or the chirp of a fledgling. How many are the miracles, which even the angels, who are limitless, cannot contain. But yearning gives no respite even when intelligence knows that the whole cannot be contained by anything other than the whole, which is the Lord. Yet even in yearning there is gladness, and for this the Lord be praised.

-And who is Gabriel? I went on to ask, when Michael had finished speaking in praise of Raphael. I saw hesitation in his face, and I understood that with Gabriel it is necessary to stop and to think. Unlike Raphael, who invites only praise, Gabriel invites hesitation, although it is clearly evident that all he does, he does at the Lord's behest.

-If I am to tell you about Gabriel, I need to choose my words with care, he replied. Gabriel bears a sword, a sharp and gleaming sword, a symbol of destruction. On him the Lord has enjoined the most onerous of tasks. His duty is to destroy what the Lord has created but is constrained to destroy in order to preserve His creation.

I listened carefully to Michael's words; he not only spoke carefully, but I could also hear him weigh out each word as he spoke it, conscious of saying nothing that would blur the fine line which separates creation from destruction. Once again I was privileged to witness the secret of contradictions, between which only the Lord can walk unharmed.

-At the time of Creation, Michael continued, the Lord took the darkness and moulded it into light, He took the dust and breathed into it the breath of life, He took the raging tempests and harnessed them to be the motive power of stars and suns, He took the void and created the skies, the continents and the seas. But all that had been before did not disappear. Those things are constantly striving to break free and return to their former condition. Gabriel's task is to patrol the frontiers between what exists and what must not, between the harnessed and the untamed, between the will of the Lord and rebellion against Him.

As he spoke I sensed he was drawing me up, promoting me from step to step, bringing me closer to the highest of degrees, closer to himself, closer to the circle in which the Lord resides.

Despite the mild giddiness in my head I asked: Is the Lord incapable then of ruling over all, the darkness, the void, the forces of destruction?

-Aziel, I cannot describe how dear you are to me, he replied. It may be that what I say to you, you are not yet capable of understanding, but it is good that you hear the word so you may ponder it and grow with it. Everything that rebels against the Lord is a part of Him, since He is both destroyer and creator.

I heard his words, and knew that opening before me was a very long road strewn with wonders and mysteries, questions with no answer, hesitations and doubts. Would I have the strength for all of this? Even today, when there is devastation all around me and the water that was created to sustain life on the land has destroyed it, I am hardly nearer to understanding the purpose of the deeds of the Lord the destroyer.

-This is the nature of the sword and this is the nature of Gabriel, Michael went on to say. He is the power, the muscle in the service of the Lord. Sometimes he even smites those who are innocent of any offence. Such power is exceedingly painful, even to the one who wields it. I do not know if Gabriel understands and feels the pain and the suffering that his sword inflicts. When I have tried to speak with him of this, he has evaded my questions, saying only, and saying firmly, that this is the will of the Lord and he does not meditate on His will.

-I was created to smite, and I smite. I was created to bear the sword and I unsheathe it, I came into the world to cast fear and to terrify. Who am I that I should think? I obey His word as you obey His word. Yours in the more pleasant part, you are his emissary for joy, prosperity, creativity, for smiles and goodness and grace. I am the emissary of his anger, his vengeance, His jealousy. I was created to serve the power and the might of the Lord. So he tells me.

-And why, I dared to ask, did the Lord not create a world that was all good, a world without evil and destruction?

Michael was stunned by my words. He looked around him to be sure no one had overheard me, and was relieved to find we were sitting alone on the bank of the river with its gentle flow and soft, relaxing sounds.

-Azi, it takes great courage to admit that you do not know. I do not know how to answer your question, and I doubt I ever will.

We were silent a long time. A wise silence, rather solemn but comforting. I already knew that with this question I had ascended the ladder of degrees. I had reached the degree of doubt.

# Chapter twenty

Of Lillith he did not speak. Why was Michael silent on this one subject? After all, he spoke at length when describing the senior angels, the Seraphim and the Cherubim, when telling me of Samael the rebel and the angels of wrath, of Asmodeus the wicked and of Satan the cunning trickster, of hatred challenging the forbearance of the Lord. Only where Lillith was concerned was he silent. Why? Perhaps he feared to revive the memory of something difficult he had experienced with her, or perhaps he wanted to protect me and to preserve my innocence. Was he concerned for the clarity of my vision, in my observation of the ways of male and female, among the creatures I had seen? Bird descends upon bird, lion mounts lioness, buck leaps upon doe and clings to her— sights, which astonished me, no more than all the other marvels surrounding me. Everything was simple, and everything marvellous. Stars of the sky in their orbits are simple and marvellous; a blade of grass is simple and marvellous. Everything astounded my intelligence and my senses, and everything was intricate and astonishingly simple, coming from the Lord and his creation.

So why had Michael omitted to mention Lillith? Had he preferred that I find out by myself?

As I thought this over, I put forward numerous questions to myself, but not one of them satisfied me. Only when I realized how mighty and prodigious was the power of Lillith, did the thought occur to me that Michael was protecting his love for me. Perhaps he feared that this power of hers seduce me, too, estranging me from him.

For whatever reason, Michael made no mention of her, and I found her by myself. Michael and I spend much time in one another's company, but sometimes he was busy with his duties for a few hours and I would wander among the paths of the Garden. I studied the behaviour of the animals, and, after meeting Adam—I would study his behaviour too. I learned from watching the ways of living things, the flight of winged creatures, the industriousness of tiny insects, the agility of fish in the water and everything that came my way.

One day, as I walked among the bushes of the Garden, there wafted towards me an unfamiliar scent. It was a pungent smell, and I sensed that it had the power to derange my peace of mind. I felt some force harnessed to the roots of my being and drawing me to places unknown to me. Concealed desires called out to me. I looked around me. Everything was as yesterday and as the day before. Flowers bloomed in their beds, bushes were in full foliage, a gentle breeze stirred the treetops and caressed the leaves. I detected nothing that I had not known before, and yet the urgency of this pungent perfume pervaded everything. I left the open path and stepped deeper into the dense undergrowth. A shady clearing drew my attention. As I approached, the heady perfume growing ever stronger in my nostrils, I saw her.

She lay upon Gabriel, he embracing and pressing her to his body. Both were moving rhythmically, up and down and from side to side, uttering sighs and moans and small groans and wordless noise. Lillith's wings were spread, stunning in their splendour.

Gold, purple, blue and yellow, periodically they twitched and fluttered to the rhythm of the groans. Her back rose and fell at regular intervals, until from the mouths of both of them issued a long, extended moan, repeated until it eventually subsided. Gabriel's sword lay sheathed by his side. I could have taken it and he would have noticed nothing, his head buried in her breasts. Engrossed in Lillith's voluptuous body, Gabriel was quite oblivious of his surroundings.

When I met Michael, I told him what I had seen. He looked at me a long time and said, So you have seen her, Azi, and now you know.

-I have seen her, I said, but what is it that I need to know?

-About Lillith and her powers, he said.

-Which powers do you mean, Michael? Didn't you say that power is the domain of Gabriel?

-Yes, I said that. But you have seen his power melt before the power of Lillith. His power is in his arm, but hers is everywhere. Her power seduces, stuns, intoxicates and robs of his senses anyone who lusts for her. With your own eyes you've seen it, and as you yourself said, that you could have taken his sword with impunity. His sword without his arm is nothing other than a useless rod of iron, and his arm without his sword is just as ineffectual. What is Gabriel without his sword? Another angel, the equal of his many inferiors. Gabriel is the only one to whom the Lord has given male potency, and Lillith is the only one in whom the Lord has implanted the powers of fertility, desire, rapture. Her power is astounding. It flows through all the channels of life. There is no living creature in creation, from the tiniest to the greatest, such as the Leviathan or the Behemoth, in which you will not find the harvest that flows from this torrential river. Lillith is the propagator of desire, of the yearning to be as one, to return to the beginning, the source of Creation, fountain of new life. At the very moment of Creation, her power is no less than the power of the Creator, and there is no escape and no hiding from her.

-In the world of the angels, he continued, she inspires envy, even wonder, as she mocks their impotence, their angelic sterility. The angels look at her and do not understand the source of her power, her overwhelming attraction, her intemperate youth, and her majesty. She is both princess and mistress. The angels look at her and they see her enticing smile, and they do not respond to it since they have nothing with which to respond. Yet every tiniest living creature knows how to respond—effervescing, running, parading its beauty, spreading wings, raising tails, changing colours, with smouldering eyes or their whole body aflame—wooing, winking, preening proudly, revealing and revelling in the secrets that the Lord has implanted in them.

The passion in his voice betrayed the desire for something he could never attain. After a short silence he continued in a more soothing tone:

-That is why they scorn her, spread rumours and malign her. When you hear it said that she is the mother of devils and evil spirits, pay no heed to all this. The Lord is the source of her power, and the Lord loves her. She is his emissary for life, she opens the way to the future of generations to come, and how should the Lord not love her, He who desires fertility and increase?

Just from the way he was talking, I understood that there was a special place in his heart for Lillith. Could this be called love? He loved her although her power had no influence over angels, and although he was not commanded to be fruitful and to multiply. Michael's love was of another kind, a love dependent on nothing, not in the desire for the fusing of body with body, as it was with other creatures of creation. They, the others, were seeking the part of themselves that was missing, the part needed to make them whole, and Lillith had the power to bring them together. But Michael loved her for her prodigious might, for her feminine beauty, for her dominion and perhaps also for her proximity to the love of the Lord. He did not envy this love, for he knew that what Lillith brings about is all for the sake of the prosperity and harmony of the universe.

-We senior angels, Michael said, we are subject to what exists now, and to this alone. But Lillith has earned the power to mould the future.

When I recall the wonders revealed to me by Michael, the Lord's concern for establishing order, for the Law of Creation and for the flame of life that is not to be extinguished, when I think of Lillith, the bearer of life from the beginning into the future, the question rises again to my lips: Lord, are you destroying all this in your anger? All these wonders—have you condemned them all to extinction?

Past and present are confused in me, memories of the past and actions in the present flash equally before my eyes. When I look at the ark, I am also witness to my beginnings in the Garden, to my love for Michael, for Lillith the enchantress, and most of all, for Adam—his destiny, his experiences, his life, his defeats, his failures throughout the ten generations that have elapsed. And his heroism that has overcome the adversities in his path.

I remember the first stone that was used as a plough, to break up the solid ground. I recall Adam's joy when he discovered new life had been created on the day that he knew Eve, his wife; and I remember their grief and pain when they saw their son Abel stiff and lifeless, when they first encountered death. I see before my eyes the first fire that Adam devised by striking flints, and the first fruits of the land, the labour of their hands and the sweat of their brow. Lord, Lord, give me understanding, that I may understand Your works and Your purpose.

## Chapter twenty-one

From the day that Michael described the power of Lillith to me and told me all of the stories and whispers woven about her, I sought her out. Although I was not endowed with the faculty of responding to her appeals or lusting for her favours, there was aroused in me a most profound curiosity; I wanted to look at her and to observe her actions. She was so extraordinary, so different, so laden with secrets and with mysteries. Of all the things I had heard about her from Michael, her pursuit of Adam since the day of his creation astonished me the most.

She is of course an angel, and cannot be seen. Adam will never see her. For him she will remain an aspiration that can never be satisfied; and as for her, she will lust for him, but to no avail. Though he will lust for her, but they can never be one flesh, as she was with Gabriel or as Adam will be with Eve. Yearning will accompany the lives of the sons of men and will fill their imaginations. Yearning will both nourish and starve their souls, inflame and deceive, awaken fantasies and desires. Yearning will disguise itself and put on jewellery, arouse tempests and speak in whispers, ignite imaginary suns, utter sounds sweet as the chanting of the angels before the Lord—and never come to fruition in the creation of life.

A few days after my conversation with Michael about Lillith, I met her again. I was on the path leading down to the river and suddenly my nostrils were invaded by the heady scent that told me she was close at hand.

I thought I would find her lying with Gabriel, and looked all around. She was hovering above the cliff that jutted out into the river, and her image was also reflected in the ripples of the water beneath her, wing above wing, body above body, splendid, proud and beautiful. And, as I looked, she continued to hover and float, hover and bath in the pure water. I could not help but stare at Lillith's beauty, feeling a painful sense of deprivation— deprived as I was of the instinct that drives and is driven towards the creative sources of life. I looked at her with sorrow. I wished I had been given the faculties to respond to her enticements.

At first I thought she was alone, hovering above the waters of the river. But Adam was there. When I saw him, I realized he, too, had been searching for the source of her powerful scent. He ran from bush to bush, looked all around him, turned over stones, clambered up the steep cliff-face and slid down into a deep cavern. He was restless, as if he must be constantly changing position— standing, or lying, his ear to the ground, gazing up at the sky. Then he took a long branch and probed the water. I saw his male member growing erect, while his female genitalia faded away to nothing. From time to time he held his member and let it go, clutching and releasing by turns, as if seeking relief. All the while, Lillith was drifting above his head, spraying him with her astonishing, intoxicating perfume, arousing Adam's fantasies and daydreams.

Adam lashed out about him. I saw tears trickling from his eyes. His lust was blended with his weariness and his pitiable solitude. With whom could he speak, to whom bring his pain?

With whom could he share his agitation and to whom turn in his distress? So alone, Lord, this most glorious of Your creatures was so alone. Did You not see, did You not witness his discomfiture?

Lillith hovered above him, all but touching his body. The final hair's breadth separating them was an unbridgeable gulf. The Lord has set a boundary between the two worlds, and only at His express command could an angel cross over it.

Adam pressed himself to the ground, and hugged it. His manhood dissolved, seed gushing from his body and moistening the handful of dust beneath him. And so he repaid his debt to the earth, from which he had been formed when the Lord had taken a handful of the earth's dust to create him.

When I told Michael about what I had seen, he said that life would not be created by this act:

-Adam's potency will avail him nothing unless he has a mate, and in all the universe there is no such thing. Only the Lord can create her, and if He does not, Adam shall be alone forever.

## Chapter twenty-two

After what I had witnessed, I reflected that I might have been his friend, if only I could have been revealed to him, spoken with him, told him of the wonders I had seen and heard from his lips of his pain and his sorrow. We could have been like brothers. But the Lord had created the world as He created it. Adam will dream of angels and angels will lust for Adam, and the Lord will divide them.

That night the moon rose full over the Garden. The shadows born of the light were short and close at hand. The light, pale as the milk of suckling mothers, drew in the colour from the green and red and blue shades of the flowers, and everything that grew and sprouted and rose from the earth slumbered in a dream. Only scents of perfume now wafted from the many blooming flowers.

Again I was aware of the pungent scent of Lillith. She hovered in the air, from time to time moving her wings very slowly, her eyes fixed on the flowerbeds and her wings embracing something invisible. From her full breasts oozed drops of milk blended with myrrh. I stopped, and on her face I saw a loving and comforting smile, a smile of charm and desire.

For whom is she waiting, I wondered? I saw her enfolding the air, the scents of the Garden and the white of the moon in her wings. I followed the direction of her gaze and saw Adam curled up like a foetus in the womb, in a deep sleep beneath a bush rich in flowers and in perfume, dreaming of Lillith. He embraced her, kissed her, caressed her body and sucked her milk, as she played gently with the curls of his hair, rocking him this way and that, singing softly:

-Sleep, sleep, my child, my child and my lord. Lillith, queen of the night, is watching over you.

In their dream they had come together and blended, becoming one flesh. I moved away; I sensed that my place was not with these dreamers. Yet, don't dreams also come from the Lord, I mused to myself? Perhaps dreams are the gate that man has opened for himself, giving access to the Lord. Or, perhaps it is through the window of dreams man can escape, the Lord's ever open and watchful eye. Angels do not dream, so it is hard for me to understand what dreaming does to mankind.

I did not tell Michael of the dream that Adam had dreamt. Would he read it in my face, as he had read the effects of my first meeting with him?

*Chapter twenty-three*

The floodwaters continue to subside. From day to day the surface of the water recedes from the mouth of the cave and soon the range of mountains will rise above them. Now the water is clear and calm. The easterly wind has dropped and is no longer stirring up and agitating the face of the water, and the ark drifts on a gentle swell. All morning Noah has been peering through the window of the ark to see if the flood levels are still falling. I've seen him look around him, waving his hand to check the direction of the wind before again taking refuge within. The patch of dry land that is now visible on the mountaintop is bare of all vegetation.

I caught a glimpse of Noah's gloomy features. In his eyes there was only weariness and exhaustion, not even a spark of relief at his own survival and that of his family. What had kept him alive those many months, enclosed in the ark, while the world around him had been utterly devastated? What had kept him going while life was extinguished and all vegetation devastated, and the ark had been buffeted around him by the waves, without the sight of landfall and without hope? Did Noah draw comfort from the knowledge that all this was the will of the Lord? Did the meagre cargo of life that he carried with him inspire him with strength?

Silence reigns in the universe. The waves and the winds are hushed. A world without voice, a world without sound and echo, a world that has died. Where are the fishes, the denizens of the deep? Have the drowned corpses of beasts and humankind poisoned the waters as well, destroying all life in them? My thoughts wander from the Days of Creation to the Days of Destruction, back and forth, back and forth. I'd like to find answers to the many questions which trouble my repose.

Again I think of Michael. Then ten generations ago, and it seems as if only yesterday I had begun to count them. I had someone to turn to in my distress, someone to give me advice, someone to lean on. The loneliness that has descended on me with the Flood is more than I can bear. Only the testimony that I must record preserves my sanity. I cannot even seek refuge in death, and now more than ever, I feel the burden and heavy weight of immortality. When will a command come from the Lord to go down to the ark, to see what has befallen the remnants of life? This, too, is my duty to describe.

I have just measured how far the waters have fallen. Perhaps a month from now there will be a greater expanse of dry land, perhaps the sun and the water will generate new plant life for the pasturing of animals. There are hard words in my heart. Bitter thoughts fill my mind, and I cannot dispel them. I do not rebel against You, Lord, for what would my rebellion achieve? But I cannot dispel these hard and bitter thoughts against You, Lord.

This silent universe is not the silent and glorious universe of the seventh day of Creation, when the angels stood and stared in amazement at Adam, the creature You had made in Your image. And then, as Michael told me, they began to sing the song of Creation, the paean of praise to life, and they sang of the glories of heaven and earth and of all their hosts. And You, Lord, looked around You and saw what You had created, and You breathed future into life, and You gave joy to all living things. You said that it was good.

And then, when the day was sinking, when the sun was setting for the sixth time since its creation, You blessed the seventh day and dedicated it to rest and repose. That day You set up the seventh pillar of the universe, the pillar of the soul, the soul and all that is in it—thoughts, impressions, hope and despair, joy and sorrow, vision and imagination, the inclination to good and the inclination to evil, lusts and desires. On the seventh day, Lord, when You finished all the work that You had done, Your spirit was fused into the soul of Adam. And You Lord rested from all Your labours.

And now, beneath the depths of the waters, thickets and forests, bushes and grassy plains all lie buried under avalanches and landslides of loose stones and boulders and rocks from the mountains that have been eroded and swept away . . . all of life in one great tomb.

Will Noah be able to emerge from all this calamity and ruin? Will his sons uphold the duty that their father has taken upon himself, of starting anew the history of mankind upon the earth?

No, Lord, I do not cast doubt on Your promise, but I cast doubt on Noah's ability to fulfil it.

# Chapter twenty-four

One day Michael said to me, his eyes bright with happiness.

-Aziel, it has come to pass!

-What has come to pass?

I did not understand why he was so joyful.

-I have been commanded to prepare you for your encounter with the Lord. Evidently that day is close at hand.

I was filled with wonder. It had never crossed my mind that one day I should be summoned to His presence. Then, a mighty wave of dread washed over my soul. I felt I was choking, and even my wings palpitated as if in the grip of fever.

I recovered sufficiently to stammer, Why me?

Michael smiled faintly,

-Perhaps it is because of the dream that you saw? What I tell you now, you *must* remember. The Lord is never seen. No one can see Him and live. Perhaps long ago, at a time before the past was the past, before the light, the chosen of the chosen saw Him, perhaps Samael, perhaps the abyss itself. Nothing is known about this, so about this we shall not speak. What we, the senior angels see, is the flame from the midst of which a voice speaks to us. Is this the voice of the Lord? It is not known. They say that the Lord has neither form nor voice. The only thing I know is that I do not know. We feel His power, we obey His commandments, heed His prohibitions and do His will. He says and He does, and all things around you tell of His greatness. The sky that hangs above your head and does not collapse, the stars that are hung in the sky and do not drop into the abyss, the sun that rises every morning at one end of the firmament and sets in the evening at the opposite end of the heavens, never erring in time or in direction. Or the rivers that spring from their sources and flow down toward the seas—the entirety of life that is singing hymns of praise around you—these are the heartbeats of the Lord, these are His footprints on the cosmos, these are the sparks of His light. The flame that you will see and the voice that you will hear are only the place and the means. They are not the Lord Himself.

Michael's voice was husky with excitement. He paused, then, slightly calmer, resumed:

-I shall accompany you. Do not fear, no harm will befall you. The Lord takes care of those to whom He turns. When you approach the flame, stop at my signal. The place where the flame burns is the holiest of all holy places. You must not step too close to it, nor breach the invisible circle. When you feel a shudder rising from your feet to your head, you will know you have reached the limit, and there you must stop. Do not utter a sound until you are called upon to speak, and do not turn your back on the flame. When you are leaving, walk backwards, facing the flame. When you are called, we shall both go down to the crystal river, to bathe and be purified. We shall wash away the dust, and you will be worthy to meet Him.

# Chapter twenty-five

That same day Michael instructed me in the art of "letters", teaching me to read and to write. It was a day full of wonders. My mentor led me to a distant place, facing a smooth and polished wall of stone. Grooves had been carved into the stones of the wall. He took from under a dense and gnarled tree a pile of tablets, on each of which was a different symbol. He called these symbols "letters".

The first word with which he started the miraculous journey towards literacy was LORD. From this we progressed further, using the letters and their combinations to open up paths of learning, which I never knew existed.

At the close of the day, as the sun inclined towards the West and suffused the wall with a mellow, kindly light, I took the tablets and put together the letters of the words I LOVE MICHAEL. When he read this sentence he burst into glorious, heartening laughter and spread his wings above my head. I was happy. I had obtained a treasure beyond calculation, and before me a door had been opened to new worlds. I had risen in the angelic hierarchy and had now drawn so much closer to the fountainhead of memory.

Michael gave me to understand that there was a hidden and closely guarded store of memories inscribed in stone; and that few were entitled to approach and to draw from the store. Only those taught to read were able to make use of the memory of things written. From this day on I was to be numbered among the privileged. Hallelujah!

I fell into a deep sleep beside Michael and at dawn we went down together to the crystal river. We bathed and were purified and were ready.

# Chapter twenty-six

Engrossed as I was in faraway memories of things that had happened in the Garden, I failed to notice that the water had receded still further. The mountain range was already spread out around me in its entirety. The traces of destruction were like deep wounds in the body of the earth. From the outset of the flood, torrents of water had swept away the soil that once covered the rocks, giving them fertility and a covering of green. Uprooted plants and trees snapped like twigs by the pressure of the water, piles of rubble and the skeletons of beasts turned a place that had once teemed with life into the valley of the shadow of death.

The ark drifts around the exposed summit. What is happening in it now? The people inside were surely waiting for the moment when Noah would dare to open the hatch and when they might emerge from the floating prison, from the home in which they had been incarcerated for so many months. Did food still remain for the humans and the beasts inside it? And when they stepped out onto dry land, would both man and beast find enough there to nourish themselves until the ravaged land again produced grass and shrubs and fruits?

Watching the devastation emerging from the depths I begin to understand the wisdom of the Lord, when he created Adam from the dust of the earth. In this dust are stored all the fundamentals of the universe: Hebrew: sun and water, light and darkness, rain and wind, heat and cold, chill rock and blazing volcano— all converge in this dust. All the wonders of the Lord's great universe are stored in a single grain, and the image and the likeness of the Lord are reflected from it. And now, when the soil is ravaged and eroded, washed into the abyss or swept away by the torrential waters to the salty seas, will this land live again? Only You know, Lord, You alone know.

The ark has drifted against an exposed spur of rock. Patches of dry land have started to appear on the summits of the hills. Soon the ark can settle on solid ground, no longer to be tossed like a leaf by every breath of wind. High up in the bare cliff face is the mouth of my cave, and from this vantage point I look out on the ark, waiting for a signal to go down and see what is happening there. The signal has not come. Not yet.

I wonder if Noah will have enough patience and enough strength to resist those who are urging him to leave the ark too soon? This scrap of land is not capable of sustaining even the few living creatures that have survived. If the survivors emerge too soon, in their hunger they will prey on one another.

Below me a window has opened. Cautiously and slowly; now a hand emerges through the window, hesitant, probing. The hand of Noah is a hand expressing wisdom, caution and patience. The Lord be thanked for the wisdom He has given to man. After the hand has probed and tested, touching the air and the wind, Noah's upper body appears at the window. I am stunned by how much he has aged, and how tired he looks. Deep wrinkles score his face, which is shrouded by the hair of his unkempt beard. All the reverence and the dignity, which had marked him out until so recently, which had earned him respect and admiration among the inhabitants of the valley of the palms, have yielded to sadness and dejection. Noah's features tell a story of a prolonged and all but despairing struggle, of exhaustion and of the supreme effort of keeping going until the very last moment. Every crease and every wrinkle is an imprint that bears witness to the past months' hardship and affliction.

I felt compassion mingled with great respect for the ark's master mariner; for the man who has endured all these things and refused to submit to them. Not for nothing did they call you righteous, Noah, a truly righteous and innocent man. For Noah, it is not only in your own generation that you are so outstanding, so perfectly innocent—but who, save for you, in all the generations that have elapsed since then, could have borne a burden like the journey that you undertook? For you never once left your God throughout this fearful voyage, and you were not bowed. The entirety of life was entrusted into your hands, my brother, all the life that the Lord—and may He forgive me my bitter words— that the Lord abhorred. For Noah, the Lord entrusted you with the burden of life, with all the good and the evil that is in it, all that is lovely and loathsome, true and false, generous and rapacious; all the instincts and the lusts, the despair and the hope . . . All these the Lord abhorred, and He disowned their creation. All these He placed in your hands, Noah my brother, and you walked with God in grace, in compassion and in justice. It is no wonder they called you "Noah the Innocent". Who else could have taken on such an awesome mission, the saving of life from utter destruction?

I love you, Noah my brother, I am filled with love for you even as I see how you struggle so painfully to unlatch the window, with the last ounce of your strength. If only I could reach out and help you . . .

In Noah's hand a black bird flutters. I see it is a raven cradled between his fingers. Noah turns to the four corners of the heavens, to find the direction from which the wind is blowing. A westerly wind, light and gentle. Noah directed the raven's head in it's direction and the raven beats its wings, impatient to break through to the wide open spaces of the sky, to the light of which he had been deprived for so many months, to the air that will give freedom and flight to his wings.

I was entranced by the spectacle of the force of such desire, and even how such desire could have lasted and been fostered despite the darkness, despite the foul and stifling air in the ark, despite the meagre food, despite incarceration. How freedom fluttered between his wings, how there could burst from his frail little body such lust for liberty and for space, how everything that had been dormant, paralysed, choked and defeated, could rise in an instant and live again. I was astonished to see how this tiny body could encompass the energy of the entire universe.

This wondrous sight restored faith to my heart. The other living creatures in the ark, on reaching dry land, on touching the pure springs of water, the blue of the sky and the brightness of the light—they too would break loose, break loose and once again fill the land with their clamour.

The raven in Noah's hand uttered a wild and abandoned shriek. Its sharp, abrupt call cleft the air with a succession of short, unembellished notes, shattering the oppressive silence, which had settled months before on the face of the universe. This was an alarm call, a battle cry, and a yelp of triumph. It rolled across the water, struck the bare rocks and returned as an echo, rolling away again and finally disappearing in the deep fissures of the sky. My heart rejoiced. Sounds of life would once again be heard, sounds other than the thunder and the roaring of the waves lashing angrily at the shore and the shriek of tornado winds—all the agents of destruction and harbingers of the end. It was as if the cry of the raven rose from the very depths of life. Suddenly the raven broke free from Noah's grasp; then it rose once, descended a little, then rose a second time, as if gathering strength, flexing its wings, and, mustering courage, set out with even more raucous cries above the wastes of water. The bird circled the ark once, and then yet again, almost landing on the head of Noah, who followed his flight with a look of concern, curiosity and love. From the expression on Noah's face it was clear that he had released the black bird with both trepidation and hope.

And the raven wheeled and circled, diving down to the surface of the water and rising again to the skies, Noah's eyes following him as if attached by an invisible thread. His long white beard stirred in the gentle breeze, and every time the raven approached the window of the ark, Noah waved his arms to send him away. The bird widened still further the range of his wheeling flight. In ever widening circles he flew, already accustomed to the light and unafraid of its intensity, searching for land and a place to alight. But the only dry ground that had risen from the depths was very high. I was afraid that in spite of this he would try to soar to heights beyond the range of his powers, flying so far away he would be unable to return. I wanted to warn him, but could not do so since I was an angel whose voice cannot be heard by mortal ears. The warning cries choked in my throat. How I longed at that moment to be like the raven, flying at his side, warning him to steer him away from death: Raven, you've survived for so many months! So much hope has been placed in you—don't fly higher than your strength permits, for you alone can ensure the future of your species! Do not disappear, do not perish, I cried, my cries remaining unheard in my heart and my throat.

The bird again uttering his screeching cries, then all at once soared away and was gone. I felt my heart constrict with fear. Had it crashed into the rocks? Had its strength given out, had he fallen into the depths, had he climbed to heights beyond his range, had his breath failed him? I looked around me, and then I saw him again.

He was bathing in the shallow water that covered a rocky outcrop. From all of this great sea surrounding him, he had found a muddy pool where he could disport himself, slake his thirst and satisfy his yearning for contact with water, which for months he had been allowed only a few drops. Again a wave of hope and of gladness swept over me. The instinctive wisdom, which the Creator had implanted in this humble creature at its creation, enabled it to navigate a course that kept it to the path of life, and avoided the perilous. It had indeed soared, but instinct guided him to stop at the correct height and not fly on to his death. After frisking for a while in the water, the raven rose, saw Noah at the window of the ark, recognised his guardian and protector and flew into his outstretched hands. Noah caressed his feathers, held him to his heart and admitted him once again to the ark.

## Chapter twenty-seven

Destruction happened quickly, but the rescue was slow. In the space of but a few days so many human lives were destroyed. The weak, the old, women and children were the first to be swept away. Those who could hurriedly scramble to the hilltops, the young and the strong, kept themselves alive a few days longer, but eventually, neither did they escape disaster. The retreat of the water was exceedingly slow.

After the raven's flight, Noah closed the ark's hatch, and again I saw the vessel sealed and impenetrable. How many days would the master mariner wait, before checking again to see if it were possible to disembark his passengers on dry land? My belief that the ark would ultimately find a secure mooring was strengthened, yet from time to time my anxieties and doubts welled up again. Supposing the rains are renewed, suppose the windows of heaven opened again? Surely, day by day, the provisions in the ark were being depleted, and surely the surrounding water was filled with deadly poison, and the creatures in the ark, scenting dry land close at hand, were liable to stampede, trampling in their path the weaker among them.

Suddenly, on the verge of the end of the ark's journey, I was assailed by doubts and by dark, menacing ideas. Just as I was recording my testimony, I also had to record the despair of waiting for deliverance.

# Chapter twenty-eight

I knew that one day the Lord would impose his mission on me. I knew the word "mission", but I did not fully understand it. Since arriving in the Garden I had learned new words every day. Every new word added to those I had learned already was connected to a thing, an action, something in my surroundings. I could understand and remember its meaning on the basis of its function or shape, and thus I learned and also remembered what I learned. But the task that the Lord was about to entrust to me was one of which I was completely ignorant and I had no conception what it might require.

-Mission? What kind of a mission?

-Mission means "sending". The Lord sends and you are sent, Michael explained.

-Yes, that I understand, but what will I have to do? Where will the Lord send me? Why have I been judged worthy of this, the smallest and meanest of his servants? If the mission is hard, will I be equipped to cope with it? And if it is very important, where shall I find the knowledge and the wisdom to ensure that I do not fail?

-Azi, Azi. Do you still not understand that in the eyes of the Lord no one is great or small, wise or foolish? If He chooses you, you will find all the wisdom you need to justify His choice, and if the burden is too heavy for you, your strength will be increased so you may bear it. It is for the one who is chosen to accept his mission with all his heart. He must be prepared to be lonely, enduring derision and abandonment, and most of all, he must not forget who sent him, where he was sent and why he was sent.

After Michael had spoken, we were both quiet for a while, thinking. Finally I broke the silence:

-Michael my dear friend, have *you* ever been chosen? Has the Lord imposed a mission on you?

-No, he replied. You see, my son? Not everyone is worthy. You are worthy. In his voice I heard both pride and regret.

I wanted to tell him that all his life was a story of missions and of choosing, that he was one of the few who served the Lord at close quarters, one of the few allowed to approach the Presence. But something inside me, something obscure, told me, Hush, do not say this, for his case is not at all like yours. He was created for his purpose, his angelic status and the place where he is situated are inseparable. Nothing startling had ever happened to him. Just as he was created, so he serves the Lord. He cannot be otherwise. He stands in the place in which he was created to stand, tall and upright and proud. This is not by choice; it is simply how he was created. Does he not long to know and to feel, if only once, that the Lord has turned His attention to him, sees him, is aware of his existence, trusts in his competence and believes in his strength, saying, He shall be my envoy, it is him that I have chosen? This is a moment to which many aspire but few attain. Whereas I, as insignificant as a mere grain of dust, expelled from the orbit of the sun, did not know and did not aspire, I could never have imagined nor envisaged such grace.

Hush, hush, lest you cause pain to your friend. Even in loving words there is the power to hurt and to wound. Silence is best when the ways of the Lord are hidden from our eyes.

# Chapter twenty-nine

One day, at the hour of sunset, we were sitting on the bank of the river, observing the halo of light adorned with the colours of the evening. The fringes of the sun all but touched the surface of the water. The two orbs of light, in fiery crimson, told the story that was repeated day by day, yet never ceased to command my enraptured attention. After all, I used to be up there, and with my own hands I drew this ball from east to west until it touched the dark sea beneath us. With my thousands of fellow Uriels I had pulled and dragged the sun and yet then I had been unaware of how much glory and splendour, fire and beauty, I was hauling day after day at the Lord's behest. Only from here, from this shaded Garden with its limpid springs and pools, from the banks of the crystal river, could I now marvel at the deed that my former brothers were performing. As the days have passed since I arrived in the Garden, so these shadowy figures have dimmed from my memory. They seem to me so far away that only the sun remains, suspended above my head, or as now, sinking with a final glow of grace and benevolence.

Had I been asked at that moment what I most wished for, without hesitation I would have replied: Let me stay forever with my friend and brother Michael, here in the Garden, where all is calm and perpetually serene!

Yet I had neither been asked, nor invited to express my preference. The Lord chooses, and He has chosen on my behalf. Suddenly, standing before us was a Cherub, one of those who are sometimes entrusted with errands in the name of the Lord. He brought us a command: both Michael and I were to make our way at dawn the next day to the Garden of Gardens, to stand in the presence of the Lord.

-The time has come, said Michael when the Cherub had departed. Tomorrow the Lord will explain your mission to you.

Although I had known this moment would arrive, I was alarmed.

-Can it be so soon? I asked Michael.

-Evidently the time has come. If the Lord is calling us, then indeed the time has come.

I was very much afraid. What lay in store for me? Perhaps all that was happening to me was nothing but a dream, and when I awoke I would find myself once more among my fellow Uriels, and, with the passing of time, all the things of which I had dreamt would fade away. I touched Michael, dipped my feet in the water, and looked again at the setting sun and its crimson flame afloat in the river. No, time moves in one direction only, and it cannot be turned back. I am here and I am now, and tomorrow will be a new day in my life.

-Michael, I whispered, I am afraid.

Michael touched me with his wings, caressed me tenderly and with devotion. For the first time since coming to the Garden, my feelings about the following day were overcast with an inexplicable menace. What sort of a menace I did not know, but I sensed its existence. I had never before sought to halt the passage of time, the time bearing me towards a new day, I had never been afraid to encounter new things, events and phenomena that I had yet to experience. On the contrary, I wanted to experience them, to enrich my soul and my spirit, to know more and more of the wonders of the universe and the works of the Creator. Yet now, shielded by Michael's protective wings, I felt I wanted to stay in this shelter, not to go out, not to face the approaching day. I could not stop myself trembling. Michael rocked me gently, calming me with a sure and soothing motion, and I slept.

He woke me before the light of dawn.

-Rise, Aziel, rise, he said. We must go down to the river to bathe and be purified. A great day is before us. A great day is before you. Today you will bid farewell to your youth, as you leave my tutelage. Today you are taking a step closer to the Lord. I shall be with you whenever I can, but from this day forth you are the responsibility of the Lord. Though I shall be your friend forever, the day is approaching when we must part company.

# Chapter thirty

Michael inspected me from the soles of my feet to the crown of my head. He smoothed my hair, caressed my wings and straightened their feathers, found aromatic plants and rubbed them on my feet and hands. Then he inspected me again and found my appearance satisfactory. On his face I saw an expression of concern and of pride. I, who had been entrusted into his hands to be educated and prepared, was at last ready for this audience before the Lord. He repeated his warning: Aziel, do not forget to show only your face. When you depart do not turn away, do not turn your back on the Lord's flame. When you are commanded to leave, for at least seven paces keep walking with your face still facing the flame. This is how you must withdraw.

When the sun rose above the horizon and the river was filled with crimson gold and molten silver, we set out on our way to the Garden of Gardens.

Michael held my hand, and for all that I had grown, still his stature and his wingspan were far greater than mine. Suddenly

I felt the wings on the lower part of my body growing larger and stronger.

-Michael, I said, see how my lower wings have increased, in size and in strength.

Michael's face was radiant. This is a sign of your maturity, my son. The Lord has raised you to the status of a youth who takes on his shoulders burdens and responsibilities. With these wings you shall cover your legs when you are summoned to show your face.

The gates of the Garden of Gardens were opened when the Cherubim who watched over them recognised Michael. As we passed by them they whispered, This is the chosen one, this is the messenger. There could be no doubt they were alluding to me. I swelled with pride. Since my coming to the Garden only Michael had paid attention to my existence. Only he saw how the changes came about in me, how I was transformed from a menial with scorched wings, cropped hair and bloodshot eyes to a youthful angel, strong and even handsome.

Whenever I looked at my reflection in the water, I found I was changing and becoming more like Michael. In my eyes he was magnificent, with his dark hair tumbling over the folds of his wings and covering his nape and his shoulders. His calm and restful features radiated not only serenity but also a profound understanding of the universe. There was abundant light in his face, as well as a smiling, loving serenity. That was how I would wish to be, I told myself.

We walked on, through paths and the beds of flowers. The Garden was filled with plants and flowers infinitely more beautiful than anything I had seen till now. All the colours of the rainbow, all the scents, all the sights I had seen—it was as if they were drawn from sources in the Garden of Gardens. Here was their origin, here they had been preserved since the day of their creation, and everything that existed outside was nothing but a faint echo of their essence. Then a vapour rose from the ground and was wafted far and wide, and there were singing voices too, blended with the sounds of unseen musical instruments. Beside the gate that opened before us stood Raphael, awaiting our arrival.

He took my free hand, and so we walked on, penetrating deeper into the groves of the Garden, until we came to a place where a great hollow sky gaped before us, broad and empty, stretching away so far that its end was invisible to the eye. A strange, unfamiliar current rose from the ground beneath my feet, reaching to the crown of my head. I understood that this was the borderline of which Michael had spoken, the borderline never to be crossed, and the great void was the habitation of the Lord.

Suddenly I realised I was standing alone. Michael and Raphael had disappeared, and I knew I was to encounter the Lord alone. Everything Michael could do, he had done. He had prepared me for this special moment in which only I, and I alone was to stand before the Lord. I was very much afraid, filled by an overpowering dread and awe such as I had never known before. In the midst of this dread I heard a voice. It sounded like my voice, speaking to me from within:

-You have come so far, Aziel the Uriel, stand here and do not fear. You have followed this course according to His will. It is His will that you come before Him, and He shall guide you.

The voice was calm, soothing.

In the midst of the great void there appeared a point of light, glowing in the distance. I covered my feet with my lower wings, and with my upper wings I shielded my face. The light grew stronger until it penetrated even my wings and the hands covering my face. Through them I saw the flame rising from the point of light, which was still growing brighter and more intense. A voice emerged from within the flame:

-Aziel, said the voice. Do not fear and do not be alarmed. From all the Uriels, from all your brothers and companions, I have chosen you.

My eyes were closed and covered by my hands. I parted

the upper pair of wings that had shielded my face. The flame grew stronger and the voice that emerged from it became clearer, as pure as crystal. The light was coming from within me. The flame burned as its light intensified, but it burned in me, as the sun is reflected in the waters of the river with all the colours of the rising rainbow. And so the flame burned within me, and the voice seemed to come back to me after crossing the skies, reaching the ultimate height, and returning laden with sounds and whispers and moans and sighs and cries of joy, and the celebration of life in all the heavens.

Fountains burst open inside me; fountains I had never known existed. I sensed the fountains rising from within me, but they were outside me as well, pouring into one another, uniting and coming back to me, and filling my soul with all the force of the universe, with the darkness of the beginning and with the light that came after it, and with the spirit of God hovering on the face of the waters and with the brooding deep, and with the perpetual tranquillity that enfolds the universe, and the storm wind and the infinite spaces stretching away within the great void, from which the point of light emerged, glowing ever brighter in the endless expanse. Void and substance seemed to join together— as creation came into being.

Then, from out of the misty vapour, rising from the ground beneath my feet, two birds appeared. The black raven that had cleft and rent the cloud, wheeling and finding no place to alight, circling round and round and trying to land on my head; and a snow white dove, an olive spray in her beak, also circling about me, gliding with wings spread and then disappearing. At that moment the voice told me:

-Aziel, my chosen one. You have seen the markers of your future. You will not understand nor know their meaning until the appointed time. I have chosen you as the witness and scribe of the things you will see, hear and experience on another star. Not today and not here shall I reveal your future. A future revealed to one who bears it within him is no longer a future, but present. The future that I am implanting in you is aspiration, expectation, searching, and curiosity. You shall bear within you the life of the world; guard it well.

The longer the voice spoke, the clearer and more lucid were the things said, as if the veils had been lifted from them. The words exposed precise meanings, clearly defined. From out of the echo the voice was heard, from out of the reflection appeared the thing.

And the voice continued: You must not deviate to the right or to the left from what you see and what you hear. As a witness you shall record everything that crosses your path, as a scribe you shall neither add nor subtract. It is not for you to judge, to sift or refine, to choose what is fit to be recorded and what is not. You are like a mirror that takes in and does not choose, a river that reflects and does not choose, like light that illumines everything around it and does not distinguish between what is comely and what is not. What you record will be as testimony before me. Yours will be the wisdom of letters that combine to form words, the wisdom of words that combine to form a sentence, the wisdom of the sentence which expresses ideas, deeds, experiences. All these are memory. You shall be the recorder of the memory of the thing that I have created, until it grows, and is capable of preserving the memory of itself.

Suddenly there was silence; silent, stilled were the voices both within me and outside of me. The flame faded, and as its light contracted within me, and I felt a hand descend on my shoulder. I opened my eyes and found Michael bending over me, as on the day that I first appeared in the Garden. He caressed my head, looked into my eyes and said:

-Today, my son, I brought you before the Lord of heaven and earth, Lord of all the worlds near and far. I am proud of you, my son, proud that you have reached this great day.

## Chapter thirty-one

That day at evening, when the sun began to incline westward and the shadows lengthened, I went to the vantage point from where I found it easy to observe Adam. He sat crouching on the bank of the river, staring transfixed at his reflection in the water. Almost motionless, he was very calm, unlike the previous time, when he had pelted his reflection with stones. The quiet in that corner of the Garden was broken only by the chirping of birds and the buzzing of bees in the fading light of dusk. All the colours of the sky were reflected, shimmering, in the smooth ripples, which bore aloft the burden of colours and shades and pictures, unchanging, yet ever changing. I was thinking to myself: What a beautiful sight it was—: river, man and angel. But the angel could not be seen and was not reflected in the river. I was sorry that Adam could not speak with me at that moment. Instead, he spoke to his reflection.

"Come to me," he whispered. "Come to me." The reflection also spoke, but its words were not heard.

"Speak aloud," Adam cried. "I cannot hear you, shout at me." But the words of the reflection were inaudible.

When night descended and the stars took up their places in the sky, I moved away from the river and from Adam and returned to Michael. He was waiting for me. Neither of us felt the need for sleep. Telling Michael what I had seen, I ended on a question.

-Do you understand, Michael, the secret purpose of the Lord in creating Adam alone, without either brother or friend?

-And do you understand the secret purpose of the infinite number of stars that are strewn about the heavens, my friend? Or the secret of life? Or the secret of the universe, and the secret of the Lord? Perhaps things exist within us and around us that are not to be understood, since our understanding is so limited. Ask no more questions tonight. Something is whispering inside me that the day will soon come when we will have to part. Since the day you were chosen to be the Lord's chosen one, your destiny has changed, and many startling and wondrous things are in store for you, things both grievous and exalted. Come close to me as before, and let us be grateful for our friendship for so long as the Lord grants us this grace.

# Chapter thirty-two

I have counted the grooves that I had carved in the stone, counted them and find that seven days have passed since the waters have begun to recede, but still they cover the earth. Only here and there have the tops of high mountains in the Ararat range emerged from the sea of the floodwaters. Quite inexplicably, I find it hard to keep wearisome and gloomy sensations from being uppermost in my thoughts. The bright sun that is beginning to dry up the waters stirs not the slightest joy in me, and even the indications that the level of the waters has dropped do not bring hope to my heart. Is this on account of the incident of the raven, finding no dry land on which to alight? The ark has disappeared from my view, but this has happened many times before. Sometimes it is hidden behind the cliff that rises sheer from the water and sometimes it drifts far, far away from the mouth of the cave, but a gust of wind is all that is needed to restore it to my field of vision. As the prospect of rescue for the those in the ark appears ever more likely, so does the sense of foreboding that I have inside me that just before deliverance—at the very last moment—there'll be some calamity. I cannot say that my fears are grounded in anything specific, but they give me no peace. Is this my role and is this my mission, to feel concern for the fate of mankind upon the earth? Surely I have no say or authority in this matter; the Lord has created, and the Lord will take away.

For a brief instant I envisaged the universe without man, and an involuntary shudder passed through me. I saw a cold universe, frozen and flat, sterile, bereft of its soul, for surely man is the soul of the universe. The Lord is its creator, but man is its soul. Man sees and hears and tastes and smells, touches and feels, exults and despairs, stands tall and bows low, takes flight in his imagination, inquires, searches, leaps and falls. He, and he alone of all that the Lord has created, remembers his past and forges a way to his future. Has the Lord forgotten that it is he who is in His image and His likeness?

My eyes scanned the horizon. Suddenly, I saw the ark, and felt a weight lift from my heart when I saw once again the clumsy craft tossed from wave to wave. The wind had driven it close to the exposed crag of the cliff. The shadow of the cliff had hidden it, but now, with the easterly wind blowing again, it was detached from the bare and sheer cliff, and it drifted in the bright sunshine. Once again the hope was kindled that the Lord would grant it deliverance, and that deliverance would be speedy, and that in just a few more days the waters would subside and the sons of men climb down from the ark, disembarking to dry land, reviving life and returning to the dead ground.

Suddenly, I saw the window of the ark open, and again Noah's hand was extended, testing the direction of the wind. Then I saw his face again. He heaved the upper part of his body out through the window and his eyes searched the heavens, his long, white beard stirring with the breeze and looking like a white stain against the blue of the sky. Again I saw his weary eyes, straining in the brightness of the light strewn across the face of the world.

In his hand he held something. I looked carefully and saw

it was a dove. She was held between his hands, pure white, and she seemed alarmed by the intensity of the light. Noah stroked her feathers and even lightly kissed her head. After many months of seclusion in the gloom of the ark, here she was, suddenly overwhelmed by a torrent of light and radiance. She hid her little head under her wing, seeking shelter from the fiery brightness. Noah caressed and encouraged her, opened his hands and even prodded her once or twice, signalling to her that she was free to fly.

Like a bundle of trussed feathers the dove lay between Noah's hands and refused to fly. She rejected the freedom that Noah tried to offer, preferring the safe haven within his hands. He held the dove close to his heart. I feared lest, in a fit of rage, he might harm her, but my fears were groundless. It was simply not in the character of this faithful old man, who walked with his God in innocence and righteousness, to commit any desperate act against life. For this dove bore within her the future of the world. He whispered words of sweetness to her, stroked her head, spread her wings to the wind. Suddenly he thrust his hands out before him and the dove fell from between his fingers. Startled, she flapped her wings and rose in the air. A sigh of relief was heard from the lips of master mariner Noah, and although my sigh went unheard, I too was relieved.

The dove turned in the westerly wind, the wind helping her wings to carry their burden over the surface of the water. She gained a little height, but her strength was insufficient to allow her further ascent. She circled around the ark, and with each circuit broadened her orbit. She seemed to be adjusting very gradually to her freedom, revelling in the open air and the intoxicating radiance. She wheeled in the direction of the cliff, and my heart was filled with dread akin to that I had felt when I watched the previous flight of the raven. Were her senses acute enough to perceive the hard rock from a distance? Would she be able to stop herself in time? The orbit of her flight grew ever wider, and it seemed likely that with only one more circuit she would collide with the hard, projecting crag and be smashed to pieces.

Not so. The instinctive wisdom implanted in her in the days of her creation was awakened once more. She almost flew into the crag, but turned back to the water, and with a glorious, swooping flight began circling again above the ark. She found no foothold on the land, so she returned to the ark. The time had not yet come.

Noah held out his hand, and the dove landed on it as if finding the nest in which she had been born. Laying his other hand on her head, and caressing her, he crooned,

"My dove, my dove, in seven more days I shall send you again. I hope you will not despair of your mission. As for me, I have all but lost faith in my mission, my dear one. I shall send you again seven days from now, and you shall be the herald of peace between the Lord and His creatures."

The dove cooed in his hands, as if understanding the words of her master and answering him in her own language.

# Chapter thirty-three

Seven more days. I am still awaiting the signal to go down and inspect the ark, which I have been expecting from my Lord. Seven more days? The provisions in the ark must be diminishing day by day, and the impatience of the beasts surely growing greater.

Oh Lord in the faraway firmament, just as You were capable of sending a great and mighty flood, is it beyond Your power to roll the waters back? You have done greater things than this in the twinkling of an eye, why are You doing nothing to save the remnant of life? Is there any purpose behind this agonising delay? Seven days lie before me; seven days of waiting that gnaw at the heart and the nerves. And in seven days the Lord created the heavens and the earth. Is it easier to create a new thing than to restore something destroyed?

# Chapter thirty-four

That starry night in Michael's company, when I heard him speak of our impending separation, I was overwhelmed by grief. I wanted to stop the passage of time, and while I was filled with pride at the thought of the mission with which I had been charged I was saddened by the prospect of separation. Had the Lord asked me if I accepted His choosing, I would have declined it and been content to remain as I was.

But such was not the will of the Lord. At daybreak, as Michael and I were still whispering together, I was again called to stand before Him.

Michael looked at me a long while, nodded his head and said:

-Go on your way, my son. Trust in your own strength. From here onward I can no longer stand at your side. From this day forth you shall follow your path alone.

I went down to the crystal river and bathed. Dawn already lay upon on the gentle swell, and the pure, bracing water refreshed me. I had had a long and sleepless night, and I could not present myself to the Lord tired and drowsy. At the entrance to the Garden of Gardens the Cherubim stood to attention and bowed their heads.

Inside the Garden of Gardens, Raphael led me to a site far removed from the centre and explained:

-This will be your regular place, Aziel. From this day your name is changed. From this day onward you shall be called Adiel. You are the scribe and the witness of the Lord, and therefore your new name is Adiel—meaning "witness of the Lord."

The flame appeared. From out of the deep abyss in the centre of the Garden the first tongues of fire emerged; steadily, without violence, curling a little, like a colourful garland of restful light. Raphael stepped a few paces back, drew back a curtain decked with flowers—and to my astonishment, Lillith appeared to me. She seemed deep in thought, her body concealed within her ample wings. Her long hair radiated dim light, and her upper wings covered her face, as is the custom within the Garden of Gardens.

From out of the flame a voice was heard, inviting, encouraging, almost caressing:

-Remove your wings from your face, said the voice. No harm shall befall you, my daughter.

Lillith parted her wings, and then I saw her in all her beauty. I never imagined that a face could hold such a limitless store of loveliness. No other part of her body was as different, as distinctive, as rich in uniqueness, as her face. Her eyes like twin pools, radiating light and reflecting the sky, enfolding in a single glance all memories, the present and the future, with strips of bright crimson framing the outlet for the fountain of speech. And above them, above the lips, the towering ridge that endows the face with both height and depth. All of this loveliness resided in the features of Lillith. Her body was covered by her wings, but I sensed its warmth and its pungent smell.

-Approach, my daughter, said the voice. It is time for us to talk . . .

-I know, she replied. It's about Adam, isn't it?

-You are not only fair but also wise, my daughter. Yes, it is of Adam that we will speak. It seems to me that you have flouted the rules governing your existence. I told you on that sixth day towards evening, when I created Adam, that he was not to be subject to your dominion. You may approach any of my other creatures, but he shall be left alone. Do you remember?

-I remember, Lillith answered. And You created him male and female, did You not? Did You think, Lord, this would satisfy his desires? Did You suppose he would not observe the beasts, their manner of procreation, and their yearning to become one flesh?

-You remember correctly, my daughter. But why have *you* flouted the agreement that was made between us?

-I have not mingled with him, Lord.

-How can you say you have not come to him? In the night, when he embraced you, when you hovered above him, when he poured out his seed and wasted it? When he kissed your breasts, enraptured, like an infant sucking his mother's breasts, he surely knew you, Lillith.

-Adam knew me, Lord, but I did not know him.

At this, the voice emerging from the flame sounded a little hesitant, a little bemused, and the first faint signs of impatience were heard:

-My daughter, you are speaking in riddles. He knew you, and you did not know him?

-Yes, Lord. So it was, and I would it were otherwise. I yearn to know him. He is so smooth, so upstanding, so different from all the angels, devils, spirits and phantoms that throng about me. I lust for him, I long for him as for cooling streams in the heat of the day.

-My daughter, it seems you wax lyrical in his honour!

-It is true; my love for him inspires poetry in me. I love him!

-I too, said the voice, and that is why I commanded that you do not tempt him. I see you have disobeyed my command.

-Not so, Lord. I came to him in a dream, and that you did not forbid me or him.

The voice fell silent. Stillness heavy with expectation reigned in the Garden of Gardens. After a lengthy pause the voice was heard again:

-You have spoken the truth, my daughter. This gate I did not lock before him. It is the truth, and what is done cannot be undone. What I wrought in the days of Creation I cannot change, and the gate of dreams shall remain open before him. I shall need to distance him from you.

-Wherever he goes, there I shall go. I shall follow him, Lord. Because I love him. I shall invade his dreams, waft around him the scents of my desire for him, light a fire in his loins. The power that You gave me to ignite the instinct for life, I shall give to him too.

-I shall divest you of your power and keep it to myself.

Lillith broke into a peal of unrestrained laughter, laughter that rolled throughout all the expanse of the Garden of Gardens and was doubtless heard in the furthest reaches of the firmament.

-How then will life be fruitful and multiply? She asked, her mirth not yet abating. Not so much as a fly will be born if you take my power from me.

-Go, mutinous one. And do not forget, daughter, Adam is mine.

Lillith stepped back, her face to the flame. The Cherubim tensed and bowed their heads in silence, and the flame took on a deep, dark, violet hue.

-Come to me, I heard the voice of the Lord. I drew nearer, trembling with fear.

-What you have seen and heard, record. This shall be your first testimony, Adiel. Here you shall begin the writing of history.

-Yes, my Lord.

-My messenger Raphael has instructed you that from this day forth you are Adiel the scribe.

-Yes, my Lord.

-And what you have seen and heard must remain secret. The things that take place in the privacy of the Garden of Gardens are not to be disclosed in the entirety of the outer Garden.

-Yes, Lord. I shall carefully guard the secrets.

-Adiel, you may go, but do not stray too far from this place. It may be that this very day you will again be summoned. Be ready.

-I shall be ready, Lord.

The flame subsided in the great void and the light in the Garden grew dim. Only the burnished sword of Gabriel reflected the last gleam of the flame.

# Chapter thirty-five

I found Michael on the bank of the river. He had been observing Adam closely, watching his movements and what he was doing. As intrigued by Adam as I was, Michael too sought answers to satisfy his curiosity, about Adam's nature and the reason for the Lord's special affection for him.

-Michael, I was looking for you, I said.

-So, you have found me. I see that on your return from the Garden of Gardens, you have grown, my brother. Already you are permitted to enter and leave the holiest places by yourself, purely on your own merit. You are no longer in need of my company.

Was there a trace of complaint in his voice? Did I hear the faintest echo of sorrow in his words, or was it pride in his achievement, having brought me thus far? After a while I said: Michael, in the Garden of Gardens my former name was taken away and I have been given a new one.

-I know, said Michael. That is the custom. And what is your name?

-Adiel.

-Splendid! said my friend, so you are the witness. I like your new name, though sometimes, out of habit, I may still call you Azi. Would you mind that?

-On the contrary—it will always remind me of who I am and from where I have come, and it will keep me from becoming too proud.

Meanwhile, the secret in my heart of what I had witnessed, oppressed me. Like an alien entity it lay heavy on my throat and my lips, but I mustered all my strength and kept silent. Was this an offence against my love for Michael? For the first time I was placed between two obligations, and my loyalty to the Lord prevailed. My sorrow grew more intense, and I embraced Michael with feeling. He sensed my distress and asked, if something painful had happened.

I was silent. I hugged him, but said nothing.

-I understand, said Michael. You cannot share your secret with me. Yet that's how it must be, Azi. You take nothing from me. I too have secrets entrusted to me by the Lord, which I must keep from you. It is the order of things.

Still embracing, we turned our attention once again to Adam, who sat not far away, looking very sorrowful and self-absorbed.

Clearly he was troubled by his thoughts; his hands supported his head with its long and tangled hair, his body was bowed and hunched, he seemed to be staring at his feet.

Suddenly I saw a creature that I had never before seen in the Garden, moving slowly and furtively, approaching the place where Adam sat. From time to time it poked its pointed head through the leaves of the bushes, and from its mouth darted a sharp, furtive tongue, lashing the air. Its body was covered with shiny and scaly skin. Had it not been in motion, it would have been hard to distinguish it from the plants through which it was crawling.

-Look, Michael, look. What is that creature, the one that resembles a branch?

-That is the serpent, replied Michael, and he is no friend to the beasts living in the Garden.

The sun was high in the sky. It was the hour of greatest radiance and of greatest light. Suddenly something unexpected took place before our eyes. Adam paced back and forth restlessly for a while, then slumped at the foot of a grassy boulder and sank into deep sleep. Four Seraphim swooped down on him, picked him up and carried him away with them.

A voice was heard in the Garden, the voice of Raphael. Michael and I were summoned to go to the Garden of Gardens.

-It has begun, Michael whispered in my ear, and fell silent.

# Chapter thirty-six

I counted the grooves carved in the wall of the cave. Every seventh day I marked with a groove double the width of the six preceding. This was the sign of the Sabbath, the day of rest for the universe. Throughout the time that I resided in the cave, I would observe this day meticulously, just as the Lord had commanded in His holiness. This day I did no work, did not move a stone from its place, carved no grooves in the wall and recorded nothing with a stylus. This day I thought a great deal of my friend Michael, communing with him in my heart, and turned to the Lord in my meditations. This was a day dedicated to matters of the heart. I counted six grooves. The day of creating all species of living creatures, I said to myself, the day of the creation of man in His image and His likeness. And on this day, will the Lord not have mercy on the most wondrous of His creatures?

Once more I returned to observing the ark, and saw it drifting on still waters. In the distance there were already patches of dry land protruding like islands in the sea. And, marvel of marvels—faraway, I could make out tall trees protruding from the water. It was a sight that kindled hope in my heart. If indeed there were trees that have been spared, perhaps the birds would yet return to nest in them and life again flourish. Noticing my own response, I thought how quickly hope flares up, and how overwhelming is the urge for life and survival, even amid devastation. Was this, too, the will of the Lord, or was it taking place in spite of His will? I quickly dispelled this rebellious notion from my heart. Everything that is done, everything that takes place, I repeated to myself, is done by His will. But in the depths of my soul I sensed that the rebellious notion had left a scar.

Seven days had already passed since Noah had dispatched the dove. Today he would dispatch it again.

I told myself: Look at the ark, just look at the ark to dispel your doubts.

And sure enough, the window opened. Again Noah, the thin and rather stooped figure appeared at the window. He held out his hands, clutching the tremulous white dove between them. This time the dove was struggling and flapping her wings, as just the smell of dry land infused her with strength. She seemed eager, anticipating her freedom, poised to meet whatever awaited her. Noah stroked her head and even kissed it. In the great silence all around, Noah's words were clearly heard:

"Fly, my daughter, fly. If you have no good tidings today, I don't know what we shall do. The food is all gone, and soon we shall all perish from hunger. Fly—fly and bring back good news."

It was as if the bird sprang from his hands. This time her flight was robust. Rising and soaring sharply into the sky, she sped away from the ark as if seeing before her a land of wonders, a land full of good seeds to eat and birds singing and other doves amorously crooning. Noah stood and watched her, a faint smile rising to his lips. Even when she vanished into the distance, his gaze was still fixed on the heavens.

Now it is my turn to wait, tense as Noah, as restless as he

is, full of anticipation and hope. What are the inhabitants of the ark doing at such a time? Praying to the heavens? Distracting themselves with unimportant tasks and trying to dispel their doubts? Or are they too weak to feel the pulse of willpower, excitement or anticipation?

The dove has disappeared from my field of vision, far, far away. Lord, Lord of all the universe, preserve this little soul, preserve this little spark on whose wings the destiny of all life in the universe depends!

The Lord must have heard my prayer. When the sun dipped westward and the shadows of the mountains lengthened on the surface of the water, with the colours of sunset shimmering— from gold to purple, from citron yellow to violet—on the waves, a tiny speck appeared on the horizon, growing steadily larger. It was the dove. As she approached and passed by the mouth of the cave I saw her in all her glory: her two wings spread, steady and strong as they had been at the start of the day, her body firm, her muscles taut, feet turned backwards and talons curled—and in her beak, a spray of olive, tidings of life, tidings of dry land coming back to life. Did I ever truly weep? In the course of the ten generations that I had spent among men I also learned to weep, but only rarely did I shed a tear. Now I felt the fountain of tears overflowing. Can joy also release the fountain of tears?

I followed the flight of the dove. She bore the olive spray in her beak like a sign and a miracle. A year of anticipation, a year of despair and hope drawing to an end. I erased from my mind all the questions and doubts that had thrown me into turmoil. But one remained: Who was the Lord in whose entourage I was privileged to serve—the Lord with the power to create worlds and to destroy them?

The dove flew over the ark. Since sending her out at dawn, Noah had returned to the hatch-window at intervals to scour the sky. Seeing the bird and the spray of olive in its beak, he cried out for joy. From his eyes, too, tears trickled. I was too far away to see the tears, but I saw him wipe his eyes with his hand. He summoned his wife Na'ama to the window, his sons Ham, Shem and Japheth and their wives were all gathered about him. Everyone who could share the burden of joy and emotion stood next to Noah. From the ark cries of exultation and even the beginning of a hymn of thanksgiving were heard.

Noah peered through the hatch again, stretching out his hands and putting his palms together to give the bird a foothold. The dove wheeled in small and ever diminishing circles around Noah's hands. When she alighted, I saw the old master mariner shaking with emotion and pressing the bird to his heart. He took the twig from her mouth and just stared at it; stared at the silvery green leaf and the golden stem that brought tidings of life.

The sun gradually sank. In spite of the glorious sunset, heralding the onset of darkness, I imagined to myself—in a manner contrary to the time, contrary to the approaching night, contrary to the rhythm of the Lord that is unceasing and unchanging—that it was dawn arising out of the twilight. How great is the power of the imagination to construct worlds as it pleases . . .

Noah took the dove into the ark and left the window open wide, no longer fearing tempestuous waves, howling winds and raging storms.

"In seven more days, seven days from today," I heard him say, "I shall send you out a third time, my dove. If you then report that the waters have abated and the land is firm once more, we shall know it is time to disembark. Having come so far, I shall not endanger the vestiges of life on earth through undue haste. At the Lord's command I entered the ark, and at the Lord's command will we leave it."

# Chapter thirty-seven

Michael, I whispered, What is beginning?

-Something new, Azi. The Garden is in turmoil. Adam is sowing grief and discontent among the creatures of Creation. He is angry and sullen, sometimes even trying to pursue the females of other species, who must flee from him. His loneliness is not only an ordeal for him, it has become an ordeal for others. The serpent never ceases to follow him, staring at him with malevolent eyes.

-What does it want, this serpent? Has he forgotten that Adam is the beloved child of the Lord, His favourite?

-Lillith does the same, Michael continued. She is never satisfied—diffusing her intoxicating scent among the Seraphim, among beasts and birds, among fishes and insects, as if she has an inexhaustible store of attractions. But of all those who pursue her charms, she has eyes for Adam alone, and gives him no peace.

Again I felt a stab of shame in my heart. The secret that I kept within me could have answered Michael's questions. I was silent. The word of the Lord had to prevail over the voice of love.

-Michael, do you think that these things are bound up in some way with what is about to happen?

I asked him this in the hope that it would silence the voices inside me, voices that caused me grave discomfort.

-We shall soon see, said Michael as we approached the gates of the Garden of Gardens.

To our astonishment, we were preceded by a whole procession of angels, Seraphim, Cherubim and animals. I remembered Michael's account of the sixth day of creation, before sunset. Then, too, in readiness for the creation of Adam, the Lord had summoned all the host of heaven, every living thing, all birds and beasts and insects, to witness the creation of Adam in His image and His likeness.

When the Cherubim guarding the gates saw us, they held back the throng and let us enter first. I took this display of respect as my due, for I was becoming accustomed to my new status, my privileged position.

The massed ranks parted as we passed through, and we soon found ourselves in the inner circle, along the invisible but unmistakable boundary line that even the highest ranking angels may not cross. Raphael took my arm and led me to the place I had been assigned, and from there I beheld the entire spectacle. Ring upon ring of angels enclosed the boundary all around, and behind them were all those created in the first days of creation, arranged in pairs. The Garden of Gardens was full, and yet there was still space, as if its limits had expanded to accommodate all the arrivals. Silence reigned over all. Not so much as a chirrup was heard, nor the lowing of cattle nor the rustle of an insect. Even the stumpy-legged serpent lay mute. Very slowly the glow of the flame appeared, rising from the abyss. The light grew stronger, gradually, steadily.

Suddenly I saw Raphael and Michael detaching themselves from the throng, as if responding to a signal issuing from a secret source. From the radiant groves at the fringes of the Garden came

a procession of Seraphim, six on each side, bearing a bed adorned
with the loveliest and sweetest-scented flowers of the Garden—
and on the bed Adam lay sleeping. His anger and resentment had
left him. His whole aspect was of joy and delight. Never had I
seen him so serene. Could this be the same Adam, the restless
youth who been so furious, throwing stones at his reflection in
the water? Was this the same Adam who had rampaged through
the Garden like an impetuous hooligan?

Meanwhile the flame had risen higher. Controlled, focused,
not emitting tongues of fire, but glowing inwardly, within itself.
A halo of light in which all colours were harmoniously combined,
complementing one another, crowned the flame. Listening carefully, it was possible to discern a faint sound, muffled and a little
sad, like a sound of farewell, a voice at the same time addressing
itself and musing:

-Adam should not be alone.

A stir passed through the packed crowd. The Cherubim and
Seraphim, the beasts and birds, all nudged one another and ex-
changed questioning looks. Did the Lord really regret His creation
of Adam? Was He about to repudiate that which He had created?

Gabriel drew his sword. The flashing blade cast fear all
around him, catching rays of light, which flickered briefly and
then disappeared.

-Why has Gabriel drawn his sword? voices were heard whispering, and then fell silent. Was Gabriel about to dispel the spirit
that the Lord had breathed into him from the body of Adam,
prone in sleep, and return his body to the dust from which he
was created? My wings shuddered, even as my eyes anxiously
sought out Michael.

-What is happening here, Michael? I wanted to shout. What
is happening!? Can the Lord repudiate what He has created? Was
there not an agreement and an implicit promise in creation,
whereby a thing that has been created cannot cease to exist?

I remembered Michael's story of the two mighty trees whose

fruit was not to be eaten, the Tree of Life and the Tree of Knowledge and the fearsome injunction that concerned them: that the
day that Adam ate of their fruit, he would die.

-Michael, Michael, Adam has not touched the forbidden
fruit, I cried out in my heart. I saw him seeking a way to escape from
his isolation, but he did not touch those fruits . . . Suddenly Michael
stood next to me. He had left his place beside Adam's bed and come
to stand with me. Close to me, his heartbeat soothed me and from
this fathomless silence I heard Michael's voice whispering in my ear:

-Try to calm yourself; you are really stronger than that. Do
not collapse, be strong and be brave. If you break down, you will
be cast into the abyss! This is your time of testing. You have to
prove yourself now, prove that you have the strength to carry out
your mission.

-Michael, I whispered against his chest. Surely it is uncon-
scionable, even for the Lord?! Adam is the crown of creation, the
crown of the Creator. Stop Gabriel's sword, stop it!

Michael pressed my face closer to his body, to stifle my
words so that they would not be heard by the crowd. Silence
reigned. Not the slightest rustle or movement was to be heard in
the void of the Garden.

-I shall make Adam a helper and a mate, the voice of the
Lord reverberated.

Gabriel approached the bed of Adam. A scented cloud rose
and enwrapped the flame, Gabriel and the bed. When the cloud
dispersed there was a whiff of myrrh in the air, like the perfume
of Lillith but sweeter and not as pungent, beside Adam's bed there
was a figure that had not been there before. It was both like Adam
and unlike him. Like Adam's face, the face was radiant, but more
gentle. The naked body had breasts and female genitals. She
rubbed her staring eyes with her hands, which were softer and
more delicate than the hands of Adam. Her eyes, too, were both
like the eyes of Adam and unlike them.

So was this the final act of creation? So was this the way

that Adam's mate came into the world? I knew this was not how man had first came into the world. Adam had been formed from the earth and from the breath of the Lord. But this one, this female, we had all witnessed as she was created from Adam himself, from his body and his spirit, from his flesh and from his loneliness. She had been born of his pain and of his yearning.

I watched her and saw how her eyes roamed about her, seeking something to focus upon. She saw Adam, stretched out on the bed, and dreaming. What was he dreaming now? I could have penetrated his dream, but I desisted. I was observing changes in the shape of his body. Completely gone were the signs of femininity and only the signs of his manhood were apparent. Now it was good to allow both of them to discover each other without anything hampering them, unmediated. I was sure that this was the will of the Lord—to allow them to be alone.

With the smell of his flesh still in her flesh she lay down beside him, wrapped him in her arms, put her mouth to his, touching breast to breast, entwined her legs in his and whispered:

"Man, man, my man." Her words penetrated Adam's sleep. He, in turn, embraced her with his sinewy arms, his muscles tensed but at ease, nestled close to her body, head to head and foot to foot and still asleep, whispered: "Woman, woman, my woman." They appeared to be one body and one flesh.

From out of the flame a voice was heard, restrained, as though addressing itself:

-Now he is parted from the earth, his mother, and from me, his father, and he cleaves to her, and so it shall be throughout time to come.

When Adam awoke from his slumber and saw the woman lying beside him, he smiled at her and said: "I dreamed you."

He caressed her body, touched her breasts, peered into her eyes, kissed her lips, ran his fingers through her hair, then entered her and knew her. Not in his dream, not in his imagination, but with awareness and with rapture.

When they were resting, their passion spent, he said to her: "I have given names to all the creatures of the world. I shall give you a name also."

She put her ear close to his lips and said: "Call me a name, beloved, call me, and this shall be my name in the mouth of the Lord and of His angels."

"You are my wife, my mate, the one that I love."

"But say my name, say my name . . ."

Adam was silent, pondered and said: "Woman. Your name is woman. Woman, this is your name."

"Woman," she repeated after him. "This name pleases me. It will show me who I am. I am woman," she said again. "Woman . . . woman."

I heard angry voices close by. I looked around to see what was happening, and there was Lillith, standing amid the senior angels, with Gabriel restraining her, preventing her from approaching Adam's bed.

Her eyes flashed in fury, her lovely face was ablaze with indignant passion: He is mine, he is mine, Lord. I married him in his dreams.

The serpent lay at her feet and laughed. I never knew laughter could be so bitter and malicious and hurtful. The angels who stood in the inner circle were stunned and confused. From the flame, a signal was emitted and the assembled crowd, instead of chanting a song of praise as had been expected, departed from the Garden of Gardens in their order of precedence. Only the senior angels, and I among them, were commanded to remain in our places. When the Garden was cleared, I saw Lillith standing before the flame, tears streaming from her eyes.

-Come hither, my daughter, said the voice from within the flame. I know that I have caused you pain. But it was not for your sake that Adam was created. To you I have given all other living things, all beasts and fishes and birds.

-Yes Lord, I know. But he is the one that I love. I cannot

be parted from him. All my strength is in him, and he, too, has been in thrall to me. I know him, I know his dreams.

-He was sad and lonely. It seems that I erred when I created him without a mate, believing that he would be mine alone. I confess, my daughter, I was mistaken. But what is done cannot be undone, and the wisdom of hindsight comes too late here. He is not yours, daughter, he is hers and mine.

-And she will be mine, I heard the serpent hiss, scuttling away into the bushes. No one else paid any attention to that faint sound.

Lillith wept bitterly, and the flame took on a violet hue, more gentle and compassionate.

-Lord, Lillith continued through the tears that were choking her, I will not leave him alone, I will follow him, and I will hate her and envy her. I will arouse discord and conflict between them. He shall never be all hers. I shall lie between them and inflame his imagination. I shall persist in his dreams.

The flame turned to a bright and almost dazzling light.

The voice sounded out:

-Lillith, have done! Not one more word! I knew you were rebellious and troublesome, but disobedient as well? Take her away, out of my sight, Gabriel, but be gentle. Do not be harsh with her, for she is sorely grieved.

Gabriel sheathed his sword, took her arm gently, almost affectionately, and led her from the Garden of Gardens.

-And you, Michael, the voice continued, take Adiel, and you too Raphael, go out into the Garden and calm down all those who dwell therein. Warn the serpent to guard its tongue.

The air in the Garden was cool and pleasant. We needed a few moments of rest after all that we had seen and heard that day. Michael laid a soothing hand upon my shoulder,

-Today the work of creation has been completed.

As night fell, the stars again told of the glory of the heavens and once more the day of rest descended on the universe, crowning it with peace and tranquillity.

## Chapter thirty-eight

Now I am confident about the future of the travellers in the ark. I glimpsed them through the hatch. Their faces were lean and dejected, with eyes sunk deep in their sockets. Beards grew wild and tangled on the cheeks of the men, and the grey hair of the older women had turned completely white. Old age had over-taken even the youngsters among them. Was it any wonder? For almost a year they had been confined within this narrow vessel, lacking air and almost without hope, cooped up and surrounded by the stench of the penned up beasts. The wonder is that they survived. Life is evidently stronger than it sometimes seems. A spark of hope for survival lights a fire that can burn for days. By the light of the approaching sunset, when I saw the people waving and crying out gleefully to the dove circling above them, falling into one another's arms and weeping for joy, I knew their despair had turned to hope. The day of disembarkation was, like the circling of the dove, within sight.

The ark floats on a radiant path of light cast by the full moon, and although it seems so small, even wretched, in my eyes it is the most precious thing in the universe. Were Michael to come to me and ask: What is the most precious thing in the universe, I would tell him that, of all things, I hold the ark dearest to me. For ten generations I lived amid mankind and I matured and learned many things, of good and evil and of the choice between them. I saw what love and hate can cause, I learned of death and of the ways of man and woman. In spite of the bitterness and the disappointment, and there were desperate days indeed, I learned that man is the Lord's most wonderful gift to the whole universe. Without him, who would recognize and sing the praises of Creation? Who could tell of the infinity of the cosmos? Or who join letter to letter and word to word, composing chronicles and epics, songs of love and exaltation, of dreams and desires?

An engorged, bright star traverses the sky, dragging behind it a train of fire. This is the sign that the Lord is sending me down to the ark to see what has befallen its voyagers. Tomorrow at dawn, when those in the ark rise from their sleep, I shall go down to them, and record everything that I see. Now I too must lie down and rest, for the memories that arise of those days, the faraway days of the Garden, are heavy indeed.

The following day, I rose at dawn, bathed in the water of the pool in the cave, turned to the east and sang the anthem of praise. Since coming to this land, all those generations past, I have kept to the order of angelic song as it is practised in the heavens. Once I tried joining in the prayers of men, but I found them vague, superficial and lacking direction. Sometimes they bowed down to gods, sometimes to the One God; sometimes they invoked the names of trees and rocks in their prayers. I understood that they were still confused, floundering amid charms and incantations, imprecations and spells. The songs of praise that I brought with me from those distant days in the Garden are distinguished by clarity, direction and order.

So I sang the song of the day and thought about Michael. It is to Michael that I have turned before every vital step in the fulfilment of my mission. I would consult him in my heart, come to him in spirit to hear a word of approval and encouragement, or to receive a critical look if I had failed in my duties. Heavy indeed is my loneliness now. I am close to the sons of men, but they are not close to me. I see them, hear their words, observe their actions, but they cannot respond to my approaches, cannot hear my questions and cannot share my doubts. Therefore I return in spirit to Michael, and imagine I hear his warm, soothing voice, feel his hand caressing my head, as if I am a child and he my elder brother.

Today I turn to you, my brother Michael, for soon I am to go down to the ark of Noah, and I am full of anxiety. What shall I find there? Almost a year has passed since they were confined within it. Inside are the few, the very few, the vestiges of the remnant of the family of man — one family alone, and just one male and female of all living things. Michael, can you imagine what kind of a burden has been laid upon these survivors? Can you understand what they have endured, what they have suffered; can you comprehend what they must have seen when the world — their entire world — was laid waste around them and within them? That is why I am anxious, although I shall fulfil my mission as I have been commanded by the Lord. I have been chosen, and the chosen are not entitled to evade their mission — for it will seek them out and find them in any place and at any time. But fear goes with me, so be with me, my brother, if only in spirit.

I have arranged everything in the cave. I gathered up the stone tablets on which I have inscribed my testimony. I dug a pit in the cave and laid them deep, safely inside. I shall surely return here after my visit to the ark. I have grown as accustomed to this cave as if it were my home. From here I saw the flood, the fearful spectacle of the death of man and of the land, the ark struggling through storms and tempests, all but shattering on the rocks. From here I have observed a year of despair and fear and a spark of hope, and from here I have been recording my chronicle with a stylus on tablets of stone.

Now that I must leave this place and my heart is heavy, as it was when I left the Garden and came to this land. This is apparently how time is constructed in the heart from deposits of pain and joy, from wounds and scars. The stylus too, which I spent a long time perfecting, which has almost become an extra hand to me during this time of writing and recording, I have hidden with the tablets in the pit. When I return here they will be waiting for me, ready to greet me, and we shall be reunited like old friends.

I realise that I have been delaying my descent to the ark, putting it off from moment to moment with all kinds of excuses. First I needed to sing a hymn of praise, and then the cave had to be set to rights. I shall take one last glance at the cave and set out on my way. I have counted the grooves, a groove for each day, and they have added up to three hundred and forty.

The sun has already covered a portion of its course in the sky, suspended there in all its radiance. The water below me reflects the sun, and it is a glorious sight. The surface of the ocean now ripples clear of the myriad corpses, of the uprooted trees and shattered branches, which have sunk to the bottom of the ocean or have been scattered far away by the wind. Here and there appear large and expanding islets of dry land. The entire chain of the Ararat mountains is now clear of the water, and the broad valleys, where once herds of antelope grazed, and ibex and roe deer, where once hawks and eagles soared, are exposed once more to the light of the sun, but a long time must pass before there is heard here again the bleating of lambs and the chirrup of nestlings. To my delight I noticed clumps of grass among the bare patches. When the creatures emerge from the ark, they will find enough to sustain them, at least until the land is fertile and fruitful once again.

I stood in the mouth of the cave, spread my wings, took a

last brief look behind me and soared away in the direction of the ark. The ark's hatch had been left open since the dove returned with the olive spray in her beak. Could Noah have forgotten to close it in his excitement? Or perhaps he felt confident that the voyage was indeed drawing to its close, and no harm would befall all his charges. Passing through the opening of the hatch, I was alarmed.

From the open spaces of the universe — from its brightness and clarity, from the purity of the air, the blue of the sky and the translucence of the water — the transition to the interior of the ark was like a heavy blow. Everywhere, darkness reigned, the faint light from the window soon disappearing, swallowed up by the heavy pall of gloom, which could almost be touched. The darkness stunned my eyes, and only after some time was I able to discern the partitions between stalls and cages where all the varieties of living creatures were quartered. I couldn't distinguish between them. Not even by their sounds, since they lay silent.

To my surprise I found animal bones scattered among the piles of excrement. Were these the bones of animals that had died of distress, of hunger? Or had they become the victims of predators? This notion made me shudder. After all, only one pair from every species had been consigned to the protection of the ark, and if one such animal had fallen prey to another, that species would disappear forever from the face of the earth. The beasts in their pens sprawled in their filthy straw and uttered only sighs and muffled groans. They didn't have the strength to cry out, to bellow or to roar. How terrible to see a world that you knew when it was living, vibrantly wild and impassioned and procreative, raging and stirring — to see all this in its death throes. A few more days and it would have been too late, they would have all been dead. Had deliverance not come soon, there would have been no one left to deliver. Where was Noah? The rest of his family? Where were his three sons, their wives and children?

Gradually, I grew accustomed to the prevailing gloom.

Stench and a vile vapour filled the air. The excrement of beasts, their sweat, the reek of their rut and their vomit, their cud and their rotting fodder, blended together and soured the atmosphere of the ark beyond endurance. Had all the survivors of the living universe lived in this putrid stench for the past year? Had the Lord been able to preserve the remnants of life only by condemning them to this filth, and would these survivors still be capable of making a new beginning? I had come as a witness, not a judge. Hush, Adiel, I told myself to stem the rush of my feelings. Hush; you must just look around and remember. This was what I had to record.

In the bows of the ship there was a storage area for food. I peered into it. Almost empty. A few wretched piles of decomposing fodder were strewn on the floor. Broken jars were scattered everywhere, some of them containing seeds that were also rotting. I went from stall to stall, peered into every corner, under every heap of straw, and even probed the reeking stools that swarmed with maggots. In one of the pens in the stern of the ark, I encountered a dreadful sight. Sprawled on the floor were Shem, Ham and Japheth and their wives. Noah and his wife were slumped against the wall in another area, uttering groans of pain. Beside them on the floor lay small children, boys and girls, eyes wide open and a look of death in their faces. What had happened? Surely only yesterday I had seen them all celebrating and waving their hands as the dove returned to the ark.

I hurried to Noah and his wife and released their bonds. My mission was clear: I had been sent because the Lord had decided that they were to survive. I knew what I had to do. I put my ear to their chests and to my relief, could make out heartbeats, weak, and irregular, but signs of life nevertheless. From them I moved on to the children and their parents, finding faint signs of life in all of them. I found a pitcher full of water among the broken jars. I bent down over the unconscious, recumbent forms one by one, breathing air into their lungs and pouring water down their throats. One after another I dragged them to the open window, so that the fresh air could revive them.

The first to regain his senses was old Noah himself. He looked around him and understood at once what had happened. He hurried to the bodies sprawled by the window but apparently it did not occur to him to wonder who had dragged them there. Did he reckon they had succeeded in getting there with their last reserves of strength? Whatever he thought, he removed the constricting belts of their clothing, then shook their heads one after the other, sprinkling water on their foreheads, and when they began to stir, tended to each one. Na'ama his wife immediately joined in the rescue effort, drawing water from the sea and tipping it over the faces of those sprawled about her. An hour passed, and the spirit of life was returning to those in the ark.

While the sick were still being tended to, I inspected Noah's cabin. On the floor lay a polished stone tablet bearing signs of writing, letters similar to those that I myself inscribe. I examined it. It was a tablet recounting the events of the previous day. From reading it I understood what had happened the day before. Evidently, after the return of the dove to the ark, the sons and their wives were in a mood for wild and unrestrained celebration. They had shouted, danced and copulated indiscriminately, man with man and man with woman. Suddenly Japheth started shouting, demanding meat. His brothers joined in the maniacal cry:

"Meat, meat, tomorrow we are going ashore and today we'll celebrate with a banquet of meat!" Noah had tried to restrain them, but his sons knocked him and his wife to the floor, pushed them into their cell and bolted the door. Then they slaughtered a pair of animals — a species that would never be seen again on the face of the earth.

After they had gorged themselves on the raw meat, they and their wives and their children, they were suddenly overcome by fits of vomiting and choking. Noah and his wife could do nothing to help them, as they were locked up in their cabin. Had

I delayed my arrival even slightly longer I would have found them all choked by their vomit.

I saw the dove perched on a pile of tablets. The olive spray lay beside her, as green and fresh as I had seen it yesterday in her beak. I lifted her, caressed her head lovingly.

-Soon, my dove, I whispered in her ear. In six more days you will fly away in search of more dry land. Take my advice and do not return to the ark. Death awaits you here. The dove could not tell who had lifted her and caressed her head, and she cooed softly. Did she know she was the herald of rebirth?

I sorted out the scattered tablets and counted. Their number was the same as the number of days of the flood and of the journey in the ark. While I wait for the dove to be sent out for the third time, I shall read these tablets. Their testimony bears witness to the survival of mankind upon the earth.

# Chapter thirty-nine

We sat on the cliff-top, side by side and close, very close to one another, the river at our feet flowing steadily, and the soothing sound of the water telling stories in its own language. Our glances met from time to time, then reverted to watching the water streaming at our feet. Perhaps the Lord was speaking to us, and we didn't understand His words . . . ? Sunset descended gradually on the water, on the Garden, upon us. Rivers of delicate and gentle light blended with a riot of colours and swirled around us. Fragrant perfumes of evening were wafted to us from every flower, from every bush and shrub, all of them speaking in their wordless tongue. Michael spoke to me:

-This is the last Sabbath, brother, that we shall spend together. Our ways are about to part, and soon you must set out upon your mission. I shall stay in my place, here in the Garden. Perhaps, perhaps we shall meet again. But for the present we must go our separate ways and accept this with love, for it is His will.

I was silent a long time, not knowing how to reply. In my

head I understood what he said, but in my heart I hoped something might yet happen that would unite us forever. I wanted to be by his side, to feel his presence, rely on his understanding and be worthy of his love. Such is the nature of the heart, which does not always agree with the instructions of the head.

After this lengthy silence I said: Michael my dear friend, I don't always understand the acts and the words of the Lord. After all, I was but a menial slave in his vast universe. The spaces are so great, the acts so astounding and so complex, the combinations so contradictory, the words so marvellous and perplexing, that I cannot find my way among them. How can I fulfil my mission, if I don't even know what it is? I have been told: be a scribe and a witness and recount the history of mankind. You taught me to write and to inscribe letters. But this is only a tool, just a tool. More than this I have not learned—what is permitted me and what forbidden, what is my destiny and what are my limits, where I start out and where I finish. For who is to teach me? Who shall guide me? I haven't yet written a single line.

Evidently, my voice must have betrayed emotion, for Michael gripped my shoulder, drew me still closer to him and said: A mission is not something that is learned, my son. It is imposed upon you and you bear it, learning as you go. You rise and fall with it, grow with it, until you fulfil it or collapse beneath it.

On hearing these words of Michael's, the thought uppermost on my mind was how much I would miss his wisdom, wisdom that draws on the past and flows into the future. But I said nothing. Night fell and cloaked both of us, and I thought of the coming separation and wondered how I would bear it.

When I woke with the dawn, Michael was no longer by my side. It was the day of the Sabbath, the day that the senior angels would assemble in the Garden of Gardens around the Presence and tell one another the tales of Creation. They would repeat the account of the beginning, constantly discovering new depths and new greatness, as if their understanding was not capable of encompassing all at once the greatness of the act and its meaning. The more deeply they would probe those depths, the more their understanding grew, descending further towards the miraculous foundations of the universe.

After I had bathed in the crystal river, I sang the praises of the day to the accompaniment of the trilling of birds and the sound of the water and the rustling of the trees. Then I set out to walk the paths of the Garden. The light and the shade rested harmoniously on the trees and the flowers between the paths, blending into the tranquillity that reigned throughout the Garden. My heart and my spirit were also eased. The grief that had been aroused in me at the thought of the imminent separation from my friend Michael had somewhat abated. I remembered the words of the Lord at the time that the woman was created: So man shall leave his father and his mother and shall cleave to his wife. And who was I to show reluctance to leave my brother and my friend for the sake of the Lord's work? I knew it was impossible to grow and to mature without sorrow and pain. In every part of my existence are stamped the traces of my past, and memory bears everything within it, all the strands of the paths I have travelled, as if a cloth woven of many strands.

On one of the winding paths I saw Adam and his wife leaning over the gently flowing water. They sat holding hands, at their ease, still adorned with the garlands of yesterday, still exchanging amorous glances. To sense their closeness all the better, I hovered above them. When I had once hovered over Lillith, as she lay with Gabriel, I detected a dense cloud of earth smells blended with the fragrance of figs ripening in the sunlight. It was a viscous, intoxicating cloud that I loved. But the scent that Adam and his wife exuded, though lighter, aroused all kinds of yearnings and cravings and visions and aspirations, as if there existed another universe within the universe, and to reach it you had to touch the soul of another, the other, and with it, take flight to the universe that is beyond the universe.

She laid her naked body on his body, her mouth to his ear, and repeated her request: "Adam, my husband, give me a name. You have given names to all other living things, give me a name too." Her eyes wide open, she waited.

"The Lord has given you a name. Woman. That is your name."

"But you are a man and your name is Adam. And what am I? A woman with no name?"

"When the Lord commands me to give you a name, a name you shall have. So it was when I gave names to His other creatures. I am only the instrument of His will and the voice of His thoughts."

The woman pondered and then said: "But He said that man should leave his father and his mother and cleave to his wife, and I am your wife."

"Indeed, so He said, but He did not say man should abandon His will and His words. Be patient, wife, be patient. He surely means to give you a special name, a name worthy of you. Let us wait until we know His will."

The woman agreed to this, then looking at the river, smiled and said, partly to herself and partly to him, "I see a man and a woman in the river. It's us. We look into the river and see ourselves."

Adam laughed heartily, grimacing and waving at his reflection. Still laughing, he told her how he had tried to catch his reflection in the river and how it had fled from him; he told her of his anger, of the stones he had thrown at it.

"Thanks to you I understand now that this is just my reflection. I needed you, my wife, to help me understand many things."

Suddenly I heard a faint rustle among the bushes. As Adam and his wife were still embracing and kissing, the serpent approached with furtive steps, on short legs, almost crawling on its belly. It was known as a cunning, wily creature, always ready to sow sedition and enmity, threatening the well-being of other beasts. Its presence aroused disquiet among all creatures. There was something repellent in his appearance. Perhaps it was his angular head, or the way he slithered around; perhaps it was his habit of approaching unnoticed and then emerging suddenly and unexpectedly from the thickets. Even now, he was advancing with conspiratorial caution, making an effort to move soundlessly. When he was close enough to Adam and his wife, he hung by his tail from a tree, closely resembling a branch himself. He did not see me, since only angels see angels. He was sure no one had noticed his approach.

He hung above the couple and listened to their conversation. Everything they said to one another he heard and understood, for in the Garden there was a common language shared by all creatures, man and beast alike. Only the Lord spoke to His angels in the language of the flame and in tongues of fire. Adam took his wife's hand and led her through the paths of the Garden. He told her the names of the animals that they encountered on their way, told her of their ways of life, taught her to distinguish between male and female, between birds and insects, reptiles and the fishes in the rivers. He told her of the great river on whose banks they dwelt, and how it divides into four rivers following the direction of the winds of heaven. He explained to her the sun's departure from the east and its arrival in the west, told her of the lights of day and of night. He explained that light was the beginning, and all that was before it is known only to the Lord, and that the countless stars are the eyes through which He watches and inspects His universe. Then Adam told her of the six days of creation, of which he had heard from the mouth of the Lord Himself, immediately upon his creation on the sixth day before the setting of the sun. And also of the seventh day, the day of rest of the Lord and all the host of heaven.

All this time the serpent was following in their footsteps. When they stopped he stopped, when they walked on, he crawled after them on his belly or swung from branch to branch above their heads. All the while I was observing him closely. I suspected he was stalking them because he was plotting something. He had something in mind, but I could not imagine what it was.

Adam and his wife walked at a leisurely pace, drawing closer and closer to the forbidden circle, in the midst of which stood the two trees, the central pillars of the Garden and of the entire universe. Their broad tops and branches created a green canopy, a haven for thousands of songbirds. The thick trunks, the sumptuous foliage, the shiny fruits of gold and purple were entrancing in the woman's eyes.

She stopped and stood still, amazed by the majesty of the spectacle and the glorious birdsong. The Cherubim, guarding the circle all around, closed ranks. They stood shoulder to shoulder and formed a solid defensive chain to prevent incursion, any approach to the trees. Only the serpent leapt from branch to branch and invaded the inner circle. Seeing that the woman had stopped, struck dumb by the sight of the trees and their fruit, he began performing prodigious contortions — sometimes standing erect and sometimes bowing low, juggling his limbs and twirling his tail in eye-catching loops. His agility was astonishing. Sometimes he resembled a thin trunk rising from the ground, sometimes a broad bough, sometimes he put his head to his tail in a hoop and sometimes lay prone, stretched out from pointed head to tip of tail, as if dozing in patches of light and shade.

"Look, husband," the woman said to Adam. "That miracle-worker, who is he?"

"Stay away from him, woman. Beware of him. He has a bad name among the dwellers in the Garden. He is cunning, a trickster. He is in a place forbidden to him. Even setting foot in that place is forbidden."

The woman looked at Adam, perplexed. "What does that

mean, forbidden?" she asked. "This is my first day in the Garden, and you are using words hard for me to understand, like forbidden. What is forbidden?"

The serpent laughed and repeated her question: "Forbidden, forbidden, what is forbidden?"

# Chapter forty

When the members of Noah's family had regained their senses, he gave them all tasks. Shem's assignment was to divide the remaining food into seven portions, a ration for every day. Men and beasts would need to subsist on the most meagre potions, the very least of the least, if they were to live to see the day when Noah could open the hatches and lead them ashore. Noah warned them all once more against harming any living thing in the ark.

"Remember our father Cain and what befell him when the Lord said: The blood of your brother cries out to me from the earth. The blood of the animals that you have murdered and devoured cries out to us from the waters, from the land and from the skies. Remember, these are the last living things in the universe. Murder a single one of the souls quartered in the ark, and you murder a creature of the Lord, one that will never again be restored to life."

His voice was firm and resolute. Despite his age and his weariness, his strength and his authority had returned. Having given his instructions, he set guards on the pens of the beasts and the birds. All his sons were to take turns watching the animals lest harm befall them, and henceforth the blood of these animals would be on the head of the sentinels. Ham was the first to stand guard, a stout club in his hand. After him came Shem and Japheth. Responsibility for the food was given to the wives, and they too were required to weigh and to measure with care, ensuring that the provisions would suffice for all.

The children were commanded to go from room to room in the ark, removing any bones they found, then scouring and cleaning up the filth, and so cleaning away the memory of that shameful act of madness and greed. Noah told them:

"Let the vile bones be cast away, and thus may the ark be purified in the eyes of Adam, our ancient father and father of the animals who have perished in the deep, and in the eyes of the Lord, his God and ours."

The people gathered around him listened to his words and averted their eyes, smitten by his strictures. And yet his commands also expunged their shame and infused them with new strength and vitality, and a determination to forget the events of the previous day, even as they made amends. Their father, Noah, had saved their lives, their father, the father of the family of survivors, their father the master mariner of the ark, their father the navigator and commander. He was their guardian and their custodian—he, who was not to be disobeyed—he would surely lead them to land and safety.

When Noah finished speaking, they turned to their tasks. The sounds of labour filled the ark. They drew water from the sea in pails, and passed them from hand to hand. The children cleared away the bones, the dung and the lice-ridden rubbish and threw it all overboard. The decks were scrubbed clean, the food divided into seven separate piles. The food for the animals was kept apart from the food for the humans, so that none would be deprived of his rightful share.

"Their lives and the lives of men are of equal value," said

Noah. "Men and the beasts of the field and the birds of the air, everything wherein there is a living soul, all are required to reach the seventh day in health and well-being. The Lord has entrusted them into our hands," he reminded them solemnly, "and to the Lord we shall return them. That which is slain cannot be brought back to life. But what remains will be saved with us."

Noah passed from corner to corner and from room to room. He went into the pens and moved from animal to animal, distributing food from the meagre rations that remained, stroking their heads, cleaning their skin and fur, brushing out their manes. He fetched pails of water and relieved their thirst. The animals, too, were in better spirits now, beginning to low and to bleat, to stamp and to skip, to sing and to growl. The ark was filled once again with vibrant life. The day that had begun in terror ended calmly. Noah's family accepted the orders of the master mariner, sensing that only with firm will and resolution would the journey be completed, bringing them all to the landfall that they craved.

While Noah and his household were still about their business, I began to read the stone tablets on which Noah had inscribed the history of the ark and its journey from when he entered it until the present day. This is what was written:

*The ark is nearing completion. I have made it as the Lord commanded that it be made. Three hundred cubits in length, fifty in breadth and thirty in height. From reeds and from gopher wood I built it, and I have smeared it with pitch inside and out. There will be a hatch above and a hatch in the side. Three decks I have built. On the lower level the animals brought into the ark will be housed, the upper level will be for the sons of Adam.*

*The people of the valley of the palms stand around me and mock me. Noah, where will your boat be sailing? On waters that do not exist? Do you not see that the riverbed is dry, that drought has consumed it to the very last drop? Today they even threw stones at us in their anger and dismay. The drought has dried up not only the sources of water, but even the very marrow of their bones. Hunger is everywhere. The forests are ablaze and a great pall of smoke hangs in the air.*

*All the members of my household who are fit to work are helping me. The children cut reeds and pile them in stacks beside the ark. My sons cut down gopher trees and fashion them into panels, planks and struts. The women take care of the provisions and go out to gather the animals, pair by pair, into pens on the bank of the river. The pure beasts and fowls are kept in separate pens. These we shall sacrifice to the Lord when the days of the flood have passed. The angel who prophesied the flood told me that God would send down rain for forty days and forty nights. What the Lord says through the lips of His messenger shall surely come to pass.*

*Today I am building the hatch. It is a cubit above the frame of the ark, so it will be possible to look through it during the voyage. The scorching wind feeds the brush fire in the meadows and the forests. Tongues of flame lick the edges of the fields; if but one were to reach the gopher-wood of the ark, the ark would burn. I trust in the Lord and in His promise. The people of the valley of the palms are fleeing towards the river. They believe that the fire will be halted on its banks. It is now no more than a muddy creek, swarming with snakes and worms. Beasts and birds have taken refuge here in the riverbed, but they lap up the fetid water and die. In the air there are borne the cries of those who have been too slow to escape from their huts in the face of the advancing fire, together with the bellows of trapped animals. At night, a giant ring of fire can be seen surging down from the mountains in the direction of the river.*

*In my dream the angel said: Seven days hence the Lord will send a flood over all the earth. Five days have passed. Perhaps the wind will yet change direction and the ark will be spared. I trust in the word of the Lord, but my sons are sceptical. They have stayed only because I have stayed. It is not in their nature to abandon their father at such a time.*

Shem said: Father, you are such a saint, you believe everything that God tells you. If He told you that the sun will rise in the west, you would believe it.

Ham said: Father, Father. You are as innocent as a newborn lamb. Do you not see that the end of all flesh is approaching? Your angel told the truth: the land is indeed full of violence and corruption and treachery, and you, in your innocence — can you still believe that God will want to raise another generation of mankind?

Japheth, my youngest son, has turned his back on my God, but I cannot reject him, for he is still my son. Yet I see with pain how he despises Him. He has carved an image with the head of a bull and the body of a lion on a rock, and he sacrifices to it and pours libations to it and bows down before it, and to me he says: "Go, Father, go and walk with your God, and see how that will help you. Will He deliver you from the drought, from the blazing fire, from the smoke that is choking our children? Go, Father, walk with your God. I bow to gods that my eyes can see and my hand can touch."

Were it not for the respect that Japheth owes me as a son, he would deride me as openly as my good neighbours do. But for my part, I remain steadfast in my faith and I am not angry with him or with the others. I shall do as the Lord has commanded me, when he sent me his envoy, the angel.

Today is the seventh day. All night the wind has blown from the west. Over these past five years the easterly wind has scorched our land and dried up the creeks and the gullies and the rivers, mountain streams and lakes. In five long years the cruel wind has consumed every drop of water in our land. Only a few meagre wells remain, and these are fiercely contended by men and beasts, by birds and insects. People are possessed by madness and by fear. They lie in wait for one another at night and steal pitchers of water one from another. But worst of all, they have started drinking the blood of animals. From the blazing hills and the fire-ravaged forests animals have fled to the parched gullies of the river in the hope of finding a little water.

*There men stalk them, slit their throats and drink their blood. The blood is life, but their thirst has made them forget the word of God.*

*Tonight the skies are covered with dense clouds. They come from the west and they bear within them the rains that have been promised. Perhaps now the neighbours will cease to mock me and my sons will once again believe in the word of God.*

*The ark has been filled with all manner of living beasts, male and female. They will sail with me and with my household and they will survive, while the God of heaven and earth destroys every living thing upon the face of the earth that is outside the ark.*

*With morning, the rain began to fall. After seven days it began to fall, no more and no less, exactly as God's envoy had foretold. Here is the sign that all that He said is the truth.*

*From this day I shall count forty days and forty nights until the rains have ceased. By that time, I am confident, the rivers and the streams shall once more be filled and the land will be replenished with water. Then I am sure that life will return to the earth with this blessed rain, and the spirit of God to the heart of men, and they shall no longer do evil in His eyes.*

*Today the ark began to rise as the dry creek once again filled with water. It no longer sprawls like a behemoth in the foul mud. Living water, the waters of the heavens, flow in the gully and encompass the ark all around. Creaks and groans were heard as the dry timbers began to swell and expand. Until noon the waters were building up to raise the ark, and when it floated on the surface of the rising waters, my heart rose too. Here is the rain, here is the ark, here is the swelling torrent, and here is the word of God coming to pass.*

*From the hatch of the ark I saw the people of the valley running from the mountains and the forests. The fire had been dowsed by the ferocious rain. Beasts awoke from their swoon and came down to the banks of the river to slake their thirst. What will happen when the water rises above the riverbanks and sweeps away everything in its path? Only now is my heart pierced by dread of the end. All these happy people, standing on the banks, whooping, celebrating, bathing, filling their pitchers with water, embracing one another and dancing—are they all doomed to annihilation?*

*Shem my eldest son, my chosen one, berated me: Father, Father, you were forewarned by God that all life was to end, and you consented? You did not appeal, you did not protest, you did not try to save them? Are you a righteous man? Righteous perhaps in one generation, in your own generation, but not in generations to come.*

*It is now seven days and seven nights that the rain has fallen without respite. The skies are heavy above our heads. Low lying places have become a broad lake, and on the surface of the water float uprooted trees, corpses of animals, household articles, shattered huts and booths. People too, those who did not escape the torrents of water, are swept down from the mountains, especially old folk, children and infants. The blessing of water has become a curse and a destroyer. My heart is filled with pain and doubts, but my lips remain sealed. This is His will and these are His acts.*

*My sons are angry and mutinous, refusing to accept His will. Japheth flung at me words that are hard even to repeat: "Is this your God, Father, a God of destruction and death, a God who created a world in order to see its devastation, who created life in order to see its annihilation?"*

*I did not answer and did not argue. My task is to lead the survivors entrusted to my care to safe landfall. This is my mission. Let my sons wrestle with God on their own account and on account of their children. The strength that is left in me is dedicated to their deliverance. By my faith I have lived, and by my faith shall I die.*

*"You are incorrigibly innocent, Father," says Ham. "Your faith is your blindness. You are afraid to be cured of your blindness and to see."*

*"God has given, God has taken away." I reply. Shem is silent.*

157

*There is grief in his eyes but his mouth is silent, his eyes cry out but his voice is mute.*

*I seal my sorrow within me, but the hard work keeps me occupied from dawn until sunset. It is my task to distribute the food, everything measured and weighed, and to ensure that the animals do not become unruly. Their fear is aroused by every jolt of the ark. The scent of the blood that they sniffed in the days of the drought has not faded from their nostrils. They must be watched carefully lest they attempt to prey on one another. Once flesh has been tasted, it is sought after again and again.*

*The members of my family are tense and anxious. Quarrels erupt over the most trivial of matters. One person looks at another's portion, and suspects it is greater than his own. In the night I heard rustling from the direction of the granary where food is stored for the humans. I surprised Ham, bearing a pilfered jar of grain. I could not believe it. Had I not, day and night, impressed upon my sons the lesson that stealing is a sin? And yet the fear of hunger in the future prevailed over the fear of sin in the present. Day by day, the superficial veneer is being stripped away from the soul, revealing anxiety, jealousy and darker desires. Will I succeed in bringing the ark to a safe shore, despite the deluge without and the passions within? God will guide us and save us.*

*A calm day. The rain is still falling but with less intensity. Clouds still cover the heavens from horizon to horizon, but it seems to me that their colour has lightened a little. Or is this just a delusion? Many things are seen in the mind of the one who longs to see them. Is it possible that there does exist both an imaginary world and a solid world? A passing thought. My hands are filled with work around the animals and the humans alike. All display the signs of distress, impatience and defiance. The animals fill the narrow space of the ark with vile smells, with bellowing, braying and bleating. Even the singing of birds, once so delightful, has turned into a nightmare. The sharp screeches, the strident whistles that seem to pierce our very bowels, the monotonous chirping that is like rhythmic and constant blows to the head—all these things are tiresome to the point of distraction. The endless rutting inflames their carnal instincts. As soon as one female calms down, another begins to stamp, to wail, to howl, to demand. The command to be fruitful and multiply is not applicable to times of flood, however loudly the males may roar. There is no room in the ark for more creatures, or more mouths to feed.*

*When the waters continued to rise, I was obliged to separate the males from the females. Later, the wives of my sons came to me and demanded that the humans be separated too. They told me that they could not conceive or give birth in stinking stalls amid piles of excrement. There is no water for purification, nor is there privacy. I have promised to speak with my sons, but will they obey me? Who can build a dam that will restrain desire, this strong and turbulent wind?*

*The water has risen high. From the last of the ranges that still stand above the broad sea, flow mighty cataracts of water. Everything that came down from above now aspires to be swept into the sea. Water to water. I thought that all human beings had drowned, but yesterday something happened that still makes my flesh crawl. On a broad trunk five children were floating, two girls and three boys, sons and daughters of our neighbours. I had known all of them from the day of their birth. Time and again I had stroked their heads, time and again they had laughed and played on the threshold of my home. Grandpa Noah, Grandpa Noah, they used to call me, when I gave them ripe and juicy dates. When the ark passed by them they began to shout: "Grandpa Noah, Grandpa Noah, save us! We are drowning, save us!" They cried out in heart-rending tones, and with the very last of their strength waved clenched fists, their faces contorted by the fear of death.*

*I closed my eyes and stopped my ears with their hands. They tried to clutch at the bow of the ark but slipped into the swelling waters. Who will avenge their blood? Will their killer take revenge upon himself?*

# Chapter forty-one

Evening. I have laid aside the tablets. The gloom within the ark was deeper than the gloom outside, and even my eyes, which can see by day and night, were unable to go on reading the writing on the tablets. The sorrow of Noah and his struggles give me no peace. What will happen if his faith is shattered—who then will guide the ark safely to shore?

The voices in the ark have fallen quiet; here and there only a sigh can be heard, here and there the faint rustling of cooped up men and beasts struggling with their insomnia.

# Chapter forty-two

"hat does forbidden mean?" the woman repeated her question, seeing Adam hesitate to reply. Adam groped for the words that could explain it to his wife.

"It means that it is possible to eat of any tree from the Garden," said Adam. "It's just from the two huge, spreading trees in the middle of the Garden, is it impossible. These trees are the Tree of Knowledge and the Tree of Life, and whoever eats of their fruit shall surely die."

The woman's eyes widened as she stared at the trees, at the ripe and shiny fruits.

"But they seem so enchanting, they look so wonderful and they're surely just as tasty to eat."

"Yes," responded Adam, "but it is forbidden to touch or to eat them. Whoever eats of their fruit, shall surely die."

"Shall die," says the woman, bemused. "Shall die? What does that mean?"

Adam was perplexed. What is *shall die*, he wondered? He knew what it meant to be alone, what a woman was, what it was when flesh cleft to flesh and became one flesh; but what *did* it mean, to die?

"I don't know," whispered Adam. "I don't know, but that is what the Lord said, and so I take great care not to touch those trees and their fruit. When I pass through the Garden, I avoid the forbidden circle; I go round it. You should be careful too. Perhaps the Lord will explain to us what it means."

The serpent curled up around himself, and shook with laughter. You shall know soon enough, he said to himself in a choked voice, You will know — and how!

I felt like hitting him, and beating the cunning and malice out of his spineless body. He was surely hatching up some mischief to harm them, I thought, but was at a loss to know what it could be. I resolved to follow him. Take care, Adam, take care, dear woman, for you are beloved of Adam. As they moved away from the forbidden circle, the woman glanced back from time to time, still entranced by the forbidden trees.

"Look, Adam, even from afar the fruits shine gold and purple like the sun. They are like little suns, a very delight to the eyes, charming to look at."

"Have done, wife, have done! I told you. Forbidden is forbidden."

"But I don't know what forbidden means," she said.

The serpent followed them and intervened in their conversation. "Eat and you shall know . . . it is good to eat of the Tree of Knowledge and to know," he said, leaving Adam and his wife and disappearing into a thicket.

I followed him. He stuck out his tongue to sniff, searching among the bushes, until he found a cave hidden in a shady spot. As a fountain of pure water gushed from the rock, it burst into a tuneful song, melodious in a language of its own. The serpent entered the cave, with me close behind him. Where was he going in such haste? In the gloom of the cave I saw Lillith sprawled on her belly, asleep. Her hair flowed over her back; her wings were folded beneath her and her legs, fine and shapely legs, parted to reveal her cleft. Furtively the serpent approached, intent on her warm body. Lillith awoke and saw it, hastily bringing her legs firmly together as she recoiled from his touch.

-Here again, pest? I told you, I'm not for you! Go find yourself a female serpent. Let her cool you off!

-But can you guess, Lillith, what the serpent is bringing you? He said in a whisper, trying to penetrate her with his tongue.

-I've no patience for you, serpent. You know that since the woman appeared Adam has forgotten me and I want only him.

-Just so, Lillith, just so. I see you're following my serpentine thoughts . . . I'll give him back to you, and you'll give me what I desire.

Lillith was suddenly extremely attentive.

-What are you suggesting, you pest?

-Listen, my wanton beauty. I will tempt the woman to eat of the forbidden fruit – and you know the punishment . . . she shall surely die. And so I'll return your bare-bottomed lover to you. He'll be yours and you'll be mine, if only for one time.

Lillith's eyes were bright at the prospect of returning to her dreams of Adam.

-Get rid of her first, she said, and then come back to me. But only the one time. After that I shall keep myself for him alone.

-So be it, the serpent replied, and as for the future, well, we shall see.

He jumped up on his stumpy legs, and quickly scuttled away to look for Adam and his wife in the Garden. He found them sitting on the bank of the river. Adam was busy plaiting stalks of reeds. Evidently they had decided to build a booth to provide them with shade. The serpent approached with stealthy tread, and whispered in the woman's ear:

"Do you like the pretty fruits?"

"Very much," she replied. "But it is forbidden to touch or eat them."

"Of course, of course," said the serpent. "Do you think that the Lord wants anyone other than He to know the difference between good and evil? The day you taste this fruit, your eyes will be opened, and the things you see will amaze you. What you see now is as nothing compared with what you shall see then. The fruit is delicious, and it will make you wise."

"But what does it mean, we shall surely die?" the woman asked.

"That is just myth and make-believe. Nothing in it. Words, words, words to frighten you."

The serpent coiled into miraculous contortions and slithered from branch to branch, the woman close behind him. Moving with acrobatic agility he approached the trees in the centre of the Garden. The woman followed in his wake, entranced, and crossed the line into the forbidden circle, to the sound of screeching birds rising from the branches and the loud protests of the Cherubim, astonished to see the woman invading their sanctum. The serpent picked a single fruit, and put it to the lips of the woman.

"Hurry, bite it, hurry. Before they snatch the fruit from your mouth."

The woman took a bite, and the serpent sprang up and hurried away to the cave to report his triumph to Lillith.

Adam was searching for his wife, looking very anxious and at a loss. When he saw his wife with the forbidden fruit between her teeth, he broke into the circle and shouted:

"Stop, stop, it's forbidden!"

It was too late. Hungrily and with sensual delight she took a second and a third bite, and pushed the fruit between his teeth.

"Eat, my love, eat, and we shall be like the Lord. The fruit of the tree is delicious; it is the giver of wisdom. Eat my love, eat, and we shall know good and evil."

"And death too!" cried Adam.

I stood at the edge of the forbidden circle, not daring to cross the line. The man and the woman stood in the middle. The fruit still between their teeth, they both looked up at once, shielding their eyes with their hands. The great light dazzled them. Slowly and hesitantly they removed their hands, first the fingers and then the whole hand, and rubbed their eyes as if trying to dispel something they had not seen before. They looked at each other, as if discovering one another for the first time. They saw that they were naked, and were ashamed. The woman hastened to pluck some fig leaves and rapidly made a covering for her cleft, while Adam, likewise, wrapped his groin in a girdle of foliage. It was the twilight hour. There was no living soul in the Garden; only the breeze stirred the leaves, and from the breeze came a voice. It was the voice of the Lord. Adam and his wife hurriedly hid themselves under the fig tree from which they had plucked the leaves.

Again the voice called out to Adam: What is this, why are you hiding in the trees?

"We are naked, and ashamed to show ourselves like this before you, Lord."

-Naked? Asked the voice, as if amazed. And who told you this?

"I saw the nakedness of my wife, and she saw mine, and we understood that we were naked."

-You have seen your nakedness, said the voice in a tone of restrained contempt. Evidently you have eaten of the forbidden tree.

Adam was stunned. Now he knew that from the watchful eye of the Lord nothing could be hidden. Now at last, with his eyes open to see and to understand, he saw it was impossible to evade the scrutiny of the Lord.

"It was not I, Lord, who plucked the forbidden fruit. The woman that you gave me, she plucked the fruit and gave it to me, to eat."

-What have you done, my daughter, what have you done?

"The serpent tempted me with his charms and his lies. You did not tell me what it means, when it is said that a thing is forbidden, Lord. How was I to know? You told only Adam, Lord. You never speak to me, you have not even given me a name."

Her voice was plaintive, somewhat resentful. I stood to the side, not knowing whether to stay and listen, or to go away. In the voice of the Lord I heard more sorrow than reproof, more the words of a father than of a judge.

I sought out my friend Michael. What I had seen was a burden too heavy for me to bear. I realised something had happened that would disrupt the serenity of the Garden. Even I did not know the meaning of "shall surely die" though I sensed it must be something momentous, separate and different from everything I had seen and learned. Only with Michael could I share the burden. When I found him, he already knew what had happened. The rumour had swept through the Garden and the Garden of Gardens. Wherever I passed, I found conferring flocks of angels of all ranks. What would happen now, now that it was not only the Lord who knew good and evil, but Adam and his wife too? And where was the punishment? For had the Lord not said that whoever touched the tree and ate of its fruit would surely die? Would that really happen to Adam and his wife, the most wondrous of the achievements of the Lord's creation?

-Michael, I said, breathless with agitation, I was a witness to what happened. I saw it all.

-I know, he replied. After all, it is your mission to see and to tell. So tell, tell me how this happened.

I told Michael of the serpent and its guile, of its charms and temptations, of its desire for Lillith and of the trap it had set for the woman.

-What will happen now, Michael? We know what the punishment is. But what is dying, Michael, what does it mean, to die?

Michael knew. He knew this from the far distant times, when Satan, Asmodeus and Samael walked amid the abysses, amid the darkness and the gloom, amid the untamed volcanoes and the cataracts of fire and the sulphurous fumes sweeping the furthest reaches of the universe.

-Death, brother, is the force opposite to life. Life builds, creates, multiplies, flourishes, draws on the water and the light, takes of the goodness of the Lord and gives its own goodness back to Him. Death is silence and stillness, perpetual eclipse and paralysis. It neither gives nor takes, does not blossom or bear fruit. Life is existence, death is oblivion. Life engenders joy, love, friendship, fellowship, tenderness, compassion. Death is perpetual isolation, eternal solitude.

I was stunned by his words. The decisive, abrupt answer left no doubt as to where his own sympathies lay. Yet I wondered if Michael had considered if the Lord remembered into whose hands He had commended all living things? If he remembered who gave them names? And to whom did He say at their creation, Be fruitful and multiply? And if they were to die, there would be no one, no man or no woman left to be fruitful and to multiply. He who saw everything, who saw the beginning and foresaw the end, had he not foreseen even the serpent's temptation of the woman, and the woman's temptation of Adam? A riot of questions erupted in me.

-Michael, Michael. If only I had been granted to remain at my post, up there in the orbit of the sun, I would not now be so torn. His deeds are beyond my understanding. If He really forbade the eating of the fruit, why did He not either stop them, or make it impossible for them to do so? Just as he made it impossible for Adam to see Lillith. After all, not a single star turns in its path, nor the most humble bird chirrups in its nest, except by His will. So how could it be that the only pair of human beings in the universe, the much-vaunted crown of His creation, could have fallen into a trap set them by a serpent? Did He really not know?

Silence. A long and heavily laden, unbearable silence. I fixed my gaze on Michael's eyes, lest he try to evade my questions. Michael, my dear friend, this time, whichever way you turn I shall be at your side, I shall not leave you until I hear you out. Perhaps there are things which you are hiding from me, perhaps you are afraid of the Lord, perhaps you are silent for some other reason entirely, but this time I want to be a full partner. Your pupil, Michael, has grown up. He has seen things for himself and earned the right to doubt and to protest.

-He knew, I heard my friend's voice, He knew, and He did not prevent it.

-Michael, is what I hear what you're really saying?! If that's so, has He not led them, by His will, straight to this terrible thing that you have described to me, to death? Can it be so? With eyes open, knowingly, as if He himself had impelled them to it?

Silence returned. Deep, uncompromising, stubborn.

-Yes, knowingly, he said at last. He didn't impel them, but allowed them to choose. And henceforward this will be their path and this their destiny. They chose knowledge and death rather than ignorance and eternal life. Only the Lord has the right to know and to live forever. What you saw was not done in spite of His will, nor according to His will. The Lord created a new thing in the universe when he created man.

-And what new thing is that? I asked impatiently.

-He created the right of choice. Now Adam knows good and evil, and such will be his acts — good or evil — as he chooses.

-And yet they have been told they shall surely die. How are they to do anything when they are still and silent, paralysed in the perpetual darkness you have described? What kind of acts can they perform then?

-You do not understand, my son. They shall die, perhaps, if that is the Lord's will, but their offspring will carry on their lives from generation to generation. Like water in the river. Drops pass away and yet the water flows. Adam and his wife will pass away, yet their lives will flow on like the river.

-How, Michael, how? If they pass away, how shall they flow?

-In memory, my son. From Adam and his wife to their children. And from their children to the generations that shall come after. The creator of life and the creator of Adam cannot undo what He has done. What He has created shall stand forever.

-And what is to happen now, now that the fruit has been tasted? What will befall Adam and his wife now?

-We shall see, my friend . . . we will know the answer soon.

## Chapter forty-three

At dawn I rose early, bathed in the waters of the sea and quickly returned to the ark. After reciting the words of the morning anthem, I made my way to the cabin where the tablets were kept, intent on resuming my reading. As I passed, I caught sight of Noah with all the members of his family around him. Closest to him sat the children; behind them, the wives and at the rear his three sons, Shem, Ham and Japheth. Noah stood in the midst of them, looking determined. The great weariness that had marked his features when the dove was sent on its mission was now barely visible. Yesterday his clothes had still been stained with blood and sweat, yet today he had been quick to put on the clean garments that had been stored in readiness for disembarkation, to keep from his body the blood of the lambs that would be slaughtered then. This was Noah as I had seen him almost a year previously, standing at the head of his family and teaching his sons and daughters the virtues of toil, justice, charity and the fear of God. This was again that man on whose shoulders the Lord had laid the heavy burden of leading what remained of life to a safe shore, the master mariner of the ship of deliverance. Now Noah addressed the scant few who had survived both the drought and the flood.

"Hear me, sons and daughters, listen to me, children of Adam and Eve. In a few more days we shall leave the ark and stand once more on dry land, in safety. You must be pure. The drought that preceded the flood was a sign, a call from God that should have rung in our ears, but we did not heed it. We closed our ears to the cries of the oppressed that filled the earth. And when the drought struck, we closed our eyes as animals; birds and men preyed on one another. Blood is the life, and blood that is spilled carries away with it the souls of the living. With our own eyes we saw the forests ablaze and the hills in flames, the rivers parched and the beasts dying of thirst, and thought that we had saved ourselves. And the flood came, extinguishing the fire and life as well. A few days hence we shall go out and inherit land that is dry but supplied with water in abundance. Rivers will flow in their courses, springs welling up in the mountains and fountains gushing forth. Shall we too not open up new paths for our lives?"

Noah paused for a moment, then removed the little bag that had been hung about his neck, displayed it before the assembled company and continued:

"See, in this bag is a handful of the earth which our mother Eve gathered from the dust which covered her son Abel. This dust is moist with his blood, and from it his voice rose to the heavens. Our mother Eve kept and treasured this dust and, at her death, passed it on to her son Seth. From him it has passed, from generation to generation, throughout the nine generations of our existence on the earth. This bag I shall bequeath to you, my sons, as both a sign and a remembrance. The voice of our brother Abel cries from it not only to the skies, but to us all as well. With this cry in our hearts, and foremost in our minds the searing memory of the fire and the flood that destroyed all life on the face of the earth, we shall make a new beginning for mankind on the earth.

Ours will be a kingdom without bloodshed, without violence and evil. Be strong and be brave."

His family heard his words, but they were listless and weary. A few dozed, others chewed seeds from the daily food ration. The animals were stirred and lowed, bleated and roared. A young child hanging on his mother's parched and wizened breast wept bitterly, finding it as dry as a desert stream.

"There's no end to his naïve innocence," Ham whispered to Japheth. "We must help him because he is our father, but let him dream his dreams alone, righteous innocent that he is."

These words did not reach Noah's ears, and he passed the little bag of dust around the assembled company, inviting everyone to touch and to feel it. I was glad he did not hear the words of Ham, for they would have grieved this wonderful old man. Would another like him ever live? The closer that the day of disembarkation grew, the greater grew my concern about the few days still remaining before the opening of the ark. Lord, preserve them, preserve them until they come to shore, to their new beginning.

I resumed my reading of the tablets.

# Chapter forty-four

*D*ay follows day, and life grows harder. The children, who in the first days of the ark used to fill it with their cheerful voices and their laughter, with quick-drying tears and mischievous spirits, are silent and indolent. They sprawl on heaps of straw, stirring only to receive their meagre rations before lapsing again into inertia. From time to time one of them develops pains, causing him to groan, to weep and to cry out. Two of them, delightful children, boys of five and six years old, died. We could not bury them, so we cast their bodies into the deep. My heart was torn to shreds. Not long ago we were dying of thirst, and now we are drowning in water. Ruin prevailed then as it does now. And what of God? Was He here then, or is He here now? Or both?

To the members of my family I show the face of one who is confident and resolute, knowing the way. In my innermost heart I am filled with fear and confusion. What if plague breaks out among us? What if suffering consumes our strength? In two more days, forty nights will have passed since the start of the flood. Will the rains stop?

*God said, through the mouth of His angel, it would be forty days and forty nights. Yet still I trust in Him.*

*The rains ceased last night. At midnight, when all the voyagers in the ark were already asleep, there was a deafening silence. Our senses had become so accustomed to the constant drumming of the rain on the roof of the ark. Suddenly there was stillness all around, with only the sound of the waves splashing against the timbers to remind us that the ark was afloat. I hurried to the hatch and looked all around me. The rain had indeed stopped, and the clouds were dispersing. For the first time since entering the ark I saw stars. Blessed be the Creator of heaven and earth and the host of the stars.*

*People were awakened by the unexpected silence. They rubbed their eyes in the gloom, as if not believing what they did not hear. They gathered around me, and took it in turns to climb up to the hatch, to see with their own eyes the sky strewn with stars and the calm surface of the waters. The moon also cast a faint light, and a little of it penetrated the ark. It carried hope. Blessed be the Creator of the sun and the moon.*

*How many more days or weeks must we wait? Hope is quick to flare up and quick to fade. They call me innocent, but they themselves, on seeing the light of the stars, believed that deliverance was at hand. Did they not see the earth drowned in the deep, the great sea that stretches around us, the mountains that have vanished? Only one peak, a tall and soaring peak, rises above the surface of the water. The angel foretold the duration of the flood, but did not say when the water would subside and diminish. My sons are angry. They believe I should have asked the angel how long we must stay in the ark. They are sure it was on account of my piety that I failed to do this. What difference does it make? If we had known that months were to elapse, would we have refused to be saved?*

*Shem, my first-born, is silent. He hides his feelings. Ham grumbles, but without ire, without overwhelming rage. He has the* depth of fine and fertile soil, absorbing the rain, the sun and the wind before bearing fruit. Such is Ham. And Japheth? Alas, Japheth is far away from me. Only the respect due to a father keeps him by my side. He looses his tongue and rails scornfully against my faith in my God. He is less patient than his brothers. A few days ago he rushed to the window of the ark, opened it and shouted: "Enough, enough, have you not done enough, angry, vengeful and cruel God that You are? Was it to kill us with thirst and hunger, in the midst of the deep, that You spared us from your flood? God, we have reached a parting of the ways, God, a parting . . ."

It took all my strength to drag him from the window. Shem and Ham came to my aid, and between us we managed to calm him down with assurances that the day of deliverance was at hand. Forgive him, God, he has suffered much; we have all suffered much. Tomorrow, if the rain does not return, I shall send the raven to search for dry land. The Ararat range is before us and a little of it is exposed. We are almost there. I imagine that this is how the universe looked the day that God separated the water from the land. We shall see that it is good.

The sending of the raven was a solemn event. Men, women and children washed in water drawn from the sea, donned festive garb set aside for Sabbaths and combed their hair. The men put on linen tunics. I combed my hair and my beard, which had both turned completely white. I took the raven in my hands, and turned in prayer to God in heaven saying: You who brought us through fire and flood to this day, receive our prayer. This bird is sent out to you, God of heaven and earth. Through him give us a sign that the waters have dwindled and dry land is once more revealed to the light of the sun.

Those assembled said, Amen; the children burst into song. I opened my hands, and the raven spread its wings and soared aloft. My heart was full to overflowing, brimming with hope and with doubt. Would the bird find land? It circled and circled, picking out a tiny foothold of land in the midst of the waters but did not stay long. It circled again and returned to the window of the ark.

*My sons were angry and censorious, telling me I should have sent the dove. Send the dove, Father, she can fly further, she will find land. Are you keeping her for sacrifice, because she is pure? Are you sacrificing our lives for the sake of this? Words hard as stones, sharp as thorns.*

*A week later, I brought the dove to the open window and released it, under the sullen gaze of my sons. I did not say a word. Their grief had put bitter words in their mouths. The dove wheeled back and forth and returned to the ark, having found no foothold. In the night I heard voices whispering. Ham was saying: "It's ten whole months that we've been languishing in the ark. We should break open the cover. The ark is already nudging the summit of Ararat, and it is time to leave it."*

*The conference continued through the night. Japheth said: The children are dying, our wives are rebellious and refusing to consort with us, the food is running out—and already we see mountains. What is he waiting for, why the delay? Why doesn't he give the order to go ashore? Shem was silent. I heard his voice only once, saying: "Our father is waiting for a sign from heaven. Perhaps that is the right thing to do."*

*Shem my firstborn, you are the only one who stands by me, the only one who understands me.*

*Ham came to me on behalf of the brothers and asked: "Father, have you received a sign from your God?"*

*"In seven more days, I replied, we shall send out the dove again."*

*"By then we shall be dead, he retorted, turning his back on me."*

*Soon after that, I saw them furtively removing reeds from the animal pens and building a boat.*

*"What are you doing?" I asked.*

*"As you see, Father, we are building a boat." They said no more.*

*One night, when the moon was full and shedding bright light on the water, they opened the window stealthily, lowered the boat, loaded it with food—but before they had even cast off, it capsized. The boat and the food were lost, my sons were saved. When I saw them the next day I said nothing, and they said nothing. In my heart I thanked God for preserving them. They are my sons, and with them I must found the new family of mankind. If they too are lost, I shall take my life and die with them.*

# Chapter forty-five

Michael was right when he said that soon we would know what was to happen. That very night the Lord convened the Sublime Court of Justice, where all the senior angels and the heads of groups of lower ranking angels are summoned. Since coming to the Garden I don't remember a single session of this court. When I asked Michael about the nature and the origin of the court, he was silent a long time before replying:

-My friend, you will know soon enough all you need to know. Do not delve too deeply into the past, for more is hidden than is revealed.

-Guide me, Michael, so that I will know how to behave.

-It is a story shrouded in the mists of time. Once, ages upon ages ago, some angels rebelled against the Lord and tried to take His place. It was then that He convened a session of the Sublime Court of Justice.

-Who rebelled, Michael? I'm no longer a novice, surely . . . I, too, am allowed to know truths from the past.

Hastily, as we made our way to the Garden of Gardens,

Michael told me of Satan and the sons of Belial who joined forces with him and tried to establish the rule of wickedness and destruction, instead of the rule of creation and of life.

-And what happened then, in this court? What did He decide?

-Satan and his band were expelled from the Garden and sent to the realm of the abyss, the land of scorching heat. From time to time, one of them returns to challenge the Lord. Even Satan is sometimes permitted to attend these sessions.

We, meanwhile, had reached the Garden of Gardens. Cherubim greeted us, there were balmy scents in the air, and beauty and splendour were everywhere. I found the place where I had sat when the woman was created, while Michael moved on to the inner circle, in the midst of which the flame had already appeared. When all those summoned to attend had taken their places, a voice was heard from within the flame:

-Raphael, you are to preside. As an interested party, I cannot preside over the Sublime Court of Justice.

Raphael commanded that Adam and his wife be brought forward. Four Cherubim, two to their right and two to their left, escorted Adam and his wife to the inner circle, who stood, with their fig-leaf girdles about their waists, their eyes downcast, anxious and grieved. The flame was enveloped in a dark, reddish-purple cloud. Raphael began the proceedings and read out the indictment.

-Adam, what have you to say in your defence?

"It was not I who ate, your honour. I was fed."

-And what say you, woman, in your defence?

"My senses were dulled, your honour. The serpent deceived me with lies and temptations. He said I would not die, but we would be like gods, knowing good and evil."

Raphael was about to pronounce the death sentence that all were expecting, but the voice from the flame stopped him.

-As an interested party, I am entitled to testify, said the

voice. The woman was right, saying that she was not warned by me. Adam was right to say that it was the woman who fed him the forbidden fruit. The serpent has no excuses, acting as he did with evil intent. They are all the creatures of my hand. My law requires that a measure of justice be tempered with a measure of compassion, and to this they are all entitled.

Raphael turned to the flame, saying: Lord, this is a judgment that is beyond my abilities. You must teach us how to steer a course between the requirements of justice and the requirements of compassion.

All those assembled in the Garden of Gardens were enveloped in utter silence. No one stirred, no Cherub, no Seraph, no angel. Tensely, all awaited the verdict of the Supreme Judge of Heaven and Earth.

The flame flared into full light, radiant with many colours. A bow blending together all the hues of the universe arched like a canopy over the Garden. The multitudes were stunned by the iridescence, by the beauty and the majesty of the spectacle. Never had such a sight been seen in the Garden. There could be no doubt the Lord was about to deliver a judgment such as had never been heard before. Was it to be death for the guilty? The Lord had testified on their behalf; did this mean he intended to pardon them?

And then His voice was heard, saying: Bring the serpent here.

Two Cherubim brought the serpent forward. As it approached, I saw Lillith slipping into the Garden behind him.

Gabriel, said the voice, cut off its legs. On its belly shall it crawl and eat dust. And enmity shall prevail between it and the man, because in his guile he sought man's death.

And you, woman, you heeded his voice and were tempted. He almost succeeded in killing you, even before you had given birth. From this day forth, in sorrow will you bear children, and in pain give them life. Your desire should be for your husband, not for serpents. He, not that perverse and cunning creature, shall rule over you.

And you, Adam, because you heeded the voice of your wife rather than my commandment, you shall return to the ground from whence you came. The good things and the abundance and the delights of my Garden were not enough for you. Go back to the land, and there will you eat of humble bread that you eke out of the earth by the sweat of your brow. Water it with your sweat, and it will feed you thorns and brambles. From it you came and to it you shall return, for you shall not live forever.

Suddenly a heart-rending shriek was heard. On learning of Adam's expulsion from the Garden, Lillith's cries could be heard, as her voice rent the air in a paroxysm of grief,

-He's mine, Lord, he's mine.

Gabriel stepped forward, ready to eject her from the Garden, but the voice forestalled him:

-Let her be, Gabriel, let her be. It is the pain of love that speaks in her.

And to Lillith the voice said:

-Calm yourself, daughter, calm yourself. It grieves me too to be parted from them.

At a signal from the flame, the four Cherubs of the escort stepped forward and produced the garments of leather that the Lord had prepared for Adam and his wife.

-Take them, said the voice. It is cold on the way to the land to which you will be sent. A long and cold road lies before you.

Two Cherubim were commanded to bring them to the gate of the Garden. Two Cherubim were sent to guard the path leading to the Tree of Life, lest they attempt at the last moment to snatch fruit from this tree and to live forever.

Gabriel was commanded to draw his gleaming sword and take his stand at the gate. All the company— angels, Cherubim and Seraphim— stood lining the avenue leading to the gate.

I knew that the time had come to part from Michael. I found him close to the gate, among the senior angels.

-Michael, I whispered, not wanting to disrupt the solemn ritual of expulsion, What is to become of us, Michael? Do we have to part now?

-Not yet, he said. I have been commanded to accompany you. As the Lord said, the way will be long and cold. But we shall travel it together.

A wave of gladness swept my heart, my eyes, my whole body. How could I begin to thank the Lord, who has been so gracious to me?

Suddenly we saw a spectacle such as had never been seen before. The Lord's flame was flashing by the portals of the gate. He Himself, He in person, was to open the gate before Adam and his wife, and bless them on their departure for the distant land. They approached the gate arm-in-arm, her head on his shoulder. There was silence all around. The flame burned ever more brightly, yet steadily, veiled in a thin cloud of gold, the very finest gold, the gold of Havilah. The two walked slowly. By the gate they stopped and took a last look behind them. The Garden was in full, glorious, riotous bloom. All the aromatic shrubs and the perfumed flowers, the herbs and the grasses and the green sward—it was as if an unseen hand had infused them with colours and scents and shapes and hues—and yet all these plants were now deprived of the Gardener appointed by the Lord to tend them, water them and nurture them. Who would inherit his place?

My spirit goes with you, said the voice, in loving tones. My spirit is in your hearts. Keep it safe. Dust shall return to dust, and spirit to spirit. The gate opened, the flame flared and sputtered. Was it weeping? I shall never know. Michael and I took the two human beings under our wings.

A moment, one moment, cried Adam.

We stopped. As the gate behind us was not yet locked,

Adam cried aloud to his wife, and to the Lord in the flame:

"Her name is Eve, for she is to be the mother of all life."
And before the gate was locked I heard the voice of the Lord
saying:

-A good name, a good and a fine name.

-At that moment I caught sight of Lillith, slipping out from
the assembled ranks and bursting through the still open gate,
with the now legless serpent entwined about her body. Lillith
disappeared, and the sentinels did not notice her. And the Lord,
who sees all, did He not see her, or did He see her and take pity
on her, allowing her to follow in the footsteps of her beloved?

# Chapter forty-six

With the break of dawn I hastened once again to bathe in the sea, to sing the song of praise for the third day of the week, and to continue reading the tablets of Noah. I remembered Adam and Eve when they were expelled and sent to this land, in their sorrow and their pain, remembered their exclusion from the Garden that was abundant in all good things and their arrival in this desolate land devoid of life.

It would soon be a full year since Noah and his household entered the ark. Noah was now six hundred years old. A thousand years before he was born I followed his ancestors to this land that is gradually emerging from the flood plain. In a few more days they shall be returning to it for a new beginning. An arch of time stretches over the earth and spans these two beginnings—one thousand and six hundred terrestrial years, ten generations. Methuselah, the grandfather of Noah, lived almost a thousand years. Yet, what are six hundred, or even one thousand years in the sight of the Lord? A fleeting instant, the sediment layer of a mountain, a breath of wind, a flash of light. And can He already have despaired of the human race? This is why I am so interested in Noah and his deeds, and those of his sons and their wives? Perhaps I shall come to understand why this destruction has been unleashed upon them.

There is yet another tablet or two remaining to be read, so I continue.

# Chapter forty-seven

*T*oday I will send out the dove for the third time. God, give
her the strength to fly, to inspect, to report. Seven days ago she returned
with an olive spray in her mouth, telling us that the waters had
receded and dry land had appeared. Let her find land where she may
dwell, and never return to the ark, and then we shall know that the
land is dry. I gathered my family around me, from the tender little
ones to my firstborn son, and I said:

"Today we all stand and are witness to the second creation of
the earth and the second coming of mankind to dwell there."

Those assembled said: Amen. I opened my hands, which held
the dove. I heard its cooing, felt its warm, trembling body, and released
it. The dove sprang from my hands, as if scenting the smell of sunlight
on her wings, the smell of the water beneath her, the smell of land
where she might roost. See how she soars, climbing higher and higher
into the very zenith of the heavens. So much more can be surveyed
from such height than from the skylight of the ark down below.

All eyes followed her confident flight; all hearts beat to the
rhythm of her wings. This little bird bore all our hopes. We, the

*vestiges of the last survivors, would we once again be able to tread the ground from whose dust we came? I commanded that it be taken in turn to watch at the window to see if the dove would return. All those in the ark, from the smallest to the greatest, man, woman and child—all took their turn at watching and reporting. We counted the hours since the bird had flown. The hours of the morning passed, and the sun rose high in the sky. Midday came and went, with radiant light reflected brightly on the surface of the water. The sun turned westward, slowing its pace and its vigour fading, and still the dove had not returned. From time to time, someone reported seeing a dot approaching from the westerly quarter, or someone thought they saw a bird far away to the east, but these were false alarms. By sunset, our anxiety was growing. Had the dove faltered, had the bird drowned? It was the wife of Shem who soothed our spirits, saying:*

*"She has found dry land. She has found earth, and perhaps even found trees that have remained, and seeds that are sprouting. She is the first of us to start a new life."*

*Those around her nodded their heads in agreement. Any glimmer of hope at a time of despair shines bright as the sun, and any straw is a raft to a drowning man. We clutched at her words as if they were the undeniable truth.*

*Those on watch at the hatch did not leave it the entire night, so that should the dove return, she would find a friendly hand to guide her in. When dawn rose and the dove had not returned, I knew she had gone for good. Was this a sign of deliverance or disaster? I will have to decide. The family is divided. Some cling to hope while others sink into despair. I know that the time has come to remove the cover of the ark. I also know that if the rains return, without the protection of the cover we shall drown.*

*I called my sons and posted them at three corners of the third deck. I stood in the fourth corner. The women and the children held the tall poles that supported the cover of the ark. I gave the signal and we all heaved together, shifting the cover with our combined efforts.*

*When the cover fell with a crash into the water, and a great light, clear and lucent as the day it was created, flooded every corner of the ark, there was a deafening roar as the creatures confined there gave voice. All around us stretched a great marsh. The waters had indeed receded, but still the land was sheer mud, mud mixed with rotted vegetation and the scattered bones of beasts and men. As you see for yourselves, I said, the land is drying but not yet dry enough to live on or to live from. We have waited nearly a year; we can wait a while longer until we find ground that is firm enough for our feet to tread upon. They saw the land for themselves and accepted my words without protest. Now we know what awaits us. Another week, or a month, and we shall disembark.*

*The first day of the first month, the day of the world's creation. As we are waiting for the land to dry I shall read to them from the history of our ancestors. This chronicle was entrusted to my care. I received it from my father, and he inherited it from his father, and so back to our father Adam, who came to this land one thousand and six hundred years ago.*

*In the ark that is now awash with light and fresh air the animals are celebrating. Birds chirrup and screech and proclaim their longing for the wide open spaces, while beasts roar and bleat, snort and trumpet. The children fill the decks with their laughter and their games. A first day of pure joy, joy nourished by the air, by the smell of the air and of the land that is being revealed before their eyes. When the sun turns to the West, I shall start reading the chronicle.*

# Chapter forty-eight

I don't know how long it lasted, the journey to the land. Time in the Garden is not the time of open space, nor is it earthly time. At a dizzying speed we passed between worlds, between cold and heat, thin air and limpid air, on the trails of stars and moons. One evening, as the sun was just about to set, we reached the land.

As the journey drew to a close I saw it from above. Plains and mountains, clefts and valleys, forests and seas. I saw rivers and lakes, deserts and waterfalls and streams of entrancing beauty. The Lord had taken pity on his children and had not banished them to a dead star with no water and no prospect of life. This land teemed and sang, it was astonishing in its wealth and its abundance. I understood why the Lord had taken of the earth of the Garden to create Man. Everything that was in the Garden was also on the face of this land: water, light and sun, plants, rivers and winds, the forces of growth—everything.

-We have arrived, said Michael, carefully laying Eve, who had been asleep within his wings, on soft ground.

-Indeed we have arrived, I replied, laying down Adam who had been sleeping in my arms. They were both asleep, since the Lord had put them to sleep. As we had travelled, were their dreams filled with the route we had taken? Or did they dream of the Garden from which they were exiled?

We found a broad valley on the banks of a gently flowing river, palms enfolding it on both sides.

-This shall be their home, I said.

-Yes, said Michael, and yours too, my son.

His words reminded me that he would soon be leaving me. This was to be our last encounter. I restrained my grief, telling myself: This must come to pass, and neither Michael nor I have any control over it. I buried the grief deep in my heart, and it became a part of me. This is the way of the heart, which stores within it sorrow and joy, union and separation, and weaves it all into one tapestry, the tapestry of life.

-Michael my friend, we shall part at dawn. A long way we have travelled together, from the day I arrived in the Garden from the orbit of the sun, to the day of my arrival on the earth from the Garden. All this time you have been to me as a father, a brother and a friend, and I am grateful to you.

-And I am grateful too. Strange, it is a new feeling to me—for you have loved me, as I have loved you; it was my first love. Before that, I loved the Lord, loved His works. But in that love I was like the sea, receiving His waters and giving nothing of myself to another. My love for you was in giving as well as in receiving. Who knows if I shall ever again experience such a thing? You are my friend, but you are different. A new world is before you now, and the people that you accompany are a mighty revelation in the universe of the Lord. They know, their eyes are open now. Who knows what they shall yet see, and you with them.

-Good and evil, Michael, their eyes have been opened to good and evil.

-Yes, to good and evil. And before I set out on my way at

dawn, I should sleep a while. There is a long journey before me, and this time I travel alone.

On the ground I came upon a sparkling stone, flashing with colours ignited by the setting sun. I kissed the bright stone and held it out to Michael.

-Take it, my friend, a gift from the earth. When you look at it up there, in the Garden, you will remember me.

Angels do not weep, and yet tears streamed from my eyes, despite my efforts to appear strong before Michael. He took the stone from my hand, wiped away my tears with it, and stowed it between his wings.

-You have learned your first lesson on the earth, my friend. You have learned to weep, like Adam and Eve. I have received a present from you, my brother, your first tears. And now let us be as we were then, the first time, the day we met.

We slept. When I woke with the dawn, he was no longer by my side. Under my head I found a feather from one of his wings, a beautiful feather, long and covered with fine down. I tucked it into my own wing, close to my heart, and I carry it to this day. It hears my heartbeats, and does it convey them to Michael?

I looked at Adam and Eve, sleeping. They slept in each other's arms. Adam knew Eve, his wife, and fell asleep in her arms.

# Chapter forty-nine

The following evening, when the beasts had been given their fodder and the humans had finished their work, the people of the ark were gathered on the upper deck, from which the cover had been removed, to hear Noah read from the history of their ancestors upon the earth. They sat in a circle, children, wives and sons, with their father, Noah, in the middle. They began with a song of praise, as I too used to do during my time in the Garden. When they had finished singing, Noah took the chronicle in his hand and began to read.

The sons of Noah were familiar with the history.

In the community of the valley of the palms, it had been customary to assemble once a year, towards the end of autumn when the fruits had been gathered in and the young lambs had been weaned and had gone to pasture. Then they would give thanks for the goodness of the land, for the bread and the water. Noah had inherited the tablets of the chronicle for safe keeping from his father Lamech. When he had entered the ark, he had taken the tablets with him and now, with the flood at an end and landfall fast approaching, Noah called his family together—the last vestiges of humanity that had survived the cataclysm, the remnant of life entrusted to his care. It was a heavy responsibility indeed, nothing less than the renewal of human life upon the earth. He read:

*"Our father Adam and our mother Eve came to the valley of the palms from the Garden.*

*A river flows in the Garden, and it divides into four streams. The waters of the river refresh the Garden, in which are all the plants of the universe, from the tiniest blade of grass to the mighty palm tree. Our father Adam tended this Garden. And in the Garden, two mighty trees, their roots bathed in the waters of the abyss and their tops in the heart of the firmament. One tree was the Tree of Knowledge, and the other, the Tree of Life. And God, the Lord of heaven and earth, forbade them to eat of the fruit of the trees. And a wicked and cunning serpent tempted our mother Eve, and she tasted the fruit of the Tree of Knowledge of good and evil. God banished our mother, Eve, and our father, Adam, from the Garden, and settled them on this good land, took from them life eternal and gave them knowledge and understanding, the choice between good and evil."*

Noah looked up from the tablets and gazed about him. Of the great congregation that had heard him read the previous time, only this tiny fragment remained. He looked at his firstborn, Shem, thinking that one day he would read the chronicle in his turn. He saw Ham, heavy-set and morose, his face weary and his eyes fixed in trepidation on the sky, fearing the return of heavy clouds portending ill.

He saw Japheth, sour and angry, his face bitter and defiant. Clearly he had come to hear the reading of the chronicle out of surly obedience to his father, but not out of any desire to subject himself to the rigours of discipline and morality.

The sons knew what was written on the tablets. Their children listened and learned. Goodness was rewarded and evil punished. But now, after the flood, after destruction, did these things still hold? Were good deeds really weighed against the reward, and evil deeds against the punishment?

Many thoughts filled the minds of the listeners, and they gazed into the face of their father Noah, trying to read his thoughts. Was *his* heart at one with the writings?

# Chapter fifty

Day by day they left the ark and tested the dryness of the land. They took Noah's staff and descended cautiously, holding hands, driving the staff into the mud and marking its depth with a notch. As time passed it was clear that the land was gradually drying. Not a cloud was to be seen in the sky. The vault of the heavens stretched clear and pure and cloudless above the land, above the mountains.

Day by day, as evening approached, they gathered to listen, and Noah continued to read the history of their forefathers.

By the twenty-seventh day of the second month there was already a goodly expanse of land, stable, dry and fit to be trodden by the feet of man and of animals. That day Noah commanded the members of his family to prepare themselves for the great day when they would disembark—they should scour all the cabins and the pens in the ark and gather the remaining food, the jars of seeds that they had brought with them, the tools and the clothing, and be ready to greet the great day. The pure beasts and birds, which he had preserved jealously throughout the days of the flood, and the tablets bearing his journal of the flood, he collected himself. He was still waiting for a sign. His sons were impatient, urging him to set out on the way, but Noah stayed them, saying,

"We entered the ark because that was the Lord's command, and we shall leave it at His command, when we are given the sign."

That day he read to them the last chapter of the history of mankind. He read of Lamech, his father, of his father's wives Ada and Zilla and of his half-sister Na'ama, of the man and the child whom Lamech killed, and the sorrow of the Lord at these wicked deeds. He chose his reading with care, so that his hearers would clearly remember, on the day of their disembarkation, why the Lord had brought destruction upon the land. When he finished reading, as all the members of his audience were meditating silently on the deeds of their forefathers, he said: "Soon we shall again tread the good land that for ten generations has produced our food, the nourishment of all living things. On account of us the earth was devastated, on account of us life was extinguished, and on account of us this good land was ravaged."

He pointed to the land. Patches of lush grass, of green sward gleaming in the light of the sun veering westward, were like a message of greeting sent to the surviving remnant, as if saying: Come to me, return and I shall give you of my goodness. Again I shall cause my fruit to blossom for you and for all the living things that are with you. The wrath of the Lord has passed, and the time has come to restart the history of mankind upon the earth.

The light of sunset rested on the land, on the ark and on its occupants. The outstretched hand of Noah showed the way, and it was as if the entire universe was preparing itself to witness and to welcome the return of Noah's children to their land. Soon they would return to dry land, and what shall they find there? The eyes of the travellers in the ark followed the outstretched hand in silence. Was this the silence of longing, the silence of memories, or of fear and confusion?

The silence of the people was shattered by the noise of the animals, sniffing the scent of land, the scent of grassy pasture, the scent of light and sun. Birds beat their wings on the walls of their cages, sang and howled and screeched, their passions aroused by anticipation of the vast spaces again open to their flight, of the freedom to soar and to dive, to nest and to roost, beat wings on the wind. Night came down and gloom covered the dry land and the water, the ark and the mountains all around. Only stars were visible above. The people took to their beds.

Only Noah remained on the deck, waiting for a sign. There was tense anticipation in his heart, but confidence too. He had upheld the word of his God. God had entrusted into his hands the most precious pledge of all, and he had kept it safe during the course of a whole year. He had watched over the beasts, watched over his sons, the wives and the children, himself. He had fulfilled his mission through storms, through despair, through sorrow and grief. Even when he saw his friends and his neighbours, old and young alike drowning in the waters of the flood, even when he saw this with his own eyes, Noah did not turn his back on his God. Nor did despair make him neglect the remnants of life.

"We are ready, he whispered to himself, and the land is ready. Now it is for you, my God, to give the sign."

Out of the stillness and the gloom of twilight, he heard a footfall, and then a voice as Shem, his firstborn, joined him.

"Come, sit with me, my son," said Noah, "sit here. I cannot sleep. I am waiting for the sign."

"And I, Father, I am waiting for you to command us to go down onto dry land. We are growing weaker; I'm not sure how long we can endure—men as well as beasts. Only the glimmer of hope that still lives in our hearts has kept us in the ark. Were it not for this hope, we would have thrown ourselves into the sea long ago."

"That is a sinful thing to say, my son."

"It's the truth, Father. The truth is no sin. And in truth, what have we done? We saved only ourselves, the others we ignored."

"No, my son. Their fate did not depend on us. God gave, and God has taken away."

"And if you had appealed, Father? If you had stood up and demanded and pleaded, Father. If you had said then, when the messenger came and foretold the flood, you had no intention of surviving alone—but only with your friends, your neighbours, and all of the community of the valley—would He not have heard your voice? We too, the sons, were silent and held our tongues, Father. A righteous man cannot be righteous for himself alone. Something is gnawing at my heart, Father; something has been sowing doubt within me, something that does not let me rejoice in our survival. My soul has not been saved. My soul is in mourning."

"Hush, my son, hush. This was His will, and these His acts. We shall never understand their purpose. There is reward and there is punishment, and you cannot demand reward in place of punishment."

"Even if we never understand the purpose of His acts, will He perhaps understand the object of our grief? Even God cannot wipe out all life from the face of the earth and demand our acceptance and consent. He too, Father, is subject to reward and punishment. I cannot give Him my reward, when within me the sorrow is wailing and keening. See how beautiful are the stars, Father, and how indifferent. How beautiful is the stillness on the face of the world, how deep is the silence that covers the dead. Father, Father. This beauty should be weeping bitter tears over our destruction, for the ruin and the slaughter. I take no pleasure in my survival, Father. This seed of sorrow that is in me I shall bequeath to my children and to the sons of my sons and daughters. Perhaps this grief will guide them in choosing between good and evil in generations to come, if such there will be. I am not yet sure that we have truly been delivered."

Noah listened to the words of his firstborn, pondered them a while and finally said:

"Shem, my son. Hearing what you say, I am filled with pride and hope. Only he who has witnessed destruction with sorrow and with pain will one day rejoice in his own life and the life of his friends."

After a long silence Shem said, "I must sleep, Father. A great day awaits us when the sign is given. You too, Father, you must be worn out after your labours of the past few days, and more work awaits us. Go rest, Father. When God gives the sign, you will hear it even in your sleep."

# Chapter fifty-one

A t dawn the sign came.

-Go, said the voice. You and your wife and your sons and
their wives and children, and all the living things that are with
you. Everything that came with you into the ark, with you will
it leave.

Noah hastened to rouse everyone, and he commanded his
sons to release the animals from their pens and cages. The small
and the weak should leave first, thus having a chance to feed
before the larger and the stronger beasts arrived. "God entrusted
them into my hands," he said, "and I shall return them whole
into His hands."

The beasts began descending to the dry land. At first they
were dazzled by the abundance of light and they paused a while,
to grow accustomed to the light and the fresh air and the feel of
the ground under their feet. Then they set off at a run for the
lush meadows and the bubbling springs, nostrils filled with the
fragrance of rich soil, the fragrance of putrefaction and growth,
of fertility, revelling in the weight of the clods and in the solid

earth, the planks of the ark's deck no longer shifting beneath them.

Pair by pair, the birds took flight. Some made straight for the open spaces while others glided, placidly riding the currents of air and submitting to their power and direction. Life returned to its familiar ways.

When all the animals had left the ark, it was the turn of the people. First came the men, checking that the ground was firm enough to bear the weight of returning humankind. Quietly and cautiously they probed the ground, testing each step before it was taken, as if not yet certain that the land truly accepted them and wished them well . . . Last to leave were the women, carrying the youngest of their children.

The sun was already high in the sky when the ark had emptied. The beasts had long dispersed in all directions. Only the people stood huddled around it, and when they finally set out, their steps were slow and hesitant. They had no idea where they were going. On their shoulders they carried tattered bundles and a few tools—hardly adequate equipment for a long journey into the unknown that they faced. They were walking in an unfamiliar land. Before the shoah in which their entire world had been consumed, they had built their huts on the bank of one of the four great rivers that flow in the land east of Eden.

Where was this land, to the east of Eden? This was not a land of great plains that they were crossing, it was a land of mighty mountains, and even the wind was alien, not the wind that they remembered from the valley of the palms. No sweet tang of fruit, no balmy fragrance, no intoxicating aroma of ripening dates was wafted on this wind. Stern and merciless, the harsh wind lashed them as they walked. Even when the light began casting long shadows behind them as the days lengthened, behind them, they knew their course was towards the west. They descended slopes of mountains, traversed thundering cataracts, clambered over boulders and uprooted trees. Traces of destruction were strewn all along the way: skeletons of birds and animals, broken household implements, shards and ruined habitations smothered in mud.

I gathered up the tablets hidden in the cave, and followed in their footsteps.

I took my leave of the cave as a man might leave a house in which he has found a haven from the heat and a refuge from the cold. This had been my home for a year and a month; it was here that I had vacillated between hope and despair, between the expectation of a miracle and longing for my beloved friend. I also longed for the spirit of God—not His angry spirit but His merciful spirit.

I followed in their footsteps and saw with my own eyes the devastation wrought by the Lord upon His earth. I knew there was no limit to the power of the Lord, but I always assumed this was the power of creation; never the boundless powers of destruction to which I was now witness. Many are the things that are learned when their time comes.

# Chapter fifty-two

The children were beginning to stumble as they sprang from rock to rock, and every now and then someone would slip, holding up the procession. Everyone was weary, and Noah again called a halt for the night. There was water there in plenty, in springs and in mountain streams. Only fire for warmth was lacking, and the garments they wore were in tatters.

They sought out a cave to shelter them all for the night. It was the season of the new moon, and the skies were studded with faintly flickering stars. Night brought them little repose. No one spoke, but everyone sensed the lurking, bitter resentment; as if each of them was thinking of whom they could complain about, or against whom could they direct the angry words that simmered in their hearts.

I've observed that when there is no target for complaint, people usually turn against one another, picking quarrels at every opportunity. And so Noah's family argued about their sleeping-space, although there was now no shortage of it; they argued about things said or left unsaid, they argued about things that happened long ago. Lord, merciful Lord, I thought, help this poor band of survivors to reach their destination. Without Your protection, Lord, they will fall by the wayside and devour each other's flesh.

I saw how Noah, with his proud and upright bearing, with the stature of a leader, was once again bowed and diminished. How again he looked as he did that day when his sons defied and abused him, slaughtering the young animals in their madness and their greed. Noah's back was bent, his eyes duller, and his face more sunken. I saw that his knees were weak. Did he fear the road ahead of him, or was it the weight of the burden behind him? In his hand I saw his staff, with the notches marking the progress of the drying of the land. For future generations, this staff will come to symbolise all that befell the generation of the flood.

Then I saw how the people sank into a deep, heavy but unrestful sleep, how the cold nibbled at their flesh, and how fear invaded their dreams. They lay curled and huddled, each family by itself. Parents gathered their children around them, trying to cover them with the fringes of their meagre garments for warmth, or man and woman lay entwined and warmed one another.

# Chapter fifty-three

Bright sunlight penetrated the cave, spilling on Adam and Eve. Two bright red and gold-tinged patches lay on the rich, brown earth. A thin trickle of blood flowed from between Eve's legs. Adam was the first to wake. He looked at his sleeping wife, at her breathing and sated body, at the black veil of her hair. The mouth of the cave was broad, and light flooded every innermost corner. Adam turned his gaze this way and that, rose, paced back and forth, felt the stone of the walls of the cave, took a clod of earth in his hand and held it to his nose, sniffed it and tasted it and threw it to the ground. He seemed at a loss, not recognising anything in his surroundings. He ran to the mouth of the cave, looked around him and saw nothing familiar in the rocks or the landscape, not even a tree or a bush by which he could have told where he was. He was utterly confused. He plucked a few sprigs from the shrubs that grew there in profusion, leaves from a branchy tree, and still recognised nothing.

He went back inside the cave and found Eve still fast asleep. She already bore in the recesses of her body the beginnings of human life on the earth; the seed that he had planted in her in the night was already growing and unfurling. He touched her shoulder, shook her body to wake her. Eve opened her eyes, swept the hair from her face and saw Adam bending over her.

"I don't know this place," he said. "I've never been here before."

Eve looked at him in astonishment. "Never been here before, you say? Then, where are we?"

"I don't know," he said, stunned and confused. "We weren't here yesterday, and I don't know where we were."

Eve stood up, ran to the mouth of the cave, looked all around and said: "You're right, this is not the place we were in yesterday, but I don't remember any other place."

An image flashed into my mind, and I knew what had happened. I saw Raphael standing at the gate of the Garden and as we passed by him, Adam and Eve still gazing back at their lost paradise, how he had pinched their upper lips, taking from them all memory of the Garden and all memory of what happened there. Only faint traces of memory still lingered in the recesses of their minds. Fragments of blurred pictures and dark shadows and the oppressive sense of things forbidden, of bounds violated— and of a burden of guilt that neither of them understood.

"Something has happened," said the woman. "My heart tells me that something has happened. My body, my heartbeat, my breathing, everything is different from what I am accustomed to, Adam. Something has happened."

Suddenly she noticed the blood seeping between her legs. She touched it, dipped her fingers in it, thoroughly alarmed. Adam too dipped his fingers in her blood, gleaming red in the sunlight.

"What is this?" he heard her voice and saw her pointing at the blood. From the recesses of lost memory rose the echo of a voice calling on him to give names to all living things.

"This is blood, Eve. Blood from your body, your life-blood.

You are the mother of all life," he said, not remembering that he had already told her this.

So this is forgetting, I told myself. I was well acquainted with memory, but I was learning about forgetting from them, even as I knew that I, Adiel, had been chosen by the Lord to be their memory; the witness to all that had taken place in the Garden and was yet to take place in the new land, the things that have befallen Adam and Eve and shall befall the generations that will follow. Heavy is the responsibility laid upon me. I must miss nothing, change nothing, add nothing and omit nothing in all that I see and hear, for the history of mankind is committed to my memory, and what I see and hear is my duty to write and record.`

I saw a man and a woman standing and staring at the broad expanse, and the landscape stretching out before them, a vista of thorns and thistles, tall grasses and trees, rivers and streams, barren earth and virgin forests. My heart was filled with compassion and love for these two people, dressed in leather tunics and all alone in the universe, banished from their past and exiled to this land. Were they strong enough to bear the burden of their destiny?

They were hungry. Adam left the cave, treading cautiously. Thorns pierced his feet and nettles stung his hands. He plucked a fruit from one tree and tasted it, then threw it to the ground, repelled by its bitterness.

Eve followed him out of the cave. The strong light dazzled her eyes. Once accustomed to the brightness, she took a few slow and cautious steps, going round the big boulder that stood near the mouth of the cave, and found a flowing spring, its water moistening the earth all around it. She leaned over it, washed the stains of blood from her legs, washed her face and hands and body. Her limbs were suffused with joy and delight, she called to Adam:

"Come, Adam, come and be refreshed by the living water that this land is giving to us." A smile appeared on her face.

Adam heard her call and approached the spring. The bubbling of the water brought a smile to his face as well. Thus the land welcomed them, and they responded with their smiles. A palm tree laden with ripe fruit rose from the moist earth. Eve picked up some of the dates that lay scattered at her feet, tasted them and found them good to eat, sweet and satisfying. She took another handful and offered it to Adam.

"Eat, husband, eat." Adam hesitated for a moment, not knowing why. A distant, obscure echo stayed his hand, but his ravenous hunger prevailed over his misgivings. He took fruit from her hand, and ate. The taste was delicious and his hunger was soon sated. He leaned over the spring, drank water and sprinkled his face.

He took a handful of soil, gazed at it fixedly and said: "This land shall be our home. I don't remember where we came from, but I see where we are. Eve, our home will be here." Adam looked around him, found a sharp stone and began clearing a path amid the thorns from the spring to the mouth of the cave. Eve uprooted weeds and moved stones until a small patch was cleared and exposed.

"This will be our first piece of land. We will earn it by the sweat of our brows."

When the sun was inclining westward, they sat in the mouth of the cave and looked out at the darkening sky and at the plot of ground cleared of thorns and thistles, and wiped away the sweat that dripped from their faces.

"There is blessing in this land," said Adam. "Of its goodness will we eat and drink. It will give its fruits to us, and we will repay it with our sweat." A distant, forgotten echo lingered in his memory. The echo of a solemn voice, full of grief and of sorrow, a voice of love and pain, caring and compassion, a voice without words, yet crying out and saying, By the sweat of your brow shall you eat bread till you return unto the ground, for out of the ground were you taken, and unto dust shall you return.

Adam asked Eve: "Do you hear a voice speaking to us?"

"No," she replied. "I hear only the bubbling of the water in the spring, and the singing of the birds that come here to drink."

I looked towards the spring, and was stunned. I saw Lillith leaning over it, while in the verdant grass at her feet lay the serpent, coiled into a knot and looking like one of the rocks. Again, the turbulent impressions of the previous day rose up before me— the image of the gate that was locked behind us and Lillith slipping through the narrow gap, the serpent wound about her body and refusing to loosen his grip.

I wanted to warn Adam and Eve of the danger lying in wait for them. I recalled how the serpent had been cursed by the Lord: Adam shall bruise his head, and he shall bruise Adam's heel. And Lillith loves Adam and will not let him go, for her love is as strong as death. Sadly, I remembered then that my words could not be heard by human ears, except at the Lord's command. And He had not spoken and therefore I was unable to warn Adam or his wife. New to me, too, was the intense feeling of discomfort that I experienced at the knowledge that I was powerless to so much as lift a finger or unfurl a wing feather without first receiving an explicit command from the Lord. So, I said to myself, their destiny is in their own hands. The Lord placed their destiny in their hands, and I have been chosen only to witness and to record.

## Chapter fifty-four

Day after day they went out at first light from the cave to the spring, to draw water and to meet the beasts that came there to quench their thirst. Since the day they realised that the spring drew to it the birds and beasts of the field, they no longer felt they were alone in the land. Adam called them names, to distinguish kind from kind, forgetting that he had done this before, when they were in the Garden. I was amazed to discover that the names he called them here, on the earth, were the names he had already given them in the Garden. Was this the Lord's intention, to leave the natural order unchanged and undisturbed in spite of the sins of man?

"Look," Eve would say happily, "what a fine creature!" pointing to the gazelle.

"It's a gazelle," he replied, not knowing where the name had come from.

"And see, Adam, look what a splendid mane covers that creature's head."

"That is the lion," he said without hesitation.

And this continued day after day, till all the beasts that visited the spring had a name. Sometimes the beasts would pass by the mouth of the cave, peering inside and sometimes even entering, looking at the occupiers while nodding their heads as if in greeting.

The plot of land around their cave was growing larger. More stones were removed, more stones and thistles cleared, revealing brown and fertile earth.

"This is our home," said Adam.

"And the home of the son that shall be born to us," said Eve.

For months now he had watched his wife Eve bearing new life in her belly. Already they had seen animals pregnant and giving birth, had seen nestlings hatching from eggs, and knew that one day soon a child would be born to them, the bearer of life and of the future.

Sometimes, towards dusk, when the toil of the day was behind them, they would sit by the mouth of the cave, as they had on their first day in the land, and watch the sun descending and the sky turning to gold and purple, citron and turquoise, Adam grinding leaves and flowers between his hands and Eve laying her head on his shoulder and feeling the movements of the foetus in her womb. Then Eve would take Adam's hand, laying it on her belly,

"Do you feel it? He's moving; he's growing and developing from day to day. Soon he will come out into the daylight, and that time is not faraway."

"Yes," said Adam, "I feel him moving," and he looked at Eve his wife with eyes full of love.

At night, when the world was wrapped in clouds and stars, and the only sounds were the gurgling of the spring and the voices of the night all around, they fell asleep. Eve dreamed of her son and sometimes spoke to him, too.

"You are mine, you are my possession," she would whisper

in her dreams. Then I saw Lillith hovering over Adam's head and whispering to him, "You are mine, you are my possession." The serpent lay at the mouth of the cave, coiled and alert, waiting for her. He fixed his malevolent gaze on the mouth of the cave, baring his tongue and hissing though his venomous fangs, "And you, Lillith, you are mine. I shall have you yet."

That night the child was born in the cave and the land around it resounded with Eve's cries of pain, the first human cries to be heard on the earth. Tenderly, Adam bent over her, holding her head, clutching her hands, which flailed about her, lashing at the ground, at him, at everything in their way. The waves of pain came and went, pounding at the doors of her womb and threatening to rip her guts to shreds, then subsiding, briefly. As the pains subsided, her face showed ever more grief.

"Adam," she gasped in her anguish, "Adam, my husband, the pains are tearing me apart. Our son will be born in grief and in pain. Perhaps he is death. Shall I live?" A fresh wave of torment snatched the words from her lips.

Adam could only repeat helplessly and incessantly the words, "You shall live, you shall live." His words were drowned by a final shriek from his wife, and the baby's head appeared. His little body was drawn from her womb, impelled by all the forces of the world. Blood streamed between her parted legs, staining bright red her body and the ground beneath her. The light of the full moon was tender and soothing.

Adam took the baby from between her legs, severed the cord connecting the little body to the mother's womb, and cried aloud, "You are no longer flesh in her flesh, but flesh of her flesh." The baby uttered the first wail of life, and his mother's moans were silenced. Adam gave him back to Eve

All the signs of pain and of sorrow were wiped from her face, and in their place came a smile. Joy and delight swept through her limbs when the baby took her breast, clamped on the nipple and started sucking.

223

Calmer now, his fears for her and for his son relieved, Adam said, "I shall give him a name, as I gave to you and to all the creatures around us."

"No," Eve replied. "He already has a name. Even before he was born I called him my possession. He is the possession that I have received from the Lord in pain and in grief."

Adam was silent and seemed unsure. Since the very beginning, since his creation, it was always he who had given names to creatures. He had even named his wife; should he not name his own son?

Eve saw his hesitation. She took his hand, laying it on her body. During the time of her pregnancy she had withdrawn within herself. She listened to the sounds of the life inside her and nourished the foetus with her blood, with her heartbeat and with dreams and with longings for the life of the world that she bore. She had retreated and withdrawn further and further from Adam the closer she came to her time. Now, with the child born, her body seemed to return to her husband. She felt the desire to shelter again in the haven of his arms, to feel his warmth protecting her and her son from all perils, from storms and from hunger and pain and oppression, and from fear.

"Husband," she whispered as the baby sucked her milk. "We need you to look after us and to take care of us. We need you to defend us."

At the touch of her living, fertile, nourishing flesh, and with the warmth of her body permeating his hand and diffused through his limbs, he felt as if he had been born with his son. He sensed that his wife Eve, this sweet and loving creator of life and of milk, had with the birth, changed him utterly, for he had never known a mother's sweetness, never clutched at a mother's warm breast, never felt in his mouth the nipple binding him to the universe, to everything that was before he was. Suddenly he felt he too had been born, with his son, of a mother's womb. He leaned over her tranquil body, put his lips to her ear and whispered, "You are the mother of all life, the mother of all life. You give him a name."

"His name is Cain," said Eve, "meaning a possession given by the Lord."

"Cain, Cain," Adam repeated the name.

The sky began to pale. With first light the beasts began coming down from the hills and walking to the spring. As they passed the mouth of the cave Adam stood in their path, offering them a handful of grass, a handful of dates, a pinch of seeds, and to each one of them he said: "We have a son. We have a son and his name is Cain."

The beasts walked on calmly, untroubled. They nuzzled Adam's bare skin and looked at him with their big eyes, bowing their heads and eating from his hand. Now and then a dove alighted with a flurry of wings, pecking seeds and kissing his hand before flying away. Adam's heart was filled with joy and gratitude. He wanted all creatures to know this was a day of celebration. For Cain had been born; Cain, the first son of the first man.

# Chapter fifty-five

The sons of Noah walked on by day and stopped at night to rest. As they went they looked about in search of food, picking up anything that might provide nourishment for themselves and for the beasts that were with them. Noah was adamant that the pure animals and birds be preserved. He delegated the duty of caring for them between his sons and their wives, also among those boys and girls who were old enough to shoulder responsibility.

"I have sworn an oath to God," he would say. "If He spares us from His wrath, these creatures shall be sacrificed. The beasts that came out with us from the ark are ours. God entrusted them into our hands for safekeeping. It was on account of us that God destroyed all living things, and it is for our sake they have survived. But the pure animals and birds are His. This is the oath I swore, and this oath I shall fulfil."

The sons heard him and grumbled. Hunger was gnawing at them all. The children wept bitterly, and the nursing mothers tried in vain to suckle their infants from parched and withered breasts.

"Was it to starve us to death in a rocky wilderness that your God spared us from the flood and brought us out of the ark?" they asked. "Better that we had drowned in the deep," added Japheth, forthright as ever. The God of Noah was not his God. Good and evil in the eyes of God were not the good and evil that Japheth saw with his own eyes; not was it clear to him that man was in control of his actions. In his view, actions were decided and determined before his birth, and whether he acted well or otherwise, fate would decree his future.

"Your oath, Father Noah, is yet another manifestation of your innocence. Let us eat these beasts and live. We must, if the children and the women are to survive until we find other sources of food."

Noah heard and did not reply. Man cannot be comforted or his hunger eased by words alone. He kept his eyes open and watched. Of his three sons, Japheth, the youngest, had always been the rebel. When circumstances allow, he might still be able to guide him to the right path. Shem, on the other hand, had remained loyal to Noah and followed in his footsteps; and Ham was steadfast, seldom complaining. He kept his thoughts to himself. Noah was not one to indulge in deep reflection; he did what he felt he had to do with determination; both flow with the time and not pausing in his path. He saw his duty in simple terms: to bring his three sons and their families back, alive, to the place from which they had been uprooted.

I'm growing old, he told himself. I have received my portion in life from the hands of God. But my sons have not yet made their way in the world. Will I succeed in leading them to a place where they can carry on with their lives?

As they continued their descent from the high mountains, they found valleys green with fresh vegetation. The air grew steadily warmer, and the chill of night was diminished. They dug into the moist earth and found roots that could be eaten. Now and then they came across olive trees that had survived the flood, their branches covered with tiny, silver-green leaves—good news for the exhausted travellers. Luxuriant palm fronds would be seen at the tops of trees, and corn stalks were sprouting in the silt washed down from the mountains. Edible plants of all kinds were to be found, and the deep discontent and grumbling stopped. Mothers could feed their young children as their breasts filled with warm and wholesome milk, and the crying of the children was no longer heart-rending; it was the weeping of life, not the weeping of despair.

As they walked among the valleys in the foothills of the mountains, they came across the ruins of houses built of stone. They were amazed. Until now they had stumbled on no human habitation, and even before the flood they had known only the place where they lived. From time to time they had heard stories told in the name of Cain, the wanderer, of the land of Nod, east of Eden. They heard of beings who had come from the clouds, who had actually fallen from the sky—the sons of God, giants and mighty warriors, who took the daughters of men to wife. These stories sounded like the tall tales of a man condemned to wander from place to place, a man never finding a home or a livelihood, stories as unreliable as Cain himself.

When they saw so many stones strewn about there, and jars and pitchers and skeletons of men among the ruins, they realised these were the remains of a city. Noah decided to stay in this place and rest. In the cool nights they found shelter in the derelict houses. In many of them they came across seeds contained in sealed jars, and in one building, which had evidently served as storehouse for the entire settlement, there were cruses of oil too. Even for the pure beasts and birds, of which they took especial care, enough food was found. God was merciful to the small community that had survived. Had they already reached their goal? Was this the place where they would stay, to rebuild their home?

They ate such food as they could find and drank water

from the many streams flowing down from the hills, and they felt their strength returning to them from day to day. The joy of the children, playing among themselves once more, brought smiles to the faces of their elders. In their enclosure, the pure beasts and birds lowed, bleated and chirruped contentedly, and the people passing by them no longer yearned to slaughter them for their meat. They were sacred, they had been consecrated by their father's vow, and soon he would surely sacrifice them to his God.

One day, when Elam, one of the sons of Shem, was playing among the ruins of a house, he came across a big sealed chest, made of stone and almost buried in the rubble. With the help of his friends he cleared away the stones and together they dragged the chest out of the mud into which it had sunk. When they had cleaned it, wiping off the dried mud that clung to its sides, they saw Noah watching them. The dimensions and the shape of the chest had attracted his attention. He approached, cautiously removed the lid and saw a stone tablet hidden inside it. His sons also gathered round. When he tried to lift the tablet by himself, it proved too big and too heavy for him.

His sons lent a hand, and together they pulled the stone tablet from the chest. The top of the tablet was decorated with carvings of interlaced palm fronds, and on the body of the tablet were inscribed lines of symbols that Noah recognised at once. This was the script that he used himself when writing his journal.

In the meantime all the members of the little flock had gathered around the stone tablet. Noah stood in the middle, the tablet before him. Again I saw him as on the day he sent out the messenger-dove for the third time, his back straight and his eyes shining.

The eyes of all the assembled company followed his movements. He stared hard at the stone, with intense concentration. Deep silence descended upon all. They watched their father as he approached the stone tablet every now and then, wiping off a speck of dust, passing his finger over a blurred symbol, then standing back and reading the whole text from start to finish, without uttering a word. His whole appearance was changing before their eyes. Once more he radiated strength and confidence, as if a hidden force was flowing from the words carved in the stone, and passing through him.

Suddenly he awoke from the reverie into which he had sunk, turned to the assembled company and said: "Remove the piles of stones and search this place thoroughly. Perhaps beneath these stones lies the key to a riddle generations old."

Those gathered there heard his words and did not understand them. To what riddle was their father alluding? Does this place where they have halted hold within it the reasons for the wrath of God?

# Chapter fifty-six

When the second son was born to Adam and Eve, their firstborn, Cain, was old enough to go out with his father to the clearings and to work the land with him. With his father, he used to rise at dawn, go to the spring to wash and to draw water, and while his father laboured, grinding seeds between two stones to make flour, Cain would add twigs to the fire that had dwindled overnight and stir it into flame. These two skills Adam had acquired from his experience of working in the clearings during the years of Cain's childhood.

From the moment he learned to walk with confidence on his little legs, Cain loved to go with his father and see things in the largest clearing. Everything was new to his eyes. Sometimes he saw a bird building a nest in the branches, at other times, a butterfly sipping nectar from flowers, once he saw fledglings hatching from eggs and another time he saw a little wet lamb thrust into the light of the world from a ewe's womb. The world was full of wonders, things born and formed and created and happening before his very eyes. And his eyes were wide open, his look attentive, his heart open and his head forever thinking, making connections, comparing and imagining, passing from one thing to another and drawing conclusions. Not that he found answers to everything that intrigued him, not even from the lips of his father, Adam. When no answer would be forthcoming, he would lapse into long periods of meditation, as if not having resolved that question was somehow holding him back and impeding his progress. An unsolved question would obsess him for days on end: How does a tree grow? How does a bird fly? How does the sun rise? Why does a river always flow in one direction and never change course? Who blows the wind and who puts clouds in the sky? Where does the rain come from?

There was no end to his questions, and they perplexed Adam and Eve. Having never been children themselves, they had never asked such questions. The world had been given to them as a gift, and Cain was their gift to the world.

When Eve was pregnant for the second time and her belly swelled, a great change came about in Cain's life. He felt his mother was not as she had been the day before yesterday and the day before that. She no longer carried him in her arms, and she seemed preoccupied. Something he did not understand divided them. Once, when he asked her why her belly had swelled like a big apple, she answered him with a laugh, "This isn't an apple, Cain my boy, it's a little brother growing inside me. You're going to have a brother, Cain. You won't be our only child anymore."

"Brother?" he asked, astonished. "What's a brother? I don't know what that means."

"A brother," Eve replied, "is another child, like you but smaller. You're going to have a brother and you can talk and play together, laugh and be happy."

Cain became closer to his father. He saw his father ploughing the ground with a stone, and tried doing it himself, saw his father burying seeds in the ground, and did likewise. Seeing his father sit in the mouth of the cave and gaze at the sky, watching out for rain clouds, he followed his example. Cain had been Eve's precious gift from God at the time of his birth, and now he was becoming more and more like his father, the man born from the dust of the earth.

When Abel came into the world, Cain stood with his father and witnessed the birth. He heard his mother's cries and was scared; cries such as this he heard sometimes at night from beasts of the forest, but then his mother would clasp him to her body, caressing and calming him. But now, as she lay writhing in pain, with Adam leaning over her and trying to soothe her with words of love and comfort, there were no open arms for him to run to, no refuge from all the fears that suddenly clustered inside him. For the first time in his life he was alone, unwanted, standing and waiting for someone to take care of him. He felt abandoned to his fears, confronting the great world, all he could do was to clutch at his father's hand and shout:

"I'm frightened, I'm frightened!"

But Adam was too preoccupied with the birth of his second son to notice Cain's distress.

## Chapter fifty-seven

Give him a name, Eve said to her husband when the baby at last lay on her breast, taking her nipple in his mouth and sucking.

"Abel," Adam replied, without thinking.

"Abel? Why Abel? I don't know what that name means."

"Nor I," replied Adam. "Perhaps it's a riddle and we shall know the solution when he grows up."

While Adam went out to the spring in the morning, with Cain beside him, Eve and her son Abel would lie on their bed asleep. Cain saw his brother in his mother's arms, clutching with his little hands at her breast, swollen with warm and sweet milk. Sometimes he longed to stretch out beside her, to grasp her breast, to fill his mouth with her warm flesh and suck from it, like his brother Abel. Adam chivvied his son, roused him from his reverie, made him forget his yearning for his mother's breasts and took him to the clearing. They had to prepare food for his mother and his brother, and for themselves.

When Abel was capable of walking, he never left Eve's side

as she worked. When she fed the fire, ground up seeds, laid out fruit to dry in the sun, went down to the spring to draw water, gathered olives to press for oil, Abel would run around her, tasting the fruit, studying columns of insects marching over the ground and inventing games to play with his mother.

Cain watched Abel's behaviour with a baleful eye: While I'm working with the sweat of my brow, scratching my hands on thistles, burning my body in the sun, bent over the ground from morning till night, what is my brother Abel doing? He felt a new sensation in his heart, a feeling of dark, painful jealousy. He didn't know what to call this sensation, didn't know what it was, but he felt its ominous power. Whenever he could hurt his brother, without arousing his parents' anger, he would do so. Passing by him, he would knock Abel down and then quickly pretend to share his pain. Sometimes he pinched him, or shoved an elbow in his little ribs.

Abel didn't know what made his brother do this to him. Father and Mother, he thought, treat me with love. Mother hugs me a lot, and Father brings me sweet fruit from the clearing, and it's only this one, my brother Cain, who treats me like this. Feeling weak when confronted by his brother, he would often call out to his mother and father to support him.

Cain's anger turned into secret hatred. He knew his parents did not look kindly on the way he treated his brother. He would hide his feelings, even trying to hide his hatred of his brother from himself. After all, they shared one father and one mother; his blood was as his brother's blood and his flesh as his brother's flesh. But the hatred had burrowed deep into his soul.

When Abel was old enough, he would go out with his father and his brother to the clearing, which Adam had sweated long hours to turn into a field. As Abel would work with them, hoeing, clearing away stones, helping to plough and sow, Cain would whisper in his father's ear, telling him of Abel's failures and mistakes, complaining of his laziness.

"He's more harm than he is use," was his constant grouse. When a sharpened ploughing stone was broken—naturally it was Abel's fault; if an irrigation ditch was blocked—this was down to his younger brother and his carelessness. Abel's eagerness to accompany his father, to appear strong, big and useful, turned to apprehension, and he stopped coming to the clearing.

Abel began to look for ways to fill his time while the others toiled; he preferred to stay in the cave or to explore its surroundings. Later, as he grew stronger, he began to wander, going ever further and further from the mouth of the cave. He found the streams, he found the river, the forest, the coloured rocks, the fruit-laden trees and the animals that sprawled, reclined, copulated, gave birth, laid eggs, twittered, roared and raged. He found them and was enthralled by the natural world and its wonders, soon becoming familiar with their habits, the paths that they followed to the springs, the caves where they sought refuge and the patterns of their behaviour. He found fruit that was good to eat, the sweet, the sour and the bitter. The living, burgeoning world was rich and enchanting, constantly changing, challenging the inquiring mind.

He would return eagerly, wanting to share the delights of his world with his parents and his brother. His mother listened and rejoiced in his enthusiasm. Adam listened, but after a long and wearisome day, his senses were dulled. He would nod as if paying attention, but sometimes his head slumped forward on his chest as Abel talked on and on. Cain did not listen at all. He would be engrossed in some work in the cave, either going out to draw water, or gathering dry branches for the fire—anything rather than endure his brother's eager prattling.

Abel soon learned it was possible to milk animals that had given birth. He tasted their milk, and finding it tasty, he used to fill stone pitchers that he had prepared and bring milk to the cave. And eggs that had fallen from nests he also picked up and brought with him. He also learned to tend a wounded animal that had strayed, falling over the cliff, a young bird that had tumbled from the nest, or a cow calving in the open clearing. And so, not many years were to pass before Abel became a herdsman. Cain was a tiller of the ground, and Abel a herdsman. One ploughed and sowed and harvested, while the other milked cows, clipped the wool of sheep and skinned dead animals, making leather garments for all the members of his family.

"Who needs your garments?" raged Cain. "Aren't these girdles of leaves good enough for us? Skins are unclean, they come from dead things," he complained, and refused to put his on.

The more Abel tried to placate Cain with his gifts, the more intense became the other's jealousy and hatred. He wants to buy his mother's heart, he thought to himself. Since he was born he has stolen her love from me, and now he wants to take my father's place beside her.

# Chapter fifty-eight

I watched the activities of the brothers; I began to fear the hatred that was rising in Cain's heart. It boded ill. I remembered Michael's stories from the distant past. I remembered the conspiracies of Samael and Satan, the wicked machinations of the serpent, and I remembered death. Something bad, something very bad is happening, and Adam and Eve do not see and do not hear the voices raging about them. And how could they know? Who was there to teach them? And who would open their eyes or warn them against the impending evil? The Lord was silent. I could not intervene, but was destined only to watch and bear witness. Every time the serpent slithers by the cave, it reminds me of days in the Garden, the shadow of the forbidden trees, expulsion and fear and death.

# Chapter fifty-nine

They all set to work on the scattered stones, digging with their hands under heavy boulders, in a combined effort to move them. Even the little children, those who were capable of moving and cleaning stones, joined in sifting through the rubble. Noah passed among them, giving instructions and supervising the work, lending a hand here and there, examining every stone with the faintest trace of a letter, or what could be a letter, inscribed on it. He set out pitchers of water, so that the thirsty could slake their thirst while working, and so that each fragment of stone could be washed and cleansed of its coating of mud. Very carefully, he examined the ruins of the house where the stone tablet was found. The dimensions of this house, greater by far than the dimensions of the others, gave him the idea that it had served as a temple. The script on the stone tablet that had been discovered also suggested this. Although he had not yet told them the meaning of the words inscribed on the tablet, they all sensed that these were things of the greatest importance, and they waited with curiosity for the moment that Noah would choose for their enlightenment.

As the sun began to sink in the western sky, Ham, working with his sons in the ruins of the big house, cried out: "Father, Father, come here, Father! We have found the skeleton of a man, and something fastened to his breastbone."

Noah came running. From Ham's hand he took a small stone, brightly polished, carved at the edges with patterns of flowers and crowns. By the light of the setting sun the stone gleamed and glittered with reddish rays like translucent drops of blood, and from the heart of the stone, from its heart of hearts, the inscription stood out:

*I am Enoch, the servant of God.*

All those gathered there knew this name; they had heard of Enoch, the son of Jared. They spoke of him and spoke of him constantly in the booths and temporary dwellings of the valley of the palms. Enoch the fair, the wise, the young; Enoch the dreamer, who had walked with God and whom God had taken—though where He had taken him no one knew. Fathers would tell their sons, and sons tell their grandsons of the wondrous exploits of Enoch the young hero. At the age of 365—a mere stripling!— he had left his home one fine day, left his home and the home of his father and mother, and tried to find his way to the Garden. He longed to return to the Garden that had been left behind by the father of his father and the mother of his mother. There, in the Garden, he would say, everything was bathed in primeval splendour, everything was pure and there was no sin, no destruction and no violence. Of the lost Garden men had told from the days of Adam and Eve to the days of Enoch son of Jared, told it on all kinds of different occasions.

In the days of the first father and first mother, they would share the blurred scraps of memory between them, images and recollections which would suddenly fly away, as if caught by a gust of wind, disappearing without trace—until the next time.

When Cain and Abel were born, they would sit through the long winter nights and remember the summer in that Garden,

and what they did not remember they gave their hearts free rein
to imagine, embellishing and embroidering as their sons listened
intently. How lovely those times in the Garden had been. Life
had been easy. How delicious was the sweetness oozing from the
plants and the fruits. The sons heard of the lost Garden and
yearned for it. And as they grew older, they were even more drawn
to the stories of their father and their mother.

By the time that Enoch heard about the Garden from Jared
his father, seven generations had passed, each adding further layers
and levels—seven reincarnations of a saga that, for them, had
begun with faint and misty memories and ended in a blaze of
glory. Enoch was entranced by the charms of the tale and he used
to tell it to his friends with great excitement, fanning the flames
of the curiosity of the children of the valley of the palms, stoking
up their desires along with his own.

Enoch's father, Jared, tried to dissuade him from his course,
telling him of the Cherubim that guard the gate, of the blade of
the flashing sword, of the perils of the long road that no man had
ever travelled. He also told him of the evil spirits and devils that
lie in wait to ensnare the pure in heart. Enoch would hear out
his father's words courteously, and then answer him respectfully
and pleasantly,

"Father, I must set out on this perilous journey, for I hear
a voice commanding me to do so. I shall go, and others shall go
with me, and we shall go on until we find our way to the Garden."

Meanwhile, Enoch's own wife and his children pleaded,
"Father, Father. You are only three hundred and sixty-five years
old! You shall perish on that road that no man has travelled."

"No, my dear wife and my sons," he answered them
equably, "Whoever walks with God walks in His way, and His
way leads him to the Garden. God will command the Cherubim
to open the gates before us, and the flashing sword will be returned
to its sheath."

Pleas were of no avail to Enoch, neither the warnings of

his father, nor the tears of his wife and his children. The voice that called him prevailed over the other voices that tried to stop him. He set out on his way, and God took him and he was no more.

Sometimes they said that Enoch was the son of Cain, who built a city and named it Enoch after his son. At other times he was said to be the son of Jared, who lived several generations after Cain. Both the beginning and the end of Enoch were veiled in mystery—and here he was lying at their feet, another skeleton among the skeletons of the victims of the flood. But his skeleton was unlike the many other skeletons scattered among the ruins: the skull of Enoch had been smashed, and a heavy stone lay beside it. It seemed that the other skeletons were of those who were caught unawares by the torrents of the flood and were buried beneath the rubble of the shattered buildings. Enoch had died differently. Enoch had been killed with intent. Someone had shattered his skull with the heavy stone. Who could have done it? Someone taking revenge on the son of Cain for the death of Abel? Someone who heeded God's command that Cain must not be touched, but had exacted vengeance through the killing of his son? Or was the secret of his death bound up in rivalry, in hatred of the servant of God? They had found the skeleton but were no closer to the answer—perhaps it would never be known, and the cause of his death would remain among God's own secrets.

By the last light of day they dug a pit for a grave, laid the skeleton in it and covered it with earth. Noah recited the words that had always been said at the burials of his father and his father's father, "Dust you are and to dust you shall return, blessed be the Creator and the Slayer."

The red rays of the setting sun were like the red flash of the stone, which Noah held in his hand throughout the burial. Shem and Ham stood to his right and his left, supporting him. Japheth, standing behind, whispered partly in sorrow and partly in scorn, "Behold the way to the lost Garden, behold the way to the grave."

Those standing beside the tomb of Enoch, son of Jared, knew only the sad conclusion to the story, but I knew the whole of it, having witnessed it from the beginning to its bitter end, and as a witness I shall tell the truth, the entire truth. Seeing the band of mourners lamenting the death of their ancestor, from generations before, I remembered Cain and his brother Abel, and Adam their father and Eve their mother, four people alone in the universe, until the firstborn killed his younger brother, and only three were left.

# Chapter sixty

The serpent was always slithering about the mouth of the cave, and I knew that wherever the serpent was, Lillith would not be far away. It followed in her footsteps with a servile, manic loyalty, like a slave, like a lovesick suitor who can find no cure for his malady. While Lillith rebuffed him, she also took care not to extinguish his ardour, since the serpent, the most cunning of all the beasts of the clearing, had promised to deliver her beloved Adam into her arms, and though it had failed so far, it might yet succeed. Eve was still as close as ever to her husband and he to her; they were as one flesh. Now they had two fine, handsome sons—lusty youths—the sap of their manhood ripening fast, and now Lillith intended to exceed the serpent in cunning. She would increase its desire; inflame its passion, until she attained her objective. After all, death lurked between the poisoned fangs of the serpent. One bite would suffice to kill Eve. All she had to do was raise him to such a pitch of madness and anger that he would not hesitate to bruise her rival's heel. Her love for Adam made her forget her fear of the wrath of the Lord. She wanted her rival dead, and the serpent would kill her.

-Go, sow discord between them as you did in the Garden, and when you have succeeded come back to me, she said to the serpent.

Meanwhile, Lillith herself began hovering at night over the sons, penetrating their dreams and stirring their seething young blood. They would sink into ecstasies of love that they had never known; sweetness such as they had tasted only in their sleep. Lillith inflamed them, but in their dreams they saw only one image of a woman, the image of their mother. When they awoke, drenched in sweat and in seed, they pulled their robes over their bodies, lest their parents see their discomfort. The shame that Adam and Eve had discovered when they ate of the fruit of the Tree of Knowledge was already in their souls.

A blind and hidden force, a force drawn up from the depths, originating in the Lord's command to be fruitful and to multiply, a force that had yet to carve out its channel and find the course that it should follow, drew the three men to the one woman. At night, when Adam knew his wife, the sons used to lie awake, listening to the sounds from the bed of their father and mother, following their actions intently, and falling asleep to dream their dreams, not knowing who was stirring their blood, who inflaming their lusts, who dulling their senses and who unleashing the fountains that gushed from their bodies with such sweetness.

Then the serpent would whisper into their ears in the darkness of night: "The woman, the woman who lies in the arms of your father—she is the secret and she has the answers." Lillith also hovered over the dreams of Eve. With the same charms and whispers that inflamed the passions of the sons, she aroused in the dreams of Eve longings and desires, fantasies and illusions. Once I saw her coupling in her dream with Cain, her son and her gift from God, another time she was fervently embracing her son Abel. I saw her clutching at Cain's hair and heard her whispering: "Your locks are like palm-fronds, your eyes like pools, your manhood like a raging torrent." To Abel, loving her in her dream, she whispered: "You have the vigour of a ram, and your body has a horn like the horn of a stag."

I knew that these were Lillith's wiles, but I could not warn Eve that Lillith and the serpent were in league to tempt her. Who would tell her what was allowed and what forbidden? And who was there to tell the sons that only their father was permitted to their mother? It was as if the Lord had put wood on the fire, the serpent and Lillith had set it alight—so which of the four would now get burned? I was the witness—but powerless to avert the disaster. With my own eyes I saw it coming, but could do nothing. Nothing at all.

So Cain lusted after his mother. He followed her actions with amorous eyes, staring at her body and watching her movements, whether bending down or standing erect. He saw her full and ample breasts, her strong thighs, her hips that swayed as she walked, and in his fantasies he lay in her arms. He feared his father and envied his brother. And the serpent whispered in his ear in his dreams that his brother was enjoying Eve's amorous favours.

Every time he went out with his father to the clearing, he was fearful and suspicious. Now, as we are in the clearing, Abel is left alone with our mother. He brings her milk, and his scent is the scent of stags and tigers, of lions and of running water, he feeds her the eggs of eagles and is rewarded with her embrace, her caresses and her love. Jealousy lights prodigious fires. Jealousy blinds the eyes from seeing and opens the eyes of the mind to false passions and illusions.

Cain began planting suspicions in his father's heart.

"Father, Father, beware of Abel your son."

"Why do you say such a thing, Cain? Surely he is tending his flock in the clearings."

"Sometimes he is, sometimes not. Sometimes he returns

when you are labouring in the clearing, ploughing the ground with the sweat of your brow, and comes to his mother in the cave, his hands full of gifts—milk, skins, wool and sweet fruit."

"He does this only to gladden his mother's heart, Cain."

"Yes, Father, and her body too. Her breasts, her loins. Who knows the desires of a woman's heart? Yesterday, when you were bent over your sowing in the clearing, I came to the cave to drink from the pitcher of palm-juice, and what did I see? Your son Abel offering delicious, juicy fruits, and my mother kissing and caressing his face and his hands. They did not see me as I came and went. In the mouth of the cave I saw a coiled serpent. It made noises that sounded like laughter and disappeared among the bushes."

I was alarmed. Was the serpent once more intent on seducing Eve, as it had in the Garden?

I sought it out and found it at Lillith's feet, staring with lascivious eyes at her cleft, as she rebuffed him, warning that until he brought Adam to her, he would not enter her.

-He shall be yours and you shall be mine, hissed the serpent.

Although I had observed his conspiracies in the past, but it was not until he revealed his plan to Lillith, that I realised the full depth of his cunning:

-I shall make Abel lie at his mother's side. I shall bring Adam from the clearing and when he finds them lying together, he will kill them. There is no limit to the jealousy of a man where his woman is concerned, no limit to his hatred of the one who steals her from him. Have you not seen how the beasts behave, how the males drive away other males trying to approach their females? Adam and Eve and their sons are no different. The instinct that draws them together is the instinct that will tear them apart.

It is a wonder in my eyes how the Lord combines opposites, how He joins together a thing and its utter reverse. Only the Lord knows how to walk between these contradictions. I understood the serpent's stratagem, and I was powerless to foil it.

Every now and then Cain would stoke the fire that he had lit, and Adam's mood would grow. He withdrew from his wife, lay in wait for her, and in the middle of a day of toil, he would come suddenly to the cave, sending Cain to dog his brother's footsteps—but none of it worked. Lillith constantly hovered in their dreams. Adam once more saw Lillith in his dreams, as he had seen her then, in the Garden. I realised that things buried deep in the recesses of his soul—desires, lusts, urges and aspirations—had remained so well hidden that even Raphael's pinch of oblivion could not fully dispel them. To Eve, Adam turned in his waking; to Lillith in his dreams.

Eve had no inkling of what was afoot. Her hands were full of work from morning to evening. She loved Adam from whose rib she was created, she loved Cain because he was created of her flesh, just as she loved Abel because he was flesh of her flesh and blood of her blood. With no parents, with no other experience, she could see no sin in the way her sons desired her, in their fumbling and fondling and caressing or in the emissions of their seed on her body. How was she to know that the things that brought such joy and delight to her and to her sons were evil in the sight of the Lord? Only Adam's jealousy made her feel uneasy.

The summer, which had been marvellous in its richness and plenty, was almost at an end. Trees were laden with fruit, and the branches of the palms bowed under the weight of the succulent, honey-sweet dates. The lambs and the whelps, born in the spring, had grown. The gentle breezes wafted sweet scents with them of ripened fruit and honey; and the blessings of fertility were everywhere in evidence, from every tree and shrub, to all the gullies and ravines. God had been good to them and they, the first dwellers on the earth, were grateful to the One who had given them all this bounty.

Adam called his sons and said: "It is time to bring our offerings to God, the Creator of the world and the giver of plenty."

"Blessed be He who gives of His goodness, and to Him we

bring our offerings and give thanks," the sons replied with the customary words for the end of the summer.

-Soon, whispered the serpent to Lillith, Soon!

Eve washed the men's garments and her own. It was a festive day, the day of oblation. She combed her sons' hair and anointed them with scented and fragrant oil. She dressed them in girdles made from the leaves of the vine and the fig, of olive and myrrh. They all put on garlands of perfumed flowers. Adam washed his body in the water of the spring three times, saying each time,

"Blessed be the Creator of the earth and the fruit of the earth and blessed be the Creator of the fruit of man."

Adam put on the cloak, which Eve had made from the strands of wool, that Abel had collected from low branches and thorny bushes. On his head Eve placed a circlet of carob and fig leaves, exuding scents of potency and masculine vigour. She was proud of her three men, the handsome heroes who gave such joy to her body and her heart.

All of them bore the fruits of their labours, Cain from the field and Abel from his herd. Cain carried a reed-basket full of fruits, and Abel brought some milk, butter, cheese and fleeces from his herd. Adam and Eve bore a basket filled with fruits and flowers and all manner of leaves and grasses. And so they came to the stone of oblation on the bank of the river where it had stood since the day it was created. I found it there when I came to this land. It was a crag overhanging the surging waters of the river. This was one of the four tributaries of the parent-river, the river that flows from the Garden to the four corners of the world. Since my coming to the land, the water in it had never ceased to flow.

The family of Adam stood by the ancient rock, seeing four reflections in the primeval waters of the river. How fine they are, how handsome! And no wonder, as they are in His likeness and His image. The serpent and Lillith were there too. Lillith hovered above Adam's head, and the serpent hung among the branches of the willow that grew there, looking just like one of the branches.

First to bring his offering was Cain the firstborn. With measured tread, with reverence, he walked to the rock. He laid his fruits one by one on the stone slab and spoke a blessing: "Blessed be the Creator of fruit from the ground." And all replied: "Amen, blessed be He."

Then Abel brought his oblation, the oblation of a shepherd. He laid his fleeces, eggs, cheese and butter on the slab and said: "Blessed be He who puts fruit in the bellies of the beasts of the clearing and the birds of the air," and they answered after him: "Amen, blessed be He."

Finally, Adam drew water from the river and sprinkled it on the offerings, on the rock, on the head of Eve, his wife and the mother of his sons, and on the heads of his sons with the blessing: "Blessed be He who gives water from the sky and from the river, rain from the Heavens and fruit from the belly." And again they answered: "All blessed be He, amen."

When they returned to the cave, they dined of all the good things of the land, and when the sun sank they took to their beds. The serpent crawled from the tree to the rock. Its sharp tongue found its way into the eggs; then it drank the milk, licked the butter and scattered the fleeces in all directions. The offering of Cain, the tiller of the soil, remained on the rock where he had left it.

-Now, now! whispered the serpent to itself, as it hastened away, to tell Lillith what he had done.

-What are you plotting, serpent? she asked. She, too, was still unaware of what was to happen.

-Cain will come, and he will see what has become of his offerings, said the serpent in glee. And in his wrath he will strike down Abel. Adam will come, and in his wrath he will strike down Cain. Eve will hear of the death of her sons and will die of grief.

I was gripped by dread. Could it be possible that Eve, the mother of all life, formed in the image and the likeness of the

Lord, was to die through the machinations of a serpent? With her sons? But it was as if I were paralysed, knowing that something wicked was about to happen but unable to warn. Only you, Lord, only you can avert disaster.

The next day at dawn, after they had eaten, Cain hastened to the stone of oblation to see if his offering had been accepted. When he saw his offering still there, and the offering of his brother Abel gone, his face fell. He clenched his fists in anger, crying aloud:

"You accepted his offering, God, and you rejected mine? I brought you the best of the fruits of your land: fruits, seeds, olives and dates, carobs and figs. The best of the very best I laid before you, I spoke the blessing, and you have not accepted my offering? The love of my mother he has stolen from me, the love of my father he covets, my father's wife he desires, and yet his offering you accepted and mine you spurned?"

He took everything that was laid on the rock and flung it into the river. Still furious, he went to the clearing to work with his father. He was sullen, not saying a word until Adam asked him if something was wrong.

"I am angry," he told his father, "so angry that my anger fills me completely. I have laboured by the sweat of my brow, and I offered the finest of the fruits of the land in sacrifice to God, and He rejected it. Yet Abel wanders as he pleases among the brooks and the pastures, gathering flocks and herds around him, resting, idle, in the shade of the trees while the sun beats down on my head—and his offering, over which he has not toiled and for which he has not sweated, God accepts. I am spurned by you, and I am spurned by Him."

Cain covered his face with his robe and tears streamed from his eyes.

Adam wiped away his tears, soothing him with words of comfort and love and wise counsel. "Beware of jealousy, my son, of rage and of anger. They lie in wait at our door. Jealousy is a burden hard to bear—and there is no need for it. All the land is before us, and the beasts of the clearing are our neighbours. With the sky above us and the ground beneath our feet we have enough, my son, there is enough for all of us."

"Yes, Father, but there is only one father and one mother for the two of us."

Adam tried to console his grieving son, saying: "Jealousy lies in wait, seeking ways to breach our defences. God gave us the strength to resist it. It is an all-consuming fire, but a fire that may be quenched. You should rule it, my son. Do not let it rule you."

Cain did not reply. He picked up the stone tools and went back to work, toiling diligently, but morosely.

Towards evening, when they returned to the cave, Eve greeted them in a mood of obvious agitation, telling them that while going from the cave to the spring to draw water, she had seen a big serpent coiled around the fig tree, staring with malicious eyes and baring his pointed tongue. She said she had picked up a stone to throw at him but he slithered away into the bushes, whispering, "Soon, soon."

Adam and Eve had vague memories of something concerning a serpent, so long ago it could have been before they came into the world, but they found nothing to say about it.

Cain remembered the words that his father had spoken in the clearing, the words of comfort and wise counsel, the warning against jealousy and rage. He turned to his brother and addressing him cordially he said:

"Come, brother, come see our work in the clearings. If you come, I shall teach you how to use the stone tools, how to clear the land, hoe and plough. Work with us if only for one day, and you will know the taste of bread."

Abel was eager to be reconciled with his brother. He loved him and respected him as he respected his father and his mother, and so he gladly accepted.

"Tomorrow I shall come, brother, and I shall bring all kinds of good and tasty things, such as milk and the eggs of fowls."

An air of conciliation reigned in the cave. Adam caressed the head of Cain, his son, glad that his words had penetrated his heart and soothed his spirit. When they took to their beds and lay down to sleep, Eve embraced her husband and whispered in his ear:

"I am scared, Adam. That serpent is disturbing my peace of mind. I remember that he brought evil with him. Perhaps you remember better than I the evil that he brought?"

"I'm tired; I have worked hard today. We can talk about it tomorrow."

Adam curled up, closed his eyes and slept, and Eve lay awake a long time, thinking about the serpent.

# Chapter sixty-one

Cain awoke before the light of the dawn reached the interior of the dark cave. On the mat beside him lay Abel, his brother, stirring at times in his sleep and muttering indistinctly. From his parents' couch he heard low voices. He listened intently, and heard Eve whispering to Adam her husband:

"Adam, the boys are growing up and there is sap in their loins. They are strong, vigorous, and extremely handsome."

"Yes," Adam replied. "Praise God."

"But there are no other women," Eve continued. "I see their lust and their anguish. Sometimes they come to me, and their white juice is spilled on my flesh."

Adam pretended he had not heard her words, a heavy lump of bitterness in his throat. Would he also fall into the trap of jealousy, the trap that only yesterday he had warned his son, Cain, about? He choked back his words, and was silent.

"We must beseech our God to give us daughters. Be with me, husband, and be with me now. Out of this sweetness I shall bear you a daughter."

And Adam knew Eve his wife.

Cain was stunned by his mother's words. He had only just awoken from an intense dream, and his life-giving fluid was wet on his bare legs and on the leaves that padded his bed. True, true, he said in his heart, when my mother bears a daughter, she would be mine. Fragments of the dream still hovering above him, filling his body with cravings and desires. Lillith I did not see, and I knew that this time it was not she who had inflamed his lust. It arose from the root planted by the Lord in every living thing.

Cain continued to indulge his fantasies, and Abel awoke with the dawn. He rose from his bed at once, as was his habit every day, took the pitcher and went out to the spring to draw water. Cain looked at Abel's powerful body; a perfect body. From head to toe he stood tall and erect, a flawless sapling. His hair hung to his shoulders, black and smooth. His eyes, his nose, his mouth—they were like fruits among the branches. When our mother bears a daughter, Cain imagined further, this one will come and steal her from me. The bitter jealousy, that he thought he had suppressed, emerged once again from its lair. Cain threw aside the night-cover with a swift movement, and called to his brother: "Wait, wait Abel, I shall come with you to the spring." Abel waited for him.

Beside the spring they found all kinds of creatures, coming as they did every morning to drink of its waters. Seeing Abel they approached him, sniffing his skin and brushing against his body, licking his hands when he offered them handfuls of fresh grass.

He has won even the affection of the animals, Cain mused. They come to him, but it's as if they don't even see me. Once more he dispelled from his heart the anger that had begun to swell there. Had he not promised his father he would seek ways of conciliation and tenderness, that he would avoid the trap of rage and envy? After the morning meal, and a thanksgiving offered to God for the food and the water, the good things and the grace, the men rose and left the cave. The sun had already infused the colours of the dawn with a full and radiant light.

"Join us in the field at noon. We'll rest a little from our work and eat bread and drink water from the pitcher, and you can see for yourself how your father and I have laboured, and how the land gives us its fruits. We have given it our sweat, and it repays us with all good things. Come brother, come!"

Adam heard Cain's words and a broad smile rose to his lips at these overtures of reconciliation. After all, he thought, there are only four of us here on this good earth. God has lifted His curse from us, and now He will remove the enmity of the brothers. "Yes, come, my son," he said aloud. "You will like what you see, and we shall be glad of your company in the field."

Eager and enthusiastic as ever, and thirsty for his brother's love, Abel replied eagerly, "I shall be there, I shall be there!" and they went their separate ways.

As noon was approaching, however, shouts from Eve could be heard from the distant cave. She had seen the big serpent crawling into the cave, and did not know how to be rid of it. Adam ran quickly to his wife's aid and Cain continued with his work.

At the appointed hour, Abel set out for the field. Deer and antelope followed in his footsteps. The animals had grown accustomed to living in his company. He helped them to keep themselves clean of thorns and worms and insects, tended those that fell, came to the aid of females giving birth, and even relieved their discomfort when their udders were filled with milk. I watched the trusty herdsman and his flocks following him as he led the way. On his right shoulder he carried a long staff, and hanging from it there was a wicker basket crammed with all good things— fruits, eggs, slices of cheese wrapped in fig-leaves, sweet dates and two jars, one filled with milk and the other with honey. In his left hand he carried a bundle of wool. These were the gifts that he brought to his father and his brother in token of his love and respect.

While still some way off, Abel called out to his brother: "I have come, brother, I have come."

Cain looked up from his work and waved his hand in greeting, calling back to him: "Come brother Abel, come. Our father went back to the cave, but in the meanwhile, let's eat in the shade of the tree."

A spirit of conciliation and brotherhood hung in the air. Cain thought to himself, have the jealousy and the hatred been stopped? As my father said, jealousy is trying to get the better of me, but can I control it? I shall control it, I shall.

"Come brother, let me embrace you!"

Abel came running down from the high hill on hearing his brother's call. For so long he had yearned for this moment, for this embrace; Cain's love was as precious to him as that of his father and his mother.

When he started to run, the animals with Abel broke into a stampede, rushing in all directions. They might have been frightened, or perhaps they simply wanted to follow their shepherd's example, but they galloped into the field. Corn stalks were trampled in their path, stones kicked up and scattered over the newly ploughed soil, fences shattered and the channels bearing the spring water ruined.

As Abel tried to confine the flock to the edge of the field, without success, Cain picked up the big stone that he used for ploughing and started lashing out at the beasts. This only scared them even more, and, panic-stricken they ran about in frenzied circles, trampling and destroying everything beneath their hooves. The rage that Cain had repressed in his heart burst out in a flood. Nothing could stop him. With the stone in his hand he struck his brother. The jars and the fruit in the wicker basket were scattered in all directions, bundles of wool fell to the ground.

Shouting, Cain struck him over and over again, "You

wanted the field as well? You stole my mother's love, you took my father's love, and even the daughter who is yet to be born, you covet."

The hail of blows went on until he was exhausted. When he stopped, Abel was already bereft of the breath of life. He lay in a pool of his blood.

When life begins its journey, it is stored in a single drop. Within this drop is the whole of existence. The first cry of the infant, the heartbeat, the smile bright as the sun, the first word and the last, the flash of the eye, the sound of the song rising from the fountain of the soul and the flight of the imagination, love and hate. This is the drop that enfolds the entirety of life, from its beginning to its end.

The blood that was streaming from the wounds of Abel was slowly returning this glorious treasury to the earth. Here, sprawled on the ground, was the first man to be given back to it. His blood spilt, with every drop that flowed from his injuries, all the strengths, secrets, dreams, thoughts, loves and desires that had filled this body were disappearing.

Abel, Abel, Abel, generations will come and go, but there will never be another like you. A star rises and sparkles forever. The sun shines on. Only you, Abel, have risen and set, and never in all the days of the history of the world, never in all the days that are yet to come, will there again be someone like you. The son of the first man is with us no more, but is bathed in his blood, in the spilt milk, in the juices of the fruit and the honey seeping from the broken jars—brought as gifts for his brother.

Cain bent over his brother's body. The blood pouring from the wounds stunned him. Never in his life had he seen this colour flowing in such spate. He had seen red in the rising of the dawn and in the sunset, seen red in the ripe fruit and in flowers, on the wings of birds, but the red stream gushing from a human, this stunned and frightened him. Nor had he ever seen death. He thought his brother was asleep. He saw that his eyes were open, his mouth agape, saw the vessels that had fallen from his hands, but Cain did not see the life slipping away. Surely it was in him, somewhere, in hiding perhaps from the blows that he received, but in him still.

He shook Abel's body this way and that, gripping his shoulders, his hands, and his head. As he shook him he cried,

"Abel my brother, Abel, get up, wake up, and stir yourself. Come back to me, brother; come back to your mother and your father. There will never again be such a thing as long as we live. I shall never again raise my hand against you, or hurt you ever."

But Abel lay still; silent, not responding.

Cain did not move from his brother's side. He stared at him, expecting to be given some sign. Perhaps he would still wake up, and he could tell him that he forgave him, that he wasn't angry with him any more, he wasn't to blame for the damage done by the animals in the field. But Abel did not move and did not stir. He lay sprawled on his back, all around him a pool of blood that was beginning to congeal. Ravens swooped on the pool, and an eagle too, and dipped their beaks in the clotted blood. Cain tried to dispel them, to keep them from his brother's open wounds, but the birds, aroused by the scent of blood, were quite undeterred, wheeling in the sky before returning to their ghoulish feast.

Abel's face was calm, unmarked and undistorted. Though his open eyes still stared at the blue sky, at the birds soaring above him, he saw nothing. His spirit had already left his body and was returning to his creator. When Cain reached out to touch his brother's slumped hand, he was shocked to find it so cold. It was colder than the water in the river and heavier than a stone.

The day ended, and the colour of blood was blended with the colours of the sunset.

"Where have you gone, my brother, where has your spirit fled, Abel my brother?" he asked again and again, until at last he began to understand that his brother was no longer with them, and would never come back.

He dug a pit, lifted his brother and laid him in the pit and covered him. From dust we came, his father had told him in answer to his question, and to dust we shall return. I am giving you back to the dust from which you came, brother. You are the first man to return to the dust, and I am the first man to bury a brother. Where has your spirit gone, how has your tongue been silenced, brother. Your open eyes see nothing. What happened to the light that has shone from them all these years? You are here but you are not. Your mouth is here but it is silent, and your ears do not hear. This must be the death of which God spoke to my father and my mother? I did not know that a blow with a stone would take their son from them and my brother from me. I did not know, I did not know.

In the dead of night wolves emerged from the forest and licked at the lumps of clotted blood. What is it, in the blood, that so attracted the eagle and the raven, the wolves and the teeming swarms of insects that wallow in it as if deranged?

In the Garden, the midnight watch had already sung the midnight anthem, but here, on the earth, a brother sat mourning by his brother's grave. He now knew he must answer his father when he asked, where is Abel your brother?

What could he tell him? Were he to tell him the truth, there was no doubt that his father would be so furious that he'd strike him and probably kill him as well. What would be gained from this truth, with both sons lying dead? How will my mother endure the death of both her sons, he asked himself? She would surely not survive alone in this great and empty world. Better for them, and far better for me, that the death of Abel remain hidden. They will think he disappeared, Cain argued to himself, they will think Abel went away to visit the buffalo, the deer and the antelope or the lion cubs. The animals are his friends; they love him as much as he loves them. This I shall tell them, if they ask me where my brother is.

As he pondered further, devising stratagems for the benefit

of his father and his mother, a voice was heard in the still of the night. It was not his father's voice, but a clear, sombre voice, issuing from a grieving heart and from trembling lips. Cain was startled, and looked around straining his eyes to penetrate the darkness. But he saw no one. Again the voice called:

-Cain! Cain!

And again Cain tried to locate the speaker. The voice called his name a third time. Although he could not see the speaker he replied: "Here am I."

-Where is your brother, Abel? The voice repeated the question.

Could this, after all, be his father asking?

"I don't know, Father," Cain replied into the darkness. "Perhaps he is in the forest with the animals, perhaps in the mountains with the eagle, or in the river swimming with the dolphins. Am I my brother's keeper?" Thoughts chased one another through his mind. If I am believed, then my father will not mourn, nor my mother go down in sorrow to the grave, and I shall be spared the vengeance of a father bereft of his son.

"I don't know," he repeated his answer. "I am not my brother's keeper, and he does not ask my permission when he goes."

-Cain, the voice cried, impatient now, angry, grim and resonant. What have you done? The voice of your brother's blood cries out to me from the ground!

Cain was stunned. Who was speaking? Who was it that knew it all? What voice could there be from under the ground? Perhaps the voice was coming from within him, crying out from his grieving heart. Could it really be—that from his gut, from the depths of his belly and his entrails came this shrieking voice that shattered the silence of the night? Cain was dumbfounded. He understood that from this voice there would be no hiding all the days of his life. It came from inside him, for God the creator of his father and his mother, the giver of life and death, was with him and would walk with him wherever he sought refuge. He understood now that God had been inside him since the day of his birth, and would accompany him until the day of his death.

"God," said Cain. "I did not know death. I was not warned, was not taught what it is, and yet my guilt is great."

The voice that cried from within him spoke once more:

-Cursed is the land that opened its mouth to receive your brother's blood. You shall work it and it shall repay you nothing. For you will be doomed to wandering in the land, and my voice will go with you wherever you try to hide from me, until you know, until you learn that I gave you the power to let live and the power to kill, the power to love and the power to hate, the power to reveal and the power to conceal.

"If you banish me this day from the land and from your presence," whispered Cain, "I cannot survive. I have nowhere to hide, and anyone who finds me can slay me. Great is my sin, but greater still is your punishment."

-I shall put a mark on you, Cain. I shall protect you from the wrath of avengers as yet unborn. Whosoever takes vengeance upon you, upon him shall vengeance be exacted sevenfold. But you are to be a wanderer and a vagrant, and people yet to be born shall learn from you, in every place you go, as far as the land of Nod, east of Eden, that life and death are in their hands, and they must choose life.

Before sunrise Cain returned to the cave. His father and mother were not yet awake, for the Lord had laid a deep sleep upon them. Cain lay down on his mat, exhausted and sick at heart.

When they rose in the morning, Adam and Eve saw the mark on his brow.

"Have you been fighting with your brother, did he strike you?" Adam asked.

"No, Father, I struck him and I killed him, though that

was not my intention. I must set out on my travels, since God has banished me from His presence."

Eve was gripped and silenced by her pain and said nothing; she sat on the ground and poured dust over her head, rending her robe in bitter silence. She turned away from Adam and would not let him approach her. She refused to eat bread or drink water, until Adam forced her to take nourishment. Her body withered and her face fell, her eyes faded and her lips were sealed in mute and immeasurable grief. Adam accompanied Cain to the edge of the forest and said sadly, "My son, you are all that we have left in the world. Take care of yourself, take care."

"Yes, Father. God goes with me."

Adam kissed his only son, his firstborn, as he set out to wander to the east of Eden.

When Adam returned to the cave, he saw the serpent coiled like a rope among the rocks. He remembered the Garden, remembered the Tree of Knowledge and the Tree of Life, remembered the wiles and the whispers of the serpent, remembered the wrath of God, and remembered the shame and his futile attempt to hide from Him. He remembered banishment to the land. He picked up a stone, meaning to hurl it at the serpent's head, but stopped himself. Enough blood had been shed already, he told himself. The serpent raised his head, peered at Adam and slithered away among the rocks.

Adam went to Eve his wife and tried to comfort her. "Do not weep, dear wife. We shall yet bear sons and daughters. We still have our vigour."

"No," said Eve. "Do not come near me, until the Lord promises us that never again shall a man kill his brother, nor shall parents bury their children."

The serpent heard her and hurried away to find Lillith. "I have done it," he boasted. "At long last I have done it. He is yours, Lillith, he is yours. And now is the time for me to claim my reward."

-You are mistaken, serpent, he is not mine, he is hers forever. The death of their son will bind them together for all eternity.

# Chapter sixty-two

After all the people around Noah had lain down to rest, at the end of a fraught and arduous day, he sat over the tomb of Enoch and pondered what he knew of him. He remembered the stories that he had heard from Lamech, his father, of Enoch's wisdom even as a boy, of his unstained hands, of his aversion for sin and all evil acts. Lamech had praised Enoch's charitable deeds, his unremitting fight against violence and wickedness.

Lamech would tell them how Enoch was mocked by men of his age and his generation: "Go, go and walk with God!" they used to call after him. "Here on earth, Enoch, the stronger has the upper hand. See, Enoch, the eagle flying high, and what of the starling? He beats with his wings at the low clouds. See, Enoch, the lion and the leopard. They go to the field to seek their food, and the doe waits until they leave. Thus God created the world, and this is His way."

Enoch did not share their opinion. He dreamed of the days of the Garden. From Jared, his father, he had heard the whole story, from beginning to end. Of the perpetual tranquillity, of the

Lord ruling with justice, of angels and Cherubim and Seraphim. And of his forebears Adam and Eve, and the Tree of Knowledge and the Tree of Life. His yearning was to return to the most ancient of ancient lives, to make a new beginning, to dwell once more without sin and without punishment in the great light of the Creator of the world, in His justice and His radiance.

"I shall go and I shall seek the way back," he would repeat to anyone who would listen. There were some who loved to hear his daydreams, some who pretended to be curious and afterwards scoffed at him, some who were excited by his words, and some who derided the very notion of the existence of the Garden.

"Stories, stories," they used to say. "Tales that old men tell their children."

When Noah asked his father Lamech what he thought, and whether the words of Enoch were the truth or just daydreams, his father pondered a while and said, "Who knows?"

"Perhaps?" Noah persisted. "Is there a Garden or is there not? Did it happen or did it not—what they say of our father Adam and our mother Eve?"

Lamech hesitated and then said in a low voice: "That is the story that is told."

He himself was a wretched man. Since Lamech had killed a child and a man, he feared the vengeance of God and of man. He stayed hidden in his tent, did not go among people, and even to his wives Adah and Zillah was he sullen and withdrawn. Only to his son, Noah, was his heart open. When Noah was still a boy, Lamech would stroke his hair and say over and over again words that made no sense to him,

"You, Noah, shall be my comfort for the deeds of our hands and for our grief. When you were born my son, two birds hovered above your head, the raven and the dove. One screeched, the other cooed. The raven is our grief, black and screeching, tearing at the heart and deafening the ear. The dove is our comfort, softly cooing and offering consolation. Look to the dove and not to the raven."

Father Lamech, Father Lamech, you prophesied and you did not know what you prophesied. The raven flew and returned without tidings, and the dove foretold our salvation. And the olive too, the green and steadfast olive. The olive that grows here too, from this land that swallowed up our father Enoch. The roots of the olive will reach down to you, our father Enoch. They will entwine about you and tell your dust of the sun that rises and sets, of the wind that blows and brings rain, of the light of the moon and stars. The leaves will absorb the scents of the world, and the roots will feed your dust with all the perfumes and the balms that God gave to our world. This shall be the Garden that you sought, the Garden that you yearned for.

Noah bent, scooped up a handful of the dust that covered the grave of Enoch, addressed it as if it could hear his voice,

"Who are you that lies in this tomb? Are you Enoch son of Cain, his brother's killer, who built a city and fled from the wrath of avengers, or are you the other Enoch, the son of Jared, son of Seth? Are you that Enoch who was thought to have disappeared, because he walked with God and He took him to Himself? I do not know this, and we shall not ever know this. Who raised a hand against you? An avenger of the blood of Abel, or a dreamer of the Garden, who set out as you did to seek the way back? If we knew, if only we knew."

Noah, you innocent and righteous man. I saw Enoch and I know his story and what I saw I shall tell, but you will not hear my voice. Angels speak, but men do not hear them. For it is only at the Lord's command that man may hear our voices.

Here is what I saw.

## Chapter sixty-three

The sons of Cain were hardworking tillers of the soil. They built homes, begot sons and daughters, honed tools of bronze and iron, took up the lyre and the harp, founded cities and settled in them. Their father Cain was a vagrant, wandering between his daughters and his sons until he came to the land of Nod. Because the mark of God was on him, shielding him from avengers, no man raised a hand against him.

When a third child was born to Eve and Adam they called him Seth, meaning that God gave them a son in place of Abel. Once more joy returned to the cave, once more the cave was filled with the cry of a living infant, once more Eve's breasts were filled with warm and sweet milk, and once more Adam looked at his wife Eve with trust and affection.

In the time of her mourning she had turned her back on him. She had laid a heavy burden of guilt on him. "Why, Adam, did you not have the wisdom to protect our son? How could you abandon him to the burning jealousy of Cain? You, husband, saw more than I could see. They went with you to the field; they were before your eyes when I was left alone in the cave. How did you not see, how did you not hear? Oh, my son Abel, my son Abel. I did not know what jealousy is, nor death. I did not know that it is the end, extinction. You, Adam, saw more than I saw, and you were blind to the jealousy of your sons."

After the death of Abel, there suddenly rose from the recesses of lost memory the recollection of punishment, of curse and of banishment. Now Eve understood her fear of the serpent, lurking constantly at the mouth of the cave, and understood her hatred of him. When Seth was born he brought with him the sounds of life, the sounds of weeping and laughter, a babbling voice. Only then did the wounds heal, and a little joy and conciliation return to the cave.

When Seth grew up, he married his sister, the daughter of Adam and Eve, and a son was born whom they called Enos. He was the child who brought new hope with his birth. He would renew the ways of men on the earth, and again they would call upon the name of God. The sons of Enos would remember that there was a spirit in men because God had breathed His spirit into their bodies, and stamped His likeness and His image upon them. For God had created the heavens and the earth, and the sons of Enos would be fruitful and multiply and fill the earth, choosing good over evil, and there would be no more slaying of brothers. And thus they believed from generation to generation, from father to son, to the seventh generation.

Everything that is marked by it tells us that the number seven is special. Seven days of Creation, seven planets, seven generations of mankind upon the earth. And then Enoch was born to Jared. On the seventh day he was born, in the seventh month he was born, in the seventh generation he was born. Could he ever forget this?

While still a boy, Enoch counted and calculated, looked at signs and searched for portents. Enoch asked questions. How did our fathers come to the earth? Why did they leave the Garden?

He swore that when the time came, he would go out and seek a way back to the Garden. All his life he walked with God. He strove to do only good to his brothers, to his neighbours and to every stranger who asked for water and bread, shelter or the word of God. He turned his back on all rivalry and pursued peace at all times.

When his years were the number of the days of the year, three hundred and sixty-five, he decided that this was the sign. He prepared some provisions for the journey, received the blessings of Jared his father and of his mother, and set out to seek his way back to the Garden.

He went from settlement to settlement, and told his story. Some listened to his words seriously, some mocked him; others warned him of the Cherubim who guard the gates of the Garden and of the shining sword.

"God will pardon his children," Enoch would say. "He is gracious and merciful and forgiving. Seven generations have passed since our fathers sinned, and at the end of seven generations the times change. Every seventh day is the Sabbath, and in the seventh generation will come the Sabbath of Sabbaths."

Wherever he spoke there were people who heeded his words and decided to join him—either because they sought to throw off the yoke of their father and mother, or they craved release from the daily grind of work, or even because they were fugitives from vengeance. But there were also many who were inspired by his dream.

They walked for days, weeks and months. They ate the plants of the fields and drank water from springs, sweltered in the sun by day and shivered in the cold by night. Many fell by the way. Others retraced their steps. Now and then, finding a place rich in fruit, with good soil and water, some would leave the band of travellers and pitch their tents on the new site. Only a very few had the fortitude to go on following Enoch, until they reached the place to which Noah had now reached.

This was a broad valley, surrounded by mountains and rich in flowing water. They settled amid the mountains and the orchards with their abundant fruit, the land bore golden stalks and ears of corn, and from the many stones scattered about they built shady houses, providing refuge from the winds and from the angry rains.

"Here shall we camp, regain our strength and continue on our way," said Enoch, and the people with him consented. Months and years passed. Sometimes someone came from afar to join the community of the city, which they called "the way to the Garden". Sometimes someone left and set out to return to his old home, sometimes two or three would set out to seek wives for the begetting of daughters and sons, and the city on the way to the Garden grew bigger still. Sons and daughters were born, and they heard from their fathers that the place they dwelled in was but a staging post until they would gather their strength, rest from the rigours of the journey, and set out to search for the way to the lost Garden.

One day, Enoch told them, they would reach their goal, one day they would pass through the gates of the Garden, while the angels cried out in their praise, and beat their wings in greeting, bringing them before the throne of glory which is wrought of the finest gold and surrounded by the flames of a fire that does not burn but only emits a marvellous light. Then God would make a space at His side, saying,

-You have returned, my children, you have returned, as was my desire. I have missed you, and here you are.

So it was told, over and over, by old men to their children. The children heard the words of their fathers, the wondrous vision, and went back to tilling their land, eating its fruits and telling children of their own that soon they would set out to seek the way to the lost Garden.

Enoch and his companions built a house of substantial size, decorated with precious stones quarried in the hills, set up an altar on which they would lay flowers and fruits every day, as they offered praise and envisaged the day that they would set out in search of the lost Garden. There were some who could sing the anthems of the Garden, others who could tell of its wonders, and at each telling the wonders grew and the miracles increased, the visions proliferated and the praises intertwined, like a great and many-branched tree.

When seven times seven years were ended from the day the city had been founded, Enoch gathered together the whole community and, in their hearing, recited the words that he had carved on a polished tablet over the course of the years. These were the laws and precepts enjoined by God upon travellers to the Garden. If they obeyed and upheld these laws and the precepts, they would attain the goal of their journey. And these were the words that he read to them:

> *These are the laws and precepts, which God has commanded, by the hand of Enoch, to the community of those returning to the Garden.*
>
> *No man shall raise a stone against his neighbour to strike him.*
>
> *No man shall slay his father, his mother, his brother, his neighbour or any living thing.*
>
> *No man shall oppress his brother or his neighbour.*
>
> *They shall not destroy or do wrong, any man to his neighbour, nor envy, nor covet, nor shed blood, for in blood is life.*
>
> *He who sheds his brother's blood, by man shall his blood be shed, for in the image of God has He created man.*
>
> *Man shall forever be his brother's keeper.*

The singers sang "Amen," and the community responded: "Amen." In a big stone chest, in sight of all the congregation, Enoch placed the tablet with its decorations of precious stones, setting it up as testimony in the big temple house, and declared:

"In one more year from this day, we will leave this place. In the year that lies ahead we must prepare equipment, purify ourselves, and imbue in our minds the words of God's commandment."

The congregation said "Amen", and went each man to his house.

But from that day onward, it was as if there was an evil spirit abroad in the community. The people were divided into two camps, those who said "Go" and those who said "Stay". If one person said: "We have reached this fertile place, this garden, and there is enough here for all of us," and another said: "The real Garden is elsewhere."

The leader of the group that favoured staying was called Haniel. He, too, said he had spoken with his god, and heard voices in the night saying: "Stay, build your homes, and beget your children, until I send angels to guide you to me."

Quarrels broke out between brothers, sons and fathers; between man and his neighbour. Work in the fields was neglected, the fruit rotted on the trees, the ears of corn in the fields with their grains had no one to harvest them, water channels remained blocked, thorns and thistles covered the fertile soil of the valley. Haniel and his followers spread false rumours against Enoch, accusing him of conspiracy and corruption, vice and violence, arrogance and incitement, of aspiring to make himself a god in place of the true God, the Lord of heaven and earth.

As the day of the anniversary approached, the few who were still faithful to the dream of returning to the lost Garden prepared to set forth. In the night, as Enoch was struggling to remove the tablet of laws and precepts from the heavy chest, in readiness for the journey, a man approached him from behind, struck him on the head with a stone and killed him. His companions, who found him the next day, covered him with a pile of stones and left the city. And the matter of Enoch's disappearance remained a mystery for generations to come.

And thus it was said that God took Enoch and he was no more. This I saw, and this I have recorded in the chronicles of mankind, and man himself will never know the secret, unless the Lord chooses to reveal it.

## Chapter sixty-four

Noah sat on Enoch's grave and thought of his father Lamech and of what he had done. Did he fear it was his father's actions that had tipped the balance in the eyes of God and led him to unleash destruction on their heads? Was it because of his father that he lacked the courage to plead with God to rescind His dreadful decree?

Even of his father's guilt, Noah did not know the whole truth. This was evidently the will of the Lord. I knew, because I had seen it, and since I am commanded to testify and to tell, this I shall do. If the Lord so wills, He shall reveal the words of my testimony to mankind.

# Chapter sixty-five

For nine generations I lived alone. I saw the deeds of mankind on the earth and the deeds of the Lord, but who saw my deeds? Who counted my nights charged with grief and longing for my friend Michael? In the ninth generation, the generation of Lamech, before Noah was born, on one particular night my longing for Michael was especially painful. So great was my yearning that sometimes I would seem to see him standing before me and smiling, and I would address him, speaking out loud, but he would just go on smiling and disappear as suddenly as he had come. Delusions and desire, delusions and grief were my lot.

That night I was awakened by the sound of wings beating above my head. Here he comes in my dream, I told myself. For when he came in my dreams, I always heard the beating of wings above me. Here he comes, and this is a dream that is not like a dream. Only in my dreams did I hear the sound of wings beating. Not like birds, not like the wind in the strings of Jubal's lute, not like the rustle of leaves in the treetops, but the sound of angels' wings. And Michael's wings I could tell apart from the thousands of wings of other angels; a steady, serene movement, strong but never hasty, always intense and always precise, like his breathing. I opened my eyes wide. If this was a dream, it was worth seeing it with eyes wide-open, in its fullness, in its entirety.

-Adiel, it is I, Michael, I heard him say.

-I know, my brother and my friend. You dwell in me, in my dreams, and I often hear your voice. Speak, if only in my dream.

-It is not a dream that you are dreaming, Adiel. It is I, and not your dream. I am here, with you, until dawn.

I could not believe what I was seeing with my own eyes, I could not trust what my ears were hearing until Michael took me in his arms, and I heard with my own ears the beating of his heart, and I felt with all my limbs the warmth of his body. Only then did I feel tears, which must have been my own, as I whispered:

-Michael, Michael, at long last you have heard the voice of my misery, at long last you have responded to my desire.

-Hush, Azi, hush . . . until the light of dawn. There is so little time, and so much for us . . .

Now, my head on his breast, listening again to the heartbeat of the universe issuing from it, I heard him say, It is at the Lord's behest that I come to you.

I listened to his voice, felt his touch, followed the beating of his heart, and brimming with emotion, told him everything of the days of my life on the earth. In disorderly, fragmentary fashion, one thing inside another, early after late, the first not the first and the last not the last, for the words were piling up on my lips and I could not choose between them or from them, I could only let my speech flow like a foaming torrent.

When I had recovered from the intensity of the encounter I asked: And what is the nature of your mission to me? What more does the Lord require of me that I have not done? There must have been impatience, even a trace of annoyance in my voice.

-Steady Azi, go gently here. Your conduct thus far has been pleasing to the Lord. It is not to tell you what to do that I have come, but what not to do!

We both laughed and the tension melted. My anxiety was soothed, in spite of the fact that the time was draining away, and it would not be long before dawn, before the hour of the first song of praise, the hour of the waking of birds. And this is what he told me.

-Ever since Lillith had slipped away from the Garden to follow Adam, her love, an evil spirit had descended on the angels who had known her. They sought her in every corner of the Garden, under rocks, in caves, among bushes and trees, on the river banks and in the rivers. Not all knew the secret of her escape, and those who did know were expressly forbidden by the Lord to talk of it. The angels who had known Lillith began neglecting their duties, showing weakness and making mistakes. They sowed disorder and unease, contention and rivalry among the dwellers in the Garden. Each suspected his brothers—perhaps one of them was hiding her in a secret place and not letting her hover, or fly like a breeze through the woods as she had done since the day she was created. Their jealousy threatened the routine of the Garden, the hours of song, the transparency of the universe to which the inhabitants of the Garden had become accustomed since their creation.

Then the Lord decided to banish them from His presence and send them to the earth, so when they saw the daughters of men, and saw that they were beautiful, they would take them to wife and forget Lillith.

The sons of God, the angels expelled from the Garden, would fall to earth as giants. They would choose themselves wives from among the daughters of men and beget sons and daughters who were mighty and strong and would live as men. While there was no limit to the lifespan of angels, the lifespan of man was still very long, too long, in the sight of the Lord. The son of

Lamech who was yet to be born would be the last of men to live to a great age. The earth was full of evil and God regretted creating man. After the death of the son of Lamech the lifespan of man would be but one hundred and twenty years. The wrath of the Lord at all the violence, oppression and murder was liable to impel Him to action, the outcome of which can barely be imagined.

I was commanded not to consort with the giants, not to deal with them or advise them in any way, since it was for them to find their way on the earth, as did Adam and Eve. From the day that they fell to earth they would not only be spirit but also flesh, like Adam and his sons. The Lord would make them forget the language of the Garden, as he had made Adam forget it. It was for them to learn everything from the start. To plough, to plant, to reap and to harvest. I, Adiel, was commanded to see and understand their words, hear their voices, yet they would be incapable of seeing me. They would forget their origin, beget sons and daughters and be like men in all respects. I was not to interfere in their lives, neither to guide them, nor prevent their mistakes and their failures.

I asked Michael: Couldn't the Lord have told me all this without an intermediary, as He has sent me signs in every other matter. Of course, I am not sorry that you are here, I added hastily. It is an unexpected gift, and I thank the Lord for it.

Michael smiled the smile that had captivated my heart and my life since the moment I first fell into the Garden.

-And don't you know that I've missed you, too? I asked this favour of the Lord, and explained to Him that this way you would better understand His words and He said: By all means, Michael, by all means. Words spoken with love leave a deeper impression.

I shall not say much more of our unexpected meeting, or of our parting. It is not my history that I am recording, but the annals of mankind upon the earth. I shall add just a few words regarding our farewell. Angels can also weep and the Lord understands their pain. Their wounds still smart too, even after they have healed. Their hearts too may be torn to shreds when a unique and special love is uprooted from them, a joy such as will never return even when a new love follows in its wake. Every first sensation has about it something of the intensity of creation, of its secrets and its perpetuity.

After we had parted, for many days and nights, the sweetness of the encounter remained with me. Even the pain of separation could not overwhelm it or erase its taste. Every now and then I would stare up at the sky, looking around, wondering if the giants had already fallen from above.

One night, a dark moonless night, I saw them descending, like sparks, from the sky. At first light I hastened to the place where I had seen them come to land. They were sprawled among the bushes, dazed and confused, exhausted after their long journey. An angel moved among them, cutting off their wings. In their long legs, the knee joints were already beginning to flex, and their appearance was changing from moment to moment, ever more closely resembling the form of men. Their faces, too, were being transformed before my eyes. Teeth sprouted in their mouths, human teeth; the sockets of their eyes deepened and their brows widened. They were in the image and the likeness of the Lord, as these are reflected in the faces of men. Of course, the image of the Lord Himself I have never seen, but for His likeness in man.

This was the first day of the giants on the earth. I did not follow them, nor did I record their history. I was not instructed to do this. When the giants, the sons of God, began taking wives from among the daughters of men, quarrels broke out among them. It was not over fields that they contended, nor springs, nor property, nor pasture, but over women, and their rivalry was furious. They pelted one another with stones, brandished clubs, inflicting grievous wounds on former companions.

More than once I saw a woman slipping out of her hut, meaning to draw water or to clear weeds in the field, going down to the river and waiting and dreaming. The giants were handsome and strong. A spark lit their eyes and their faces shone with the vestiges of the radiance they brought with them from the Garden. There was indeed a strange charm about them, the charm of the unknown, and attraction of a curiosity that inspires and challenges to solve riddles, to delve into secrets, to discover new sources and to strike out beyond the limits of the known. This is the way that the Lord had created man, and these were his qualities.

The women used to sit a long time after the pitchers had been filled with water, not knowing themselves why they had not risen to take them back home. Sometimes one of the giants would come down from the hills to bathe in the river, naked, his vigour and manhood exposed to the eyes of those waiting on the river bank. The women would leave the vessels in the fields and follow the muscular stranger.

Once I saw Zillah, wife of Lamech, walking down to the river, her hair combed and anointed with aromatic oils, her white robe adorned with flowers, and a spark of lust in her eyes. When one of the giants happened to come that way, she lowered the pitcher to the ground and sat beside it. The man took the pitcher and went down to the river to draw water. He came up from the river and set the pitcher down beside Zillah, the wife of Lamech. She was silent and he was silent, even as he hugged her about the waist. She took his hand and laid it on her breast, and was silent. He drew her head to his head, her face to his face, her mouth to his mouth, and then they both laughed. She understood the language of his laughter, just as he understood the language of hers. And when they coupled, I saw the look of eager consent on both their faces. Afterwards, Zillah took the pitcher of water, looked back once and smiled at the big, broad-shouldered man, whose hair was gold and eyes bright green. On his face, too, flickered a light that was not there before.

When her belly swelled, Lamech understood that it was not by him she had conceived, since she turned her face away from him. The fire of jealousy was inflamed in him. He was a man of violent temper, easily enraged, and was known as such to his neighbours and his family. Jealousy fanned the flames of his wrath beyond control. When Zillah crouched to give birth, the infant was drawn from her womb and given to Lamech. One blow of his hand was sufficient to kill the child.

Still angry, still intent on exacting revenge for his dishonour, Lamech set out to lie in ambush among the rocks, waiting for the next giant to show himself. When he spied a giant passing by on the path below him, he rolled down a great rock and smashed his skull. Seeing the big man slumped in pools of his blood, he climbed down to him from the cliff, dipped his fingers in the blood and made a mark on his forehead, and said: "Cain shall be avenged sevenfold, and Lamech seven and seventyfold." He hastened to his wives, and in a scornful and arrogant tone related what he had done. He commanded his son Jubal to take up his lute and play before him as he sang: "I have slain a man for wounding me, and a child for shaming me," a song of jealousy and vengeance. All this time Zillah was bending over her green-eyed infant, weeping bitter and silent tears for his death.

"Oh my baby, oh my child, oh my son." She paid no heed to the words of Lamech. Even his account of the death of the large man passed her by, for all that she heard was the cry of her baby, the cry of his coming into the world and his leaving it. She took the little body, wrapped it in her robe and buried it in the manner of all who enter and depart from this life.

# Chapter sixty-six

Noah spoke as if he were trying to break through the
veil of the night, through the clods beneath which Enoch lay
buried, and with him the secret of his life and death. But the
ground was silent and the rocks were silent, and only the rustlings
of night and the breath of the wind in the trees spoke in a language
of their own. And I too, Adiel the scribe, shall speak in my
language, the language of angels that is not heard by the ears of
men.

In a corner of the ruined temple, near the stone chest
containing the tablet of precepts, a minute light was ignited, like
a spark flashing in the night. A light breeze arose in the air,
bringing with it scents that recalled to me the Garden of Gardens.
I had not sensed this fragrance in the Garden or on the earth,
nor in the orbit of the sun from where I had descended so many
aeons in the past. Only in the Garden of Gardens had I once
caught the scent of such an aroma, when the flame appeared. I was
amazed. Could I be dreaming? Was it possible that my yearning for
Michael, which had not abated for one single day or one single

moment, was it possible that this yearning had caused the scent to rise so poignantly in my memory?

The flame grew, stronger and brighter, and already it was a little blaze, casting a light that could not be ignored. Noah was aroused from his contemplation, saw the flame, and thought his grandchildren had lit a fire. The children had learned from their parents the art of making fire, and they found this an enjoyable pastime, as well as a means of warming themselves when nights were chilly.

Noah approached the flame. A voice that was familiar to him, calm and fatherly, whispered:

-Noah, take off your shoes and draw near to me.

Noah removed his shoes, thinking as he did so, that since the day that they had all emerged from the ark, that God had not made his voice heard to him. In his mind, he addressed God directly.

"You let me wander wearily on without knowing my destination and without knowing if You were still by my side, You granted no sign to show that the road I followed was indeed Your road. Have You hidden Your face from my suffering? Do You regret, do You repent of the terrible things that You have done?"

Noah's thoughts coursed through his head at the speed of lightning, one upon another, one inside another, intertwining, blending and vanishing. Again the whisper was heard from within the flame, thin as silence:

-Noah my son, it pains me to see you in your grief.

"My God," Noah replied. "I am grieved for our forebears Cain and Abel and for our father Enoch. Shall the stone consume for ever, taking life for ever? They were Your creatures. The one who slew and the one who was slain."

-I know, my son. The inclination of man's heart is evil from his youth. In my heart I wish I had never created them, but what I have created cannot be revoked.

"Pardon me, my God, and do not perceive my words as

insolence, but they are Your creatures and whatever is in them, they have received from You. Even their evil inclination, from their youth."

-Yes, my son. But I also gave them the choice between good and evil.

"And how are they to know what is good and what is evil?"

-When they ate from the Tree of Knowledge I thought they knew this. But I was mistaken. When their eyes were opened to know good and evil, it was for them to seek after the good. Evil came of itself, impelled from the dark abysses. I did not teach man to choose good and to spurn evil. It is for you to learn this for yourselves. Never again will I smite all living things because of what mankind does: the day shall be for light and the night for darkness, the winter for cold and rain and the summer for growth and fertility. Never again shall times and seasons be confused. And you, my children, I shall not destroy. Be fruitful and multiply and replenish the earth.

Noah listened to the words of God with rapt attention, and he understood that God had made a terrible mistake. He had punished mankind and all living things without discrimination. They had been banished to the land which lay under God's curse, empty-handed, with dark and powerful instincts in their hearts, and in their heads the knowledge of good and evil—but not the faculty to distinguish between them.

After a pause, Noah found the courage to reply:

"No, my God. No, God of heaven and earth, in a world such as this we shall not raise new generations. Neither I nor my sons. In this lawless world it will not be long before the land is once more filled with violence, or before You punish us once more with destruction."

Noah felt anger and sorrow in his heart. As if he had discovered that he had survived by mistake, while others perished by mistake. The grief of God came too late, he reflected. If only He had regretted His deeds before they were done, if only He had repented before He brought ruin on the world, before Cain slew Abel, before Enoch was murdered, before his father Lamech killed a man for insulting him and a child for shaming him. What is done cannot be revoked.

-Noah my son, I have spoken and I have promised. Do you not hear me?

"Yes God, I hear You and I wonder, why was I saved? My own father killed a man and a child and boasted of his deeds. Blood has been spilled on the very threshold of my house."

-I have chosen you, my son, because you found favour with me, and I have tested you. You withstood the test well. And now, be fruitful and multiply and fill the earth. I shall not smite it again on your account.

"Forgive me, my God, but I fear Your anger. What happened once may happen again. I cannot beget children after what my eyes have seen. I cannot bring new life into the world. Let the universe go on without us. You have enough, God, without us. We shall breed no more children."

In the flame, red tongues were ignited. I knew these tongues of fire. I had seen them often and had learned the meaning of the various hues. Anger was signalled here, restrained but real anger nevertheless. Before Noah was aware of this, the flame had already turned to soothing blue and sober violet, showing readiness to teach and to explain.

-I shall not uproot you again, my son. I shall not strike nor punish, neither the earth nor its people. This is my promise. Be fruitful and multiply, for life shall endure for ever.

"God, it is not my intention to defy You. But one who has seen children drowning in the deep, old men crying out for help, mothers screaming in terror as the flood waters sweep them and their infants away, one who has stood helplessly and watched as the horror unfolded, unable to extend a rescuing hand—such a one does not believe it is possible to renew human life upon the earth. The earth is no longer our safe haven, the skies above our heads are not as they were, for they have rained death."

-There will never again be such a thing, my son. Summer and winter, day and night, seedtime and harvest, all these will come in their time, and I shall never again destroy life.

Noah was silent. He pondered the words of his God, wrestling with Him, and as he grew more courageous, the confident tone in his voice grew stronger.

"How shall I convince my sons that this is Your promise? In their eyes I am a simpleton who believes every word that You say. How can they be sure of Your promise that life shall endure forever? The young men are stubborn. They have learned to doubt, to deride, to ask questions."

-I will give you a sign, Noah, I will give a sign to the world, that seedtime and harvest and day and night shall not cease; that the world shall never again be devastated nor shall life be ever extinguished.

"And what is the sign, God, that others may see and believe?"

-A bow in the sky will be the sign. Go back to your sons and tell them that tomorrow they will see the sign. It is to be a covenant between me and you, between me and all living things, between me and the world forever. Noah my son, be fruitful and multiply and chose life, embrace life, you, your children and your children's children.

And Noah responded: "I thank you, God, for all your words are the truth."

As the flame began to subside, the voice of God was again heard.

-Noah my son, why did you not entreat me not to destroy the world, when you were forewarned of the flood? Had you wrestled with me then as you have wrestled with me now, I might have heeded you.

Noah was silent and the flame vanished into the darkness.

# Chapter sixty-seven

꙰

Noah saw the flame receding and disappearing from his sight. Once more he was left sitting on one of the stones of the spacious, ruined house. Behind him stood the stone chest and inside it, the inscribed tablet. The sky above was clear of clouds and studded with stars. He looked up, and it seemed to him that he saw a tiny flame moving amid the stars, a flame that gleamed like a flickering spark, diminishing until it was all but invisible.

Yes, my God, I see You. Even if You go as far as the furthest star, I shall see You. However distant You may be from my eyes, You are within me, my God. We have made a covenant, and tomorrow my sons shall see the sign that You have spread above us.

When the day dawned, Noah made haste to gather together the members of his community. They sat around him on the scattered stones, and he addressed them:

"Last night I heard the voice of God speaking to me. He commands us to be fruitful and to multiply and to fill the earth. Life will never again be brought to an end upon the earth on account of our deeds. In summer the sun will shine, and the fruit ripen, and the fields bear their crops and life emerge from every living thing. In winter the skies will darken, and the clouds drop rain in its time and in its proper measure, and the rivers shall be filled with water and the streams flow. The day will not be engulfed in darkness, and the night shall bring comfort and ease. This is the word that God has spoken to us.

"And we, the sons of Adam, shall not eat flesh when the spirit of the animal is still quick in the blood. Every man shall safeguard the blood of his brother. No man shall shed his brother's blood, for we must regard ourselves as our brothers' keepers. Blood that is shed will not be forgiven, and the bloodshed of innocents will be avenged by God. He who sheds the blood of man, shall his blood be shed, for in the image of God was man created. God shall give to man life eternal through his children and his children's children, generation after generation. Never again shall the earth be ruined nor life destroyed.

"Today we make a covenant with life. We shall not abuse it, nor destroy it. What we have received from His hands, to His hands we shall return it. The breath of life that He breathed into us, to Him we shall give back. From dust we were taken, and to dust our bodies shall return in time, and our spirits to the Lord of the spirit."

The congregation sat and listened in silence. The voice of Father Noah was very calm, as if his God was speaking through him.

Na'ama stood at Noah's right hand. She took his hand and put it to her eyes, and then kissed it, saying:

"Noah my husband, you have lifted a great fear from my heart. We women had resolved never again to bear children, if it meant to give birth to them only to have them succumb to destruction and death. Now that God has made a covenant with us never again to destroy the world, I make with Him a covenant to be fruitful and to multiply."

The women in the congregation replied, "Amen". The wife of Shem rose to her feet and said: "Truly, this was what we vowed to one another, each woman to her sister. That we would bear no more sons or daughters to see them drowning in the deep, choking and dying, nor give life to children doomed to be snatched from us before they learn the meaning of pain and joy, of grief and gladness. How can we know, Father Noah, that you have spoken the truth?"

"God has promised and He will keep His promise. Now go to the spring and purify yourselves, be cleansed and holy. Change your garments and wear your ornaments, wash your children, and every living thing shall hear and see the sign that God gives us."

His family made haste to do as Noah commanded them. As they did so, the skies darkened above them and a gentle rain, the first that they had seen since leaving the ark, began to fall. The rain was steady and benign, not raging or aggressive, but caressing like a mother's fingers.

When the people gathered once more around the stone tablet in the chest, Noah stood in the middle with the six pure beasts and the six pure birds which he had brought with him in the ark to be a sacrifice to God. They brought out the tablet from the chest, built an altar around it and placed on it a big polished stone that had been found in the spacious house, the former temple. On his chest, Noah hung the talisman that had been attached to the breastbone of the skeleton, inscribed with the words *Enoch, servant of God.*

Then, suddenly, the sun appeared and a beam of light burst from the clouds and fell on the stone inscription, which blazed as bright as fire, and Noah again seemed to see the flame from which God had spoken to him in the night.

As the members of his flock stood about him in silence, he took the six birds, one by one, and set them on the altar. The birds did not fly. He led forward the six pure beasts and said:

"These are a sacrifice to God, the Creator of the heavens and of earth, and the giver of life." He clapped his hands together, and the birds spread their wings and flew. He prodded the beasts with his staff and they began trudging towards the meadows of verdant pasture all around.

"These beasts are a sacrifice to God the Creator of life."

The clouds parted above the heads of the congregation gathered about the altar and a huge rainbow arched across the sky, like a hoop enfolding the world from end to end, it came alight in the sky. The bow gleamed with a riot of colours and hues: red for life, green for fertility, blue for joy, yellow for growth, purple for love, orange for fellowship and violet for peace.

All who stood there looked up and cried: "It is the sign! The sign!"

Noah laid his hand on the shoulder of his wife, Na'ama, and she embraced Shem, her firstborn, and he embraced his wife and children, and they in their turn embraced Ham and his sons and daughters, who clung to Japeth and his family, and so they stood, hugging one another and weeping. They wept as they remembered those who were no longer alive, those who had drowned, as they remembered the children from the valley of the palms who had clung to the bows of the ark and pleaded to be rescued. And they wept for joy, as well, as they thought of those who would come after them, with the bow of the covenant to protect them.

My eyes, too, have misted with tears, and here I cease my account of the history of mankind upon the earth. The grief and the joy that are blended in my heart would only distract me from the task.

The further annals of mankind will be set down by men themselves.

# Chapter sixty-eight

I wait to be called to return to my beloved, to my father and my brother, to my companion, Michael.

# About the Author

*Shlomo DuNour*

Shlomo DuNour was born in 1921, in Lodz, Poland, and immigrated to Palestine in 1938. None of his extensive family in Poland survived the Holocaust. One of the leaders of the *Aliyat Hanoar* Movement, he taught in the Departments of History at both the Hebrew University and at Haifa University for many years.

In 1978, DuNour's first book, *Yet Another* was awarded the Newman Prize. *Adiel*, published to great critical acclaim, won the Jerusalem Literary Prize in 1999.

He has been married to the author and translator, Miriam DuNour, for over 50 years, and lives in Jerusalem.

*The fonts used in the book are from the Garamond and Gill family*